DAVINA

3

TIJAN

To all the readers who loved Davy from the beginning and stuck with me, waiting for Davina! You guys are amazing and have been so supportive. Thank you for being patient. I truly hope you'll love the conclusion.

1

They started the chanting again, and I closed my eyes before I bent my forehead to rest on my arms. Would it ever end? They'd been trying for six months now, or so it seemed. I had tried to keep count, but every day melted into the next. Some of the times when I would wake, I didn't know if it was the same day or a different one. There were six flies instead of two on the sandwich some vampire slid into my cell. I hadn't touched it then and still hadn't, but I guessed that an entire day had gone by. With every day, the flies multiplied in numbers. Tomorrow there would be twelve or fourteen.

"There, there, no appetite for the human-no-longer?"

Lucan squatted next to my head outside my cell. He wrapped a hand around one of the bars and bent low to peer into my eyes.

I didn't flinch or look away. "I'm still human, Lucan."

"No, you aren't. You would've been dead a long time ago."

I sighed. It was the only thing I could do. Time and time again, his witches would chant. He'd get excited, as human as he ever was, and he'd stand by for The Immortal thread. It had been his plan since I turned him into a human. He wanted the power so he was determined to get it. He really thought he could be the next thread-holder; he refused to believe there would be no more thread-holders. It was only The Immortal now. I had tried to explain this to him, but since there was no lore about The Immortal, he never believed me.

And then one day, I grew tired of the torture, and said to him, "Do you miss him?"

Lucan grew still beside me. He loved to sit beside me and feel my pain. I knew every time he thought they would break me, when the thread would join him, but it never happened. He still sat beside me every day.

"You two look so much alike."

"Shut up."

I thought it would take more for his reaction. "Roane is all about duty. He's sworn to protect people who he feels are right no matter who it's against."

"Shut up," he snarled again.

"He'll come after you, you know."

Lucan shot to his feet, but he didn't go anywhere. He didn't leave. He didn't threaten. He just stood there and waited.

"He loves me. Do you think he won't come for me now?" I saw how he stood there. "Do you think he won't go against you for me?"

He jerked on his feet, but settled back.

I said further, "He loves me, Lucan. He loves me more than he does you. You've hurt me. You continually hurt me, and that's only going to make it worse for you. Every time you hurt me, he'll hate you more for it. Are you ready for that? Can you handle his hatred?"

"Shut up," he whispered this time. It had been a snarl before, but not now.

My eyes glinted in triumph, but I knew it was short-lived. He'd do what he would do. Lucan was like Roane. Both believed in their own courses, and neither would change for anyone. They both felt they were right.

It was now a matter of who would win, and my heart was on my lover.

"Again!" he roared, and the chanting began again.

I rested my forehead against one of the metal bars. The pain would start in a few seconds.

ROANE

ROANE JERKED his head up when his office door slammed open. His senses should've alerted him before the intruder had breached his inner sanctum, but when he saw who stood before him, he knew why they hadn't. She wasn't human. He sniffed the air and knew she wasn't a vampire either, nor a werewolf.

He stood slowly. "What are you?"

The girl cocked her head to the side. She had long black hair with blue tips. A large mark covered the side of her face and she stood in a warrior's stance in blue leather. She stood confident. A sword was slung across her back.

She sneered at him, "I am Saren. I am not from your world."

"What are you?"

"I am not from your world; it is not your business. I am here to help you rescue Davy."

"Davy? What do you know about her?"

She stepped back, a slow and methodical step. "She was taken by your brother, and she's held in a fortress. He's surrounded himself with Mori vampires. You have no hope of getting in there and getting her out."

"But you do?"

Her chin raised a fraction of an inch. "I am only visible to your eyes because I choose it. Do not push me, Vampire."

"How do you know Davy is there?"

"Because I am more than you can understand." She cocked her head to the side in a defiant stance.

Lucas regarded her. He didn't know who she was, but she was there. And she had information about Davy. He had little choice but to accept her word. He also smelled the sense of recognition. She did know Davy. He felt it in his gut, and she was as concerned as he was. All other questions would have to wait.

He jerked his head in a nod. "Tell me what you know."

"You have power, but your Hunter tattoo is turned off. I can sense how your powers are leaving you. You're going to need help. You can't depend on me, but I will be there. I will hold my own. I will be the one to find Davy. You will follow behind with help."

"My help?" He moved around his desk. "My best warriors were taken with her."

"Except for your fastest one and you have already sent a request to the Christane wolves."

His nostrils flared, and Roane stopped abruptly. "How do you know that?"

"I am not of your world. Do I need to repeat everything I say to you? Davy is being held—"

He waved her off. "I heard that part, but when you say 'I'm not from this world,' it doesn't explain how you knew that I'd sent word to Christian."

"Christian Christane is your friend. He is a powerful Alpha Werewolf. It would make sense for you to enlist his assistance. All members of your army are needed here." She tilted her head to the side with an absent look in her eye.

A corner of his mouth curved down. This thing wasn't something he had foreseen. "If you know Davy, why didn't she tell me about you?"

"Because I told her not to." She turned and started to leave.

Lucas jerked forward. "Wait. Where are you going? How do I get in touch with you?"

"You don't." She left the room and never looked back.

His door never opened.

Lucas sat back down and remembered a time when Talia had been the ghost Davy could see. She'd talked to her, but this Saren was something different. Then he sighed and picked up his phone. It seemed that he'd need more than the Christane wolves.

BROWN

BROWN HELD her breath and rubbed her shaky hands down her legs. Vampires roamed past her and stood before her as she inched down the hallway. Davy's boyfriend had called for her and a car had picked her up when they ended the call. Now she was back in the bar she had once been excited to go to. Her legs wavered, and she hoped she wouldn't lose her bladder this time.

She glanced around and found herself hoping for a glimpse of the Viking giant, but then, as a sea of vampires parted and Roane moved forward to greet her, she saw the strain on his face and remembered what had happened.

Gregory was gone, along with all her friends.

She struggled to keep a tear from falling and tried to steady her chin, but her lip trembled anyway.

Roane's eyes skimmed over her; his eyes were sharp as a hawk's. Brown knew that he saw it all. He probably heard how her heart started to race.

"My office?" He spoke in a gravelly voice.

Thick with emotion, Brown moved ahead of him as he held out an arm, down a hallway.

As they moved away from the crowd, she noticed glances that nearly every vampire cast her way. Before they moved into his office, a few of the lingering ones in the hallway glanced also, but their eyes moved over her shoulder. They weren't watching her. They were watching Roane. She saw respect in them, and all of them stood taller. They squared their shoulders back when Roane moved past.

This was their leader. She had never considered him before, during the brief moments when she heard him converse with Davy, but she was overwhelmed with butterflies now. Her palms got a little sweaty and her eyes went wide. When he closed the door behind him, the air seemed so intimate, so private. No wonder Davy was head over heels.

This vampire was unlike any others that she had met, not that she knew many. There had been that one with orange hair— never mind. She wasn't there to daydream. And Davy's boyfriend started to look impatient, like he was waiting for something. Then it clicked.

"Did you ask me something?"

A shadow of a smile graced his features. It transformed him. He had seemed intimidating before, but with that slight hint of amusement, his features were breathtaking. Sharp cheeks, intense eyes, a full mouth, and that cleft in his chin.

Brown swallowed and looked away. Davy's boyfriend. She needed to keep telling herself that.

Then, again, she realized the room was heavy in silence.

She closed her eyes in frustration. "I'm sorry. What did you say again?"

The smile faded, and he clipped out, "Have you worked on your magic since the attack?"

Her stomach twisted over. The 'attack' had been months ago, long, long months ago. Every day she tried to get her magic back, but nothing worked. Even the slight amount she could use before was gone. She felt human, *only* human. No magic. Nothing. She was useless.

"No, I haven't. I've been trying, but I think I used it all up. I don't think there's any more in me." Her lip trembled.

Roane narrowed his eyes. From what Davy had said, the girl had an unlimited supply, getting to it was another matter.

"Somehow," he murmured, "I don't think that's the case. Keep trying."

She glanced from under her eyelids and quickly looked away. "My sister is the one with magic. Only one of us gets the family blessing."

"Look." He sighed. His hand curled around the back of the chair he stood behind. "You have magic. Davy said that it's in you. I trust her. You should, too."

She squeaked, and her eyes widened. "I do! I trust Davy with my life or I would if she were here. When is she coming back?"

He never blinked, and he never looked away.

She hung her head. "I was wondering if you had found her." She looked back up. Hope shimmered over her face. "I'd like to help. Can I help?"

"If you have magic. That's why I called you here."

"Oh! Yeah, that makes sense. I was wondering, well, I wasn't wondering but I don't know. I mean . . . I'll keep trying. I'll always keep trying. I feel it's there. Davy said it is, and I do trust her. She's my best friend. I know she has that other girl as her best friend, but she sorta betrayed her, so I don't trust—"

"Stop. Talking."

She clamped her mouth shut.

"It's why I called you. Your magic is blocked, and I have another witch for you to meet. He might be able to unblock your magic."

"Really?"

He nodded and the door opened. A man with long brown hair, frizzy and curly, floated into the room. He wore a gray tunic, and long strings of beads wrapped around his neck. A jewel was placed above his lip, underneath his nose. His eyes were dark, and black makeup was encased around them. He studied her, up and down.

"Mavic, this is Sarah Bright."

She thrust out a hand. "You can call me Brown."

The man ignored the offered hand and turned his head. "You insult me, Changeling. I am no more a witch than you are a blood-sucking creature." The young man gave her a gentle smile. "I am a sorcerer, but Lucas refuses to acknowledge my status. He feels it is too threatening to the world."

He brushed back a wave of curls and tucked it over his shoulder. He offered his hand and Brown gasped when they touched. A night sky filled her vision with shooting stars that soared at her. Underneath them the ocean roared and waves crashed against each other. Her nose twitched. A whiff of a campfire mixed with incense teased her nostrils.

"You're a sorcerer?" Goodness.

He nodded and then cast Roane a hard look. "You didn't tell me she was a Bright."

"Does it matter?" Roane held his gaze steadily.

A look passed between the two, and Mavic sighed. "I guess not."

"She has magic that needs to be unlocked. You said you're the best."

"You tease me, Lucas. I should curse you for that."

Roane laughed and patted him on the back. "This will be your biggest challenge. Imagine how your reputation will soar if you've freed a Bright witch."

"There will be ramifications."

A hard look came to him. "She's friends with the thread-holder. That can't be coincidental."

"Then the thread-holder should free her."

"She's a thread-holder. The Immortal powers are not available to her. You know how they are."

The sorcerer gave him a grim look. "You insult me again, Roane. Stories of an Immortal have been in the wind and much more as of late. Why do you ask for my help if you continue to insult my ability?"

Roane sighed. "It's not your abilities I am insulting. It's you."

Brown closed her eyes and hung her head. She dared not make a sound. The air was thick with tension; tension that she knew not to ignite. Not the slightest movement.

Mavic sighed again. "Why do I put up with your disrespect? I have many who worship my teachings. Many who would give their siblings' lives to learn from my hands."

Roane took one step closer. His eyes never moved away and he gave him the slightest smirk. "You are here because you dare not make me an enemy, and we all know how you love gossip. You've been given a window to see if those slight murmurs of an Immortal are true. We both know your ego is not so grand that it will get in the way of even the possibility of meeting an Immortal."

Brown counted her breaths. One. Two. Three. Neither man spoke. Neither man moved.

"The witch will come to my dwelling. I will train her there."

"You will train her here."

"Lucas, I cannot. All my supplies, all my books, everything is at my home."

"You packed a bag. You knew I wouldn't allow it. She will remain here and she will be under watch." Roane stepped close, so close his nose nearly touched the sorcerer's. "If you harm her or my men in any way, I will hunt you down." His eyes turned lethal. "And I am the best there is." He stepped back and cast a sweeping gaze over both of them. "Start her training now. I want it done as soon as possible."

And with those parting words, he swept out the door. Two vampires entered behind him. They both took their guarding position, just inside the room.

Mavic lifted closed fists in the air and cursed under his tongue.

Brown frowned, it was in a language she had never heard, but she wanted to learn it. She wanted desperately to know everything this sorcerer knew, even if Roane didn't trust him. If she was going to get her magic back to help Davy, this witch was her best shot. She gave him a bright smile. "Where do we start?"

2

E verything was a blur when I opened my eyes. Then the light blasted me and I screamed, lurching backwards in retreat. Anything would do to hide from it. I had to get away. My skin started to boil from the inside out. I felt it starting to peel away, layer by layer. That light, it was all because of the light.

A deep baritone laughed. He was enjoying my pain.

Lucan.

I gritted my teeth and tried to think of a retort, anything to shut him up. But then, I realized it wasn't him. He annoyed me, but this voice hurt me. When he laughed again, pain flared through my body. Millions of tiny knives were slicing through my skin. Each one took its time. I screamed again and tried to writhe away, from him, from the light, from everything.

It hurt to breathe. The knives pierced my throat. I drew in a breath, and they slid deeper.

Then, nothing. Everything stopped.

I gasped and shot upright. There was no one in the room with me. My cage was still in the center, encased in darkness. There was no light anywhere.

The door opened and Lucan strolled inside, a satisfied smirk on his face. Blood was on his hands, but he made no move to wipe them clean.

"What new game was that?" I rasped out.

"What game?" He lifted his head and inhaled deeply.

I caught a whiff of the blood, and my stomach knotted. That was Kates's blood. I didn't want to know how that had happened, what sick game they played with each other, or even how I knew it was hers.

"What game?" he repeated and came closer to my cage.

I glanced at the door. "Do you have a new witch on your staff? One that can do that?"

I expected them to come in. They usually traipsed behind him, ready with chanting spells. The door stayed closed today.

Lucan frowned. "What are you talking about?"

Though my Immortal powers had been stripped away, my empathic abilities were still a part of me. I felt into him and read his confusion. A dark suspicion was starting to form in him and an ugly smirk appeared again. I wanted to jerk out, but I didn't. I needed to know whatever he thought, though painful and disgusting it would be.

"It's working. The thread is starting to unravel. She's starting to inflict her own pain, delusions, too. Sarach never told me this would be the first step. It has to be the beginning."

"You will never get the thread. The sooner you realize that, maybe you can figure out a way to kill me."

His smirk vanished. "You are a mere thread-holder. It will work. I've forced the thread out of others, I can do it again."

"They were thread-holders. I am not. I am The Immortal."

His hands curled around my cage bars and he leaned forward. His face pressed between two bars and his smile was blinding. He looked so much like Lucas at that moment, handsome with sparkling eyes alive with life. My heart skipped a beat, and pain of a different sort speared through me. It hurt to breathe again.

1

Lucan reveled, "If you were The Immortal, my witches couldn't touch you. You are not The Immortal. You cannot be because there is no Immortal. No human can handle that amount of power. Your body cannot endure it. You are more powerful than the others. I will give you that, but don't think that it's not because Lucas's blood is in you. You drank from him. It's the only reason you have more power than the others do. That is all."

How did he know that?

He laughed. "It was written all over your face." His voice became husky, intimate. "I know my own brother. He's always shared blood with his lovers. It gives him a connection that humans could never experience, not without vampire blood."

I swallowed back the pain. I wasn't just some lover to Roane. I knew I wasn't. "The Immortal thread has only been in humans, it has *only* ever been in humans. No vampire-wannabe is going to get it. And that won't be you. You're not good enough. The thread picks the person it goes to. If, by some miracle, you do get the thread out of me, it won't go to you."

"I'm the only human here."

"Besides Kates."

He moved back and raised a hand to the side of his cheek. Her blood trailed across his lips, and his tongue swept out to lick her blood from the rest of his hand. "That'll be remedied soon enough. Thanks for pointing that out, Kates's best friend."

My stomach dropped again. "What a nice boyfriend you are. You get her to betray her best friend and then you kill her. No matter what she's told you, I know her. She doesn't want to be a vampire. She's a slayer. Everything inside of her wants to kill your kind. That's what she was built for."

A dark hint of amusement filled his eyes, and he turned to stroll out. "Who said she was going to become a vampire?"

I rushed forward, smashing against the cage. I needed to get out. Gritting my teeth, I closed my eyes and concentrated. I needed to be free. Free. Be free. The cage never gave way. Lucan's laugh raised a notch, and the door slammed shut behind him. I could still hear him as he went down the hallway. The laughter faded, but my chest still rose up and down sharply. No matter what she'd done, Kates didn't deserve to be killed at his hands. By my hands, but not his.

———

GAVIN RESISTED the urge to break through the bars. He could hear her screams. Every day, every night, every hour. He heard them, and he couldn't do anything about it.

"You can't help her." Gregory sat forward on the bunk bed. He watched his cellmate pacing. "And get away from those bars. I don't want a repeat of the last time."

Wren laughed huskily from across the hall. "Oh, come now. Burning vampire flesh. What's a better smell than that? I know it helps me meditate. What about you, Trace?"

The tall blonde vampire glanced from her leaning stance, but didn't respond. She crossed her arms and looked back through the small window again. A bored look was on her face, but her eyes were sharp. From their basement position, their windows allowed them to see foot level of the ground above. It seemed like millions and millions of Mori moved past their dungeon.

Wren sighed and stood to stretch. Her black leather stretched with her. As she arched her back with her breasts pointed in the air, she glanced backwards.

Tracey never looked away from the window.

Wren sighed again, but this time in disgust. "Give it up, Gavin. You can't help Davy. None of us can, and unless you have magic in that tight ass of yours, there's no way we're breaking out of here."

"Why do the Mori have magic? Why can't we?"

Gregory's bunk groaned in protest when he pushed down to

stand, but when he stepped forward, a deep thud came from the ground.

"Stop." Tracey looked now. "The Mori didn't build this place for vampires of your size. They're light footed and slender in build."

"Yeah," Wren bit out. "You could help us escape, make the bars crumble. Let's not do that."

Tracey shot her a look. "He could bring the entire building down, and who knows who he might kill in the process."

The dark-haired dominatrix bared her fangs at her cellmate.

"You are being immature, Arwena."

"Shut up, you two," Gavin snapped and started to pace again. "It's been months, and you two have been at each other's throat the whole time. I thought you were lovers, you used to love each other."

"'Used to' is the operative phrase." Wren sat on her bunk bed. Her shoulders slumped forward. All fight seemed to have left her in that moment.

A strand of golden hair fell over her shoulder and as she moved it back in place, Tracey flashed her deep blue eyes at her lover. A small frown appeared, but she didn't allow it to last long. Wren seemed to be losing her fight every day they remained in captivity. And the regal Roane warrior knew one thing; they would all need to keep their rest for when they would fight free. They would get free. They had to. She glanced back out the window. If anything, she'd get free to find Talia's daughter. She knew Lucan had taken her a year ago. She would have to be there, somewhere. She would find her sister's child and take back what was left of her family.

Gavin had been watching the blonde. He saw the thoughts fly through her head, and then he saw when she dismissed Wren's emotions. His own eyes hardened. He growled, "It doesn't matter, Wren. Maybe you're better off."

Tracey's chin tightened, but she never looked away from the window.

Gregory's jaw clenched as well and he sat back down. His bunk shifted underneath his weight once more.

Gavin turned back and saw how his friend's shoulders drooped. A sad expression came over him, and he knew the blonde Viking was missing the scatter-brained witch, for not the first time.

He stopped pacing and stood there, in front of the bars. They hummed with magic, and though his fingers itched to tear them apart, he knew he couldn't.

Then he heard her scream again, and he gritted his teeth. One of these days he would find a way. He would help Davy. He had to.

DAVY

WHEN THE LAST scream left me, my body collapsed on the ground. The witches had been chanting again. This time, with each of their chants, my body lifted off the floor and rose in the air. I had fought it at first, rallying The Immortal inside of me to fight back. Nothing worked. No magic could leave my body. So now I let them try. I let them fling my body back and forth, up and down, upside down at times. I no longer cared.

It never worked. They never won.

They left again, quieted and confused.

I rolled over and tried to lift myself up. My arms fell underneath my weight and my face slammed back down. My nose hit the bottom of the cage with force and I groaned, but the pain was almost welcoming. It was nothing compared to what I'd endured.

When I pushed myself to a sitting position, I felt the blood that came from my nose. I touched it with gentle fingers and found that it still remained intact. I hadn't broken my own face, yet.

A soft laugh escaped at that thought, but I groaned instantly from the pain.

"You have hurt yourself."

My head whipped up, but no one was there. There was no Lucan to taunt me.

"What is this?" I asked. It'd been a long time since I had a voice speak to me in my own head.

He laughed. *"I am not The Immortal speaking to you."*

My shoulders sagged forward. "That'd be more helpful."

He laughed again, softly. *"They have been trying hard, have they not? The thread must be buried deep inside of you."*

"Can you help me?"

There was silence.

I heard my own breathing. In and out. Inhale, exhale. They were shallow breaths. They grew shallower by the second.

Then I heard his response. "I cannot."

"You're powerful enough to speak to me, to see what they are doing, but not enough to free me? What kind of a sorcerer are you?" My tone was loathsome.

There was a sharp intake of air and a powerful explosion immediately after. The force of it threw me against the far wall of my cage. For the first time, I didn't feel the impact. As soon as my body fell down to the metal bars, I lifted my head once more and gazed around. He had gone. I knew that, but my eyes quickly searched for anything. And then I saw it. A small amount of smoke still floated in the air, near the top corner of the room. He had been watching from there and the next time he came, and I knew he would.

The door crashed open, and Lucan raced inside. "What was that?"

I frowned. I would've expected him to be angry, but as I

searched his face, there was no rage. When I felt into him, there was concern, but no anger. I murmured softly, "It was nothing."

"Don't lie to me!" He grabbed the cage and lifted it, shaking it.

My eyes grew wide. My cage was big enough to encase an entire bedroom and he lifted it without breaking a sweat. There was no resistance, as if he lifted a bag of books.

Lucan set my cage back down immediately and backed away. His eyes caught and held onto mine.

"You are not a normal human." I rushed to the end of the cage beside him. "What are you? What have you done?"

He was quiet, staring back at me. Then he left, just as quietly.

When the door closed behind him, I sat back. He wasn't human. He was more. I didn't know what that meant, but it meant something. I felt it in my bones. I could use that to help me escape. I just had to figure out how first.

3

The voice never came back. It seemed like a month had passed. And Lucan stopped taunting me. He stopped coming to sit by me. I didn't know if they corresponded, but something had happened. Perhaps his magical palace wasn't so magical after all. Perhaps the enchanted Mori weren't so impervious. I didn't know, but after that day, things weren't the same. Lucan wasn't so mad crazy. He had stopped enjoying my pain.

The witches continued their chanting spells, and he still insisted the thread could be pulled out of me, but I caught his stares a few times. He was scared, but he wasn't scared of me. It had to be whatever had happened to me, whoever that voice had been.

Then one day, Lucan sat beside me again.

I tensed and waited as the witches left again. Was this the day he started taunting again?

"I can see why my brother loves you."

I laughed. "Really?"

He didn't look at me, but sat beside and stared at the wall ahead of us. It was bleak, made of cement, and the night had fallen. The room had grown dark; soon the cold would come.

"You're beautiful. You don't know it so you're not a high maintenance girl."

"You can tell that here?"

"I could tell before, and you were Kates's friend. They both love you—"

I gritted my teeth. My fingernails pressed into the palm of my hand. It wouldn't be long before blood would start to drip down.

He continued, "—He loves you because you love him. Even now, you see his face every day, but you don't flinch. You hate me with passion. You should've broken by now. You should be pleading with me, begging for your life. You haven't done any of it."

I clenched my jaw. Blood splattered onto my legs now. It made its way slowly down to the floor.

"Lucas was the quiet one when we grew up. Did he tell you that? Mmmm. I suppose not. I was the outspoken one, the leader. We had a group of friends and they did whatever I told them to do. Lucas didn't like it. He said that I didn't think ahead at times. He might've been right. I know he thought he was, but I never cared. I could've thought ahead, but there was no fun with that. There was no adventure. We weren't tested then. We couldn't rally and see who we could really be." He laughed softly. "Our friends were weak. I never cared about them, but I loved watching my brother. Every time we'd get in trouble, Lucas would make everything okay. He always stepped in and got us out of trouble. He grew and grew every day. He became who he is today because of me. I made him. I created him."

"A Roane vampire sired him."

He sighed and stretched out his legs. "He has their blood. He became a vampire because of them, but he's the man he is because of me."

"Because he fixed your problems?"

"Because I tested him. Every time he didn't think we could

come back from whatever trouble we were in, but we did. He always found a way. I did that. I raised him."

"You're crazy."

"I love my brother. He's the only one I love."

"And he's going to kill you." I looked over.

He did, too. Our gazes met.

I finished on a harsh note, "Because he loves me. He doesn't love you."

I waited. He'd become the enraged vampire again, but it never came. Instead, he smiled at me. "I would be honored if he was the one to kill me, but it won't happen. He's not coming, Davy."

I looked away.

He leaned closer. His voice whispered to me, it teased over my skin. "He would've been here by now if he was coming. On the night I came for you, the Roane Army was at Benshire. They attacked the town when we were leaving. My brother is dead."

This was a new torture. It had to be. "What are you doing?"

He stood and looked down at me.

I couldn't look away. He wasn't telling the truth. He couldn't have been. Roane was alive.

I felt it. I felt *him.*

Lucan smirked. "You can be with him. Just give me the thread." He squatted at my head. "You see, I've started to think that maybe you're the one holding onto the thread. I thought before that it was attached to you, but it's the other way around. Isn't it? You won't let go of it, because of my brother. You think he only loves you because of the thread, don't you?"

Shame filled me, but I couldn't look away, not even when a tear came to my eye.

His voice grew soft again. "He loved Talia. She had the thread. He loved you. You had the thread. But you see that now it doesn't matter. You don't need the thread. And if you give it up, you can be with him again. He's waiting for you, Davy. He's been watching the whole time, waiting for you. He wants to be with you again."

My stomach dropped. I'd been dormant for so long. My empathic abilities had died two weeks ago. I'd grown numb, but something sparked again. It was as if a hibernating monster had been poked too many times. It was starting to stir again. The Immortal was still inside of me. She was unable to get out, but she was there. She was angry again.

My body started to shake.

He didn't notice. "I know my brother. He'll still love you. If he had been alive, it might've been a problem. You know, if you hadn't had the thread in you. Then again, he wouldn't have even noticed you. There's really nothing breathtaking about you. You're beautiful, or you were before, but I think it was the thread that made you beautiful. I saw you before, too, when you went onto that roof with Talia. There wasn't anything special about you. Meek. Dull. Your body is boring, but the thread makes you shine. Even now, you still shine."

My hands started to jerk. My arms were starting to flail out. She was coming. She was rising.

"He will love you in the afterlife. If you die now, you'll have his love forever. But if you don't, it's a matter of time. The thread will leave you anyway. I will get it one of these days. I can feel how close I am. Give it up, Davy. Let it go. Let go and you can have my brother again. You can be in his arms again."

I was rising. My feet lifted off the floor, the toes barely touched. I stared at him. Waiting.

Lucan smirked to himself and lifted a hand to push through his hair. Silk strands of black hair slid against his fingers. They fell back in place, slightly ruffled. The bottoms touched underneath his ears. "I never told you before. I thought you'd die too soon and I had to get myself ready, but I'm ready now. I've been ready. It seems you aren't. You can't let go so I'm giving you that last push. It's time to let go, Davy. My brother will love you in the afterlife, thread or no thread. He won't care anymore. He's dead."

Something hot shot through my core. It jerked my body

upright. My arms flew out to the sides and my back arched upward. The cage was big, but I slammed against the top. My chest, chin, and nose smashed against it.

Lucan was finally quiet.

Then my body started to shake again. The fury was white hot. My blood was boiling.

"*Kill him,*" a voice hissed in my head.

"I can't," I gasped out loud.

She hissed back, "*You can. The channel is there. Open it. Do it.*"

"I don't know how!"

"*Kill him! You want to kill him.*"

Lucan was yelling in the distance, but the voice hissed over him. She wanted to break free. She wanted to murder, maim. Her hold over my body wasn't like it'd been before. The Immortal had been a part of me, but it had always been me. Davy. I was in charge of myself, but this element was something different. Her fury and power was so much, she wanted to overtake me.

Something flashed in her eyes. A white light blinded me, and she smiled at herself. It was evil, filled with rage, and she reached inside. Her hand stretched out and started to cup something in the center of me, possibly my soul. The white light began to become infused with it. It was absorbing it. She was taking control.

Then she was jerked away. The white light slammed back into darkness, and my body crashed to the floor.

My head rolled to the side. Lucan's shoes were in front of me. I heard the witches behind him, but I heard her whisper to me, "*We will be free. Vengeance will be ours.*"

Then there was nothing.

SAREN

SAREN JERKED BACKWARDS. Her feet slid against the floor, but the pull stopped as quickly as it had happened. She closed her eyes and reached out to Sireenia. *"What has happened?"*

"The Immortal is impatient and angry. She is trying to break free on her own."

Saren's head moved to the side. *"The Mori magic will not allow that."*

"Not yet, no."

"Then what would happen if she continues to try?"

Saren heard the sadness in her sister's thoughts. *"Davy will die. The Immortal will become its own entity."*

"Then what?"

"Chaos."

Saren sighed and thought to her, *"I will stop it."*

"We are all fused together. You are our body and we are the spirit together. Go to our last sister. She needs us, more than ever now."

"No, child, you must open all your senses." Mavic's frustration was heavy.

Saren returned to her body form and looked to a field below her. The little witch was learning from the traitor sorcerer. They had taken camp in a valley protected by the Independent Army. He was attempting to help the little witch open her mind, body, and soul. Even from her vantage point above them, Saren knew he was only achieving with her ears. The little witch was listening, but she wasn't doing anything else.

The wind picked up at the moment and swept Saren's black, blue-tipped hair behind her. Her sword was clasped tightly in front of her, as if she would jump into battle that very moment. Then she sighed. Questions flew around in her head, and she knew the right person to answer them was not in that valley. Though, she would deal with the traitor later, and she would enjoy that moment.

BASTION RETURNED from his scouting route and stood beside Roane. He waited until his arrival was acknowledged before he informed his leader, "They are coming. Due south and headed at a quick pace. They will be here within the hour."

Roane nodded. Grim. He knew his friend had more on his mind. "You don't approve of this alliance?"

Bastion chose his words wisely. "The Christane wolves are honorable."

"You don't approve of Christian?"

"He loved her as well."

Then Roane smiled, for the first time in four months. "And you think he still holds a grudge?"

Bastion looked away and stood tall. His lean form showcased his muscles, all developed to help him as the fastest vampire any had seen. His buzzed head had a black feather tattooed on the right side. The left side showed another tattoo written in a language he had spoken to no one. Lucas once asked, but Bastion responded that only one person would know the meaning of that tattoo. He had never spoken of it again. Lucas had never asked.

Over the last four months, Lucas depended more and more on his fastest warrior. He was tempted to ask again about the tattoo, but he always held his tongue. Bastion would share if he chose to.

The vampire responded now, "I think he could love this one, too."

Lucas was not normally taken aback, but his eyes widened a mere fraction. "You think he will fall in love with Davy?"

"You two have similar tastes." Bastion moved over, a slight inch.

"Christian fell in love with Talia because he spent two summers with her. I was gone, training for the Roane Army. He will not fall for Davy, and even if he did, it doesn't matter. He knows she is mine."

"I hope as well."

Lucas frowned at him. "If that is my biggest worry, then I gladly embrace it. I am more worried about finding her alive."

"She's alive." Confidence emanated from the lean warrior.

"You are sure of that?"

Bastion nodded his head in an abrupt movement. "You would feel it if she were not."

"And as of yet, I have not felt it." Then Roane frowned. He cast a sweeping look to his left and searched into the shadows. They stood in a valley, alone for miles except for his men, but a slight tingle warned him of a new arrival. And then, though nothing moved and no one reacted, he knew this new person was coming toward him. When a shadow separated from the rest of the night, he knew who it was. She had evaded Bastion's scouting.

Saren approached. She had watched as the vampire felt her arrival. Not many could detect her, let alone know before she wanted them to. This vampire had gone up a notch in her opinion, but she should've expected as much. Davy would choose her love wisely.

Roane spoke first, "Do you share in Bastion's concerns?"

Saren's nostrils flared.

Bastion's head whipped to the side. His own flared, but in a different emotion.

Her voice was curt. "I care not about your human emotions. Love or jealousy, both are wasteful to non-human species."

"Such as yourself?"

Her eyes narrowed, but not before a flame leapt in them.

Roane didn't react, but the sight made him pause. This thing was becoming more and more than he knew what to do about. His gut was telling him that she was a fighter, probably the best he would ever see. An ally like her was priceless, but her presence didn't sit well with him. He couldn't factor her in, she was a variable given to him, perhaps a gift or perhaps a curse. They would all have to wait and see.

Bastion spoke, "They are here."

"They moved faster than you thought."

"I said within the hour."

"It's been a minute."

Saren's eyes skirted between the two. She tilted her head to the side. "Do you always argue as comrades? Is this another wasteful emotion?"

Roane's arm shot out before she could react. His hand grabbed her throat and lifted her in the air. He growled, "I don't know who or what you are, but the only reason I don't kill you is because I can smell her on you. And I can smell that you're as scared for her as I am." He settled her back on her feet. "So you can keep your ridicule to yourself. I am in no mood to hear it."

Her eyes were cool as she reached up and untangled his hand from her throat, one finger at a time. Their gaze never broke, but the flame increased in her eyes. The fire touched the air and the smell of smoke swept around them. When his hand was free, she moved back one step. "You will not touch me again, vampire. The only reason I have not killed your kind is because I know how she cares for you. If she did not, I would slaughter all of you."

"You don't like vampires." Roane nodded, but his gaze shifted to the tree line before them. He had smelled the werewolves when they were five miles away and they were near now, very near.

"I don't like anything."

"You like Davy."

Saren's lips clamped shut, and then she took a whiff of the air and turned. Her arms were flexed, ready for a fight, and her legs were bent, ready to leap forward. The wolves had arrived. They sat watching them, their heads outside the tree line and their bodies hidden in the shadows. All of them were in their wolf forms except a group in the center. The young man was Christian

Christane, leader of the Christane Pack. The young girl smelled of Davy. Saren knew this had been the girl that Davy considered a friend, who had helped her. The other two, both older men, reeked of their power. They were ancient wolves, each a lineage amongst themselves. Still, though they were old and powerful, both adhered to the younger man. They remained behind as the other two moved forward.

Roane stepped forward to meet them.

4

Christian Christane stepped forward with blond locks that the wind whipped back and forth. He had blue eyes, as clear as the aqua colored Mediterranean, and he strode forward with confidence and authority that emanated from him. Large muscular shoulders and a trimmed waist, not many men could measure against the Alpha Christane, but many would try. An air of sharp intelligence gave others an impression that Christian didn't care what others thought of him; the only item of importance was what he thought about others. What he deemed is what was.

Pippa approached behind her brother by a step. Her reddish hair was no longer worn in two braids, but flowed freely around her face. It tossed around her shoulders, the same as her brother's, but both ignored it. As they continued to approach Davy's boyfriend, her fingers twitched. She lifted her hand to adjust her coveralls strap, but they stopped short on her shoulders. She no longer wore those coveralls anymore. When she had returned home, their older sister burned every piece of clothing Pippa owned. Her closet now housed clothing that she had only ever seen on models, such as now as she wore a white cashmere sweater that showcased her slender body over custom tailored jeans.

Pippa no longer looked like the awkward freshman she had been. Lola Christane wanted her little sister to be the beautiful woman that she knew was in there. Unfortunately, at tense moments like these, Pippa longed for her coveralls and braids. She would've felt more comfortable.

"Pip?" Christian stopped and glanced over his shoulder. He could feel his sister's nerves.

She forced herself to relax. "I'm fine. I'll be fine."

He patted her on the arm. "We'll find your friend. Roane is the best hunter I know."

She nodded. "I know."

Then they turned together, Pippa beside him, and stared across a space of fifteen feet.

Roane, Bastion, and Saren stared back.

Christian's eyes swept over the blue-leathered girl and frowned. He couldn't remember this vampire, and from the condescension on her face, he knew he would've.

He nodded to her and asked, "Have you sired a new warrior?"

Roane narrowed his eyes and stepped forward. He blocked the Alpha's view of her. "Thank you for coming, Christian."

His blue eyes snapped to Roane's. "As if I had a choice. I could not ignore my sister's friendship with this new thread-holder."

Roane's lips curved upward, but the half grin was gone in a second. His face was emotionless again. "Of course."

"Of course."

"It is nice to see you again, Pippa." Roane's voice was guarded, his body tense and on alert.

She gave him a tentative smile and said faintly, "I'm sorry about Davy."

A dark emotion flashed in Roane's eyes, but it was gone again instantly. As Christian watched, if he hadn't been told by Pippa how much the Hunter cared for his lover he wouldn't have been able to judge it for himself. Lucas Roane had never given him any window to his emotions. At one point the two might've called themselves friends, but it'd been shattered. While he respected Lucas Roane, he would never trust him enough to let down his own guard.

Christian spoke curtly, "Should we be going then?"

"How many wolves have you brought?"

His eyes narrowed further. "Around forty."

The blue-leathered girl sneered at him. "He has seventy-five men. Only thirty have come forward to intimidate us, but he has more behind them. He wasn't going to let you know about the last forty-five."

"How do you know that?"

Her eyes narrowed, and a flame leapt in them. "I counted, dog."

Bastion glanced at Roane, both hid their amusement as Christian threw his head back in a snarl. His body flipped in the air, and a werewolf with sleek white fur landed in front of them. He pounced on Saren, ready to hold her captive with his large paws. She reacted before he could grab her and leapt higher in the air. Her knees bent forward and her arms stretched out as she lifted higher and higher in the air.

Christian roughly landed on the ground, but his head reared back, and he was after her in the next second.

"Christian!" Pippa yipped at him.

He looked back, and his werewolf transformed back to his human form. Two of his men ran forward, and he emerged from behind them with clothes on instantly. When he stood in his place beside his sister again, Saren returned to her place.

Roane looked at her. "You are not helping here. Leave."

She growled.

"Now!"

Pippa shifted on her feet and clasped her hands as the two

were locked in a staring battle. After a moment, the girl warned, "I will be back, vampire. You will need my assistance."

"I'm sure we will. Come back. Later."

Saren took one step backwards and vanished from their sight.

Pippa's eyes went wide, and she gasped.

Christian's eyes narrowed even further. "Who was that?"

Roane sounded weary. "She is an ally. She cares for Davy, as we all do."

"She knows Davy?" Pippa's voice squeaked.

"I will not travel with an ally I do not trust."

Roane studied him a moment. "You don't trust me, but you will fight for my cause."

Christian fell silent, studying him in return.

Bastion moved forward a step, closer to his leader.

Roane didn't look away.

Pippa stepped between them and held up her hands. "I don't know the history between you two, but I can see now that there is some. But I'm here for Davy. Chris, you know how much I care for her. She's the only friend I have."

"You have other friends."

She sighed. "They aren't my true friends. They're nice to me because you're my brother, because I'm a Christane wolf. Davy liked me even when she thought I was there to hurt her. I respect her, and we need to go help her. She gave us Pete back, Chris. Don't forget what she's done for you, too."

At the reminder, his shoulders relaxed a bit. "My sister is right. We should start. Traveling to the Mori will be long and taxing. We don't have time to fight amongst ourselves."

Roane extended his hand.

After a pause, Christian reached for it. They clasped their hands around each other's wrists and shook once, a firm and final shake. Pippa watched the two and felt something new in the air. It was something powerful, hopeful, inspiring. It filled her with new energy, a new adrenaline rush of excitement. And something told her that she'd see more moments such as this to come, many more.

DAVY

WHEN I OPENED MY EYES, I was still on the floor. Some new food had been placed in a dish beside me, but too many flies buzzed around it. The smell of citrusy garbage made my stomach clench and vomit regurgitated out of me. I hadn't the energy to move, and so it came out as a cough, then it dribbled down my chin to fall on the floor. I couldn't move away and I couldn't stop when another cough shook my body. More vomit came out, then another and another cough. Each time it was slower than the last and each time my body shook harder and harder.

My stomach was violently assaulting my body. I was helpless to stop it. After an hour of it, my eyes started to droop. The unconscious started to beckon me. Slowly, so slowly, I heard my breaths grow shorter, shallower, and then—

"Wake up!" a voice boomed.

My eyes snapped open, and I jerked upright. A scream ripped from my throat from the pain in my limbs. A butcher knife felt like it was embedded in my spine with little knives and razors inside my body, all over. Each ligament felt like they were being cut with each movement I made.

"Who—" I doubled over, and another wave of nausea hit me. Fresh vomit spewed out again.

Then the door opened. When I tried to lift my head, another scream came out of me again. My neck felt paralyzed. I couldn't move it. A pair of shoes came to my head and they squatted down.

I had expected Lucan, but this was a female. She had long red hair, brown eyes, and white skin. A memory flashed in my head, and I remembered the Mori, when they had followed Bennett to my college. She looked like them. This was one of them.

Her eyes were blank as she watched me, then she reached through the cage and touched my head. It was a gentle touch. If I hadn't watched her do it, I wouldn't have felt the touch. But then a surge of heat raced through me. My heart started pumping fast. I gasped as my back arched again, my lungs filled with something warm, and every ligament of my body tingled.

She said softly, "I have given you life now, stand."

And I could. It was a miracle. Then I remembered. "Magic."

She stood as I did, my eyes parallel to her the entire time until I was able to stand tall again. When I squared my shoulders back, the Mori did the same. When I took a deep breath, the vampire copied again. She was copying everything I did.

"What are you doing?"

"What are you doing?" She stepped closer and wrapped a hand around one of the bars. Her head tilted to the side, all the way until I thought she would turn her head upside down.

"I'm a prisoner. What are you?"

She touched her chest. "I am Jiyama."

"You are a Mori."

"I am Jiyama. You are prisoner."

I frowned. "My name is Davy. Your name is Jiyama—"

"—name."

"—You are a Mori. I am a human."

"You are a prisoner."

"No, I'm a human—"

"Human. Davy. Prisoner."

"Yes." I surged forward eagerly. She was getting it.

"I am human, prisoner. Jiyama."

"No." She sighed. "You are a vampire."

Her lips lifted, and fangs appeared.

"Yes, see. You're a vampire. I'm a human."

The fangs slipped back in their place, and she closed her mouth. "Davy. Jiyama."

"Oh God." This was going to take a while.

The door burst open again, and Lucan stomped in. "Jiyama, what are you doing? Get away from her."

She turned, but not before I saw her grin. "I am learning English."

He stopped and frowned at her.

I expected him to rip into her, chastise her, but when he said nothing, her mouth dropped open. Instead he looked at her in confusion, like she was a puzzle that he couldn't figure out.

When he continued to stare at her, a laugh ripped out of me. "I can't believe this."

His eyes grew dark, and he pointed a finger at me. "You shut up. You don't understand a thing. Jiyama, we need to go."

She turned back and reached through the bars again. "Davy. Prisoner."

The same surge of warmth spread through me again. I gasped and my vision blurred this time. She had healed me before, but this time her magic helped me. Life—something took root in me. The Immortal stirred inside of me, wakened once more. I seized the magic and absorbed it eagerly.

"Don't!" Lucan yelled.

Jiyama jerked away, but I grabbed her hand before she could pull it out. I yanked her back to me.

Jiyama yelped, but I was blind from greed. I needed more of that magic. The Immortal's power was starting to build again. It was spreading through me. The more Mori magic I felt, the more my power rose. This time I wasn't afraid of it. I could do something with this magic. The channel could be opened again. If only—

"No." Lucan caught my hand.

I salivated for more, but crashed against the cage.

Jiyama stared at me. Her face still looked blank, but something was stirring in her eyes. They had turned from brown to red, a dark red. "I gave you a gift. Something you could not have had, you have now." She looked down. "But you must protect your gift." She held her hand out, and another burst of magic came from her. It shot through me, sealing something, but The Immortal slammed against me. She wanted to get out. She wanted the Mori.

"Stop!" Lucan pulled her back. "Jiyama, leave. This is not the one you can learn English from. I have others." He placed a hand between her shoulders and led her to the door.

She went, but looked back over her shoulder. "Others?"

He nodded. "They are below. They are not dangerous. This one is dangerous. Do not come here again."

She finally nodded and went into the hallway. His shoulders sagged in relief as he shut the door.

I held onto the cage bars. "You are not their leader, are you?"

His shoulders tensed immediately before he swung to face her. Resigned.

I saw his answer. He didn't have to say a word. A smile came to my face and I couldn't stop it. I didn't want to stop it. "You are a guest, aren't you? They have no idea who I am, who the others are, or that we're even here. What are you to them?"

Lucan frowned at me, studying me. "The Mori saved me years ago. Lucas nearly killed me once. They found me and took me in. They healed me and became my family when my real family turned on me."

"You don't really believe that, do you?" I laughed. "They have no idea who you are, what you're trying to do."

"What am I trying to do, Davy?" he asked, softly. A keen look came to him, and he started to advance forward. With each step, he asked, "What is it that you think I'm really trying to do?"

"Kill me. Take ultimate power from me. Rule all the vampires."

He stopped, but sent me a dark look. "I am trying to better the vampire race. I am trying to make it so that we don't have to hide anymore. Humans can know that we live among them. We won't have to worry about a war with the werewolves. We will be safe, once and for all. And yes, that means the Mori, too. They can finally come out of their hiding. They can show the world who they are."

"You're mad," I murmured. "I don't think you even know anymore what you want."

Everything changed in that instant. His shoulders stood upright. His smirk came back, and he gave me a radiant smile. "I want The Immortal thread. And I won't stop before I get it, Davy. One way or another, I will figure out how to rip it out of you. When I do, you will die slowly, painfully, and I will enjoy watching it."

5

There was no sound, no change in the air. I didn't smell anything new, and the hairs on the back of my neck didn't stand up, but when I lifted my head, I knew who I would see. And I was right.

Jiyama stood in front of the cage. There was a determined look in her eyes, and she squared her jaw as she reached through the cage to me.

I stood from my sitting position and stepped close.

The Immortal slammed inside of me. She wanted the Mori. She was salivating like a newborn vampire for blood.

I held her back. "What are you doing?"

Everything in me wanted to go closer, to grab her hands, and take what I could. The Immortal was snarling, an angry tornado, but I stood firm. What would happen if I took those hands? The Immortal wanted it so bad, I wasn't sure I could control myself. And that was when I realized I was scared. Not of myself or the situation, I was scared when The Immortal would take over, and in the next second, I admitted a second truth to myself. The Immortal *would* take over. I didn't know when, I didn't know how, but she would.

She was too strong, and she was no longer a part of me. She had separated from me.

Her eyes flashed, and she jerked forward. Her hands caught mine, and before I could react to pull away, The Immortal surged inside of me. She burst through our connection, and I saw the Mori's head get thrown back. Her mouth opened wide, and a bright light burst from her. Her eyeballs were like flashlights, and even her fingertips burst forth with light. It was a blinding white light.

"Your magic and mine are sister threads."

I frowned. It was the Mori. She was in my head, and her English was perfect.

"It's our connection. I have obtained everything from you, as you have taken from me."

Images flew at me, of Jiyama as a child. The first time she found a dead body, but it wasn't dead. It was Lucan. She poked it and kicked at his foot. He rolled over and her heart stopped. Then she yelled for her father and his men picked up the weird man's body and took him home with them. There was another image when she was older, twelve maybe. She sat at a bonfire and was trying to stitch something together. Lucan sat beside and showed her how to do it. He was gentle, patient, and kind.

He wasn't the Lucan that I knew.

Then she grew older. Lucan was always with them. He taught her many things about the other world, how to read in other languages except for one. English. He showed her books, and as she read them every night, they were from the human world. He told her nothing of the other vampire species. And then he was gone.

My last image was when she stood and watched him go. He gave her a gentle smile and kissed her cheek. Jiyama wrapped both her arms around him and lifted high on her tiptoes. She pressed against him and told him in their language that she loved him. He swept back her hair and promised he'd come back. Then he kissed her on the mouth.

As I hurled around inside of her, I couldn't believe this was the Lucan I knew. If he'd been like that with me, I might've fallen in love, too.

Okay—reality check. I shuddered. That would've never happened.

"He is not the monster you feel he is."

I jerked my eyes back to her. Our hands were still clasped together. The Immortal was back inside of me and purring like a cat that had gotten the cream, and Jiyama's eyes had a white rim around them now. They'd been so dark before.

"You don't know how I know him." My eyes were darting all over. Did she know? Could she read my mind now? I didn't like this one bit.

Her mouth tightened. *"You have an incredible power inside of you. Our magic comes from the earth. Yours come from the life itself. It is a new power, no one is aware it exists."*

"Except for all the thread-holders before me."

She tilted her head to the side and chewed on a lip. *"What are you concerned for?"*

"You want a quick answer or the real one?"

"You fear Lucan."

"He's not good, Jiyama."

She stepped back. When our hands let go, the connection was gone. It was instant, and I reeled inside from it. The Immortal blared again, angry once more. She wanted the connection back.

"He's good to me and my family."

I grew silent. She didn't want to hear about the real Lucan and from what I saw inside of her, what I felt—she was in love with him. It was powerful and it gripped her so tightly. Then the door burst open and Lucan strode inside.

"What are you doing in here, Jiyama?"

She turned and gave him a faint smile. "You shouldn't have kept her from us."

He drew up short and watched her warily.

"You want to know what he's doing?"

"Davy—"

"He's trying to kill me."

Jiyama turned to me with intent eyes.

"He wants to take that power out of me, and if he succeeds, I'm dead. He doesn't care. If he's this good and great person, the one that you love so much, would he do that?"

"A man should be ruthless to protect his loved ones."

I snorted. "Are you blind? Or just dumb? Your family saved his life. You have power in you that he wants. Of course, he's not going to show you the real Lucan. He's ruthless, but he's also a psychopath. Every day his witches come in here and torture me. Every day." I swung my gaze around. "And where's Kates? Does she know about her? Why do I always smell her blood on you?"

"Enough!" Lucan growled as he launched himself at me. He ripped open the cage and was inside the next instant. His hands wrapped around my throat as he flew us against the back end. When the cage tipped over and his hands loosened a fraction, I shot my hand against his chest.

"Stop."

Then everything halted.

My heart skipped a beat, and I blinked. Nothing moved. No one breathed, no one twitched. Nothing. I'd frozen time again and I turned toward Jiyama. Her eyes were wide, fearful, but her hands remained at her side.

She wasn't scared. I wedged myself out of Lucan's hold and edged closer to her. There was a look in her eyes, deep in them. Confidence. A shiver broke over me and something whispered in the back of my mind that I hadn't uncovered the tip of the power inside of her. But from what I had seen and felt, it sent chills down my back.

"Uh." Lucan's finger cracked the air. He was fighting against the time freeze.

I didn't have much more of it so I whirled around and was in the hallway. Everyone stood in place. I had done that. It hadn't been contained to only my room. Then, with my heart pounding, a loud rushing sound in my ears, I stopped and tried to concentrate.

I needed to find the rest. Even Kates. The Immortal rattled inside of me. A small burst of air came from me. It formed a tiny cloud and as it started down the hallway, it bounced back to me. Slowly, with my heart pounding and my limbs shaking, I started to follow.

It took me down another hallway, through door after door, until a last one opened. A dark stairway led downstairs and I went down, weak in the knees. These were the moments when I needed Roane to hold my hand. He would know where to go, how to do it, and I would never feel my fear.

I felt it now. It railed inside of me. And that was when I realized I had merged with The Immortal, but it was only a tiny bit. She was angry and hissing inside of me. She was screaming for me to hurry, but I didn't. I inched downwards, step after step, and prayed the time freeze wouldn't loosen.

It wasn't far after that until the small cloud darted around another corner. There they were.

Gavin and Gregory were held on one side while Tracey and Wren were across from them. They seemed so tired. My heart pounded even more and I hurried past them. Nothing. There were more cages, but none with Kates. Where was Kates? And why did I care? But something told me it wasn't right. She should've—he had her blood on him. Every day, he came to me with her blood on him. I shuddered as I remembered the look of twisted delight in his eyes. What was he doing with her?

Oh goddess. What do I do?

I ran back to them and tried to open the door. Nothing. It

didn't even jar against my force and I closed my eyes in defeat. My blood was pumping furiously through me and I sagged against the cage. I couldn't do it. I couldn't do anything.

"*I can.*"

I steeled myself and shook my head. There had to be another way.

"*I can free them. You know this.*"

I whimpered to myself, "No. There has to be another way. Not like this—"

"*Let me, Davy!*" The Immortal screamed and lunged herself at me. I gasped and my arms flew out. She was battling for control again, and she was winning.

"No!"

"*Yes!*" She lunged again. And again. Each time she drove farther into me.

As I readied myself for another launch, I already knew the battle was done. So I turned my head in slow motion and looked at Gavin. Worry lines circled his eyes. His shoulders had drooped, maybe in frustration? His own surrender? I swallowed a painful knot in my throat. I hadn't considered what torture they had done to them. Then there was a bleak emotion in me. Did I want to know? Would that give The Immortal more power over me? The angrier I got, the weaker in my compassion I became, the stronger she grew. She was taking over.

"*Now!*"

And it was done. Everything shot through me at once. Visions blasted in my head. Lucan had cracked another finger through the time freeze. Jiyama was freed, but she watched him in a calm curiosity. I felt Gavin's fury and his determination. Gregory was worried for his friend, who sat in front of him. Wren was anguished. I felt her fear for Roane, her loyalty to him, and the love for the blonde vampiress beside her. And Tracey—she shifted inside of herself and met my gaze. She was frozen on the outside, but she was aware in the inside.

She gave me a haunted smile. A tear slipped down. *"My niece is here. Leave me."*

I jerked in shock. We were communicating on another level of consciousness. *"We can't leave you behind."*

"I will be fine. Tell Wren that I love her." She bowed her head to me. *"I must stay for my niece. Talia would want me to do this."*

It was done. She had decided. I nodded. *"This is why you came to us, isn't it? To find Talia's daughter?"*

Tracey gave me a sad smile. *"It is, but it was healing for me to connect with Wren once more."*

"Once more."

There it was, the finality. I had no idea what was going to happen in the future, if we would become free or not, but I felt it. Tracey wouldn't be returning, no matter the outcome. She had another road to follow.

It went without saying. I said it anyway. *"Wren loves you."*

"She does, but she needs Roane more than my love." She glanced over and would've caressed the other vampiress's head if she could've. *"Her belief in him grounds her. She needs that and she knows it. She'll always choose him over me."*

Tick. Tick. Tick.

I felt the clock beneath our feet. The time was coming. I had to make my move. I had to do it now.

The Immortal rallied again. She snarled at Tracey, *"Leave us. You do not help, you will only hinder."*

Tracey's eyes shuddered, but she surged away in retreat.

I felt Lucan's anger. It was broiling to the top. Soon he would break through the time freeze so I hurried to the cage, closed my eyes and let go.

The Immortal gleamed as she lifted a hand. There wasn't a command, just the will. The door unlocked and Gavin and Gregory were also unlocked from the time freeze.

"Wha—Davy!" Gavin launched himself forward and started to scoop me up.

My eyes flashed at him and he braked. The Immortal's whites shined at him and he took a breath.

Then I waved my hand to the other door. Wren was unfrozen. Her head jerked up, and her nostrils flared. A wild look shifted over her, and her fangs protruded at me.

Then she stopped and turned back.

Tracey was still frozen.

She swung her head to me. "Undo her."

The Immortal sneered at her. "She wishes to remain. So be it."

"Undo her!" Her hands lifted, and her body started to arch.

She would've thrown herself on me, but I waved a hand. Her body slammed to the wall from my will. When she would've fallen to the ground, I lifted my palm. She rose in the air, and my grip was at her throat. "She remains for her niece. You knew this."

She snarled again. "Unfreeze her—I will not—"

"You will." I let her body fall to the ground with a thump. "Or you will die. I will not go against her wishes, not when they rally with one of my sisters."

"Sisters?" Gavin murmured behind me.

Then I felt the crack beginning. The time freeze thread was starting to unravel. "We must go or all will be lost."

"Kates?"

I clasped my eyes shut a moment. The Immortal allowed me this weakness. Something broke inside of me. "We must leave her. I don't know where she is—"

"Davy!"

Lucan was coming.

I whirled to Gavin and gasped, "I'm weakening. I can't—"

Gregory was at the door, then through it. Gavin started to follow, but turned back. He saw the problem and with a hardened mask over his face, he swept past me. Picking up Wren, he carried her to the door. I started forward, still leaving Tracey frozen when Wren shouted, "At least let her escape on her own, or do whatever she wants. At least—" The growl melted into a forlorn look. As Gavin paused, right before the door, her shoulders dropped. She finished, "At least, let her decide."

I felt inside of myself. I didn't have much magic, but I nodded. "Go!" I yelled at them and unfroze Tracey at the same time.

She jerked out of place, but she knew what was going on. A resolved expression crossed her face. She nodded to me. "Go."

"Wren is—"

"Go." She surged forward.

I wavered on my feet. The magic was leaving me so quickly. My knees were weakening, an entire wave of exhaustion was rising up over me. It was going to crash soon. I felt its impending arrival.

The blonde vampire saw my dilemma and she cursed under her breath. I felt Lucan coming. He was roaring my name through the building, making even the cages shake from his fury. I looked back at the door. I knew then, I wouldn't be able to make it. If Gregory, Gavin, and Wren got free, that was good. I wasn't going to be with them. I had nothing in me to evade Lucan and his army.

Then, abruptly, Tracey soared to me. She grabbed me up and was running with me. I looked up at her. Her head was down and focused, but as she darted through the door, her eyes shifted to mine. She was getting me to safety. I nodded, thinking in my head, *"I'm sorry."*

Her lips pressed together. She didn't say anything, but I felt the sadness inside of her, and she thought to me, *"Rest, Davy. I'll carry you the way."*

We raced down a hallway and soared past a door. I was so tired. The wave was crashing down on me, but I lifted my head. I felt Lucan coming toward me. He sensed my presence. He knew we were going fast, but Tracey wasn't fast enough. He was coming —the door exploded in the air and he was there. He was barreling after us. I closed my eyes and transcended above us.

The Immortal was quiet, more than she had been the entire time. I didn't have enough energy for this, so I knew she was doing this.

We weren't as one anymore. We were almost two separate beings, and she felt my distress. She was lifting me up. My body was in Tracey's arms, but I was up and I could see Lucan racing to catch up.

We were doomed. He was faster than Tracey was, but I had to try to help. I had to try, at least.

"Rest, Davy." I felt The Immortal's words. The anger was there, but held off. It was as if she knew I had tried, and then, my head started to fall back. I watched myself as my body grew limp in Tracey's arms. She glanced down, her alarm picked up, but she didn't stop. Her fear gave her a small boost of speed, but it still wasn't enough.

Lucan was almost there.

"Davy." The Immortal was at my side again. She laid a hand on my shoulder. *"Rest."*

And, as if her words had magic over myself, the world started to grow black. My eyelids fell, suddenly so tired, but I saw The Immortal gazing down where I was in Tracey's arms. Wind began to pick up. The walls of the hallway started moving around, and then we were gone.

I had fallen asleep.

6

Christian stared across the bonfire at the man he never understood. Lucas Roane was a vampire. They were all alike, but this one never did as he predicted. He loved a woman. He left her. He lost her, so he fell in love with the new thread. Next he chose to declare a war for the woman. And when she was taken from him, the old vampire he knew would've found another woman. This Lucas Roane sought an alliance with his enemy. They went together for this Immortal, for the woman the legendary Hunter thought he loved.

And then he glanced to his side. His sister sat there, content, as she munched on a chicken leg he roasted over the fire for her. Pippa was the younger sister no one understood. She scurried away from fights, hid in the shadows when confronted, and was so eager to escape away to a school far away. Then she called for them and she wasn't the same woman. She had grown. She stood upright when spoken to, she met each attack with her own fierceness, and she rallied them all when she heard a friend was in need.

It was the same woman. They both loved the same woman, though not in the same way.

Christian looked down at his lap and gripped his water again. His confusion didn't matter. He would go to this woman. He would rescue her and he would do it without protest. His sister believed in this woman and he would forever be grateful. He was given a new sister, one who loved herself, was proud of herself, and who made him proud as well. He would fight for whoever managed that feat.

"You're thinking too loud." Pippa glanced up as she bit into the chicken leg again. She grinned.

"That's what being older and wiser means. We think a lot." He draped an arm around her shoulder and pulled her close. A tender smile came to him. "Good thing I have you with me."

She nudged him with her elbow. "I keep you on your toes."

"You do."

"I do." She was solemn as she held her older brother's gaze.

From across the fire, Lucas watched the exchange. A part of him tore inside, but there was no outward reaction. He sat as a statue and his face never moved. He was a stone, had been since Davy was taken. But something softened in him as well. Davy would've liked to see her friend happy, and she seemed to be with her older brother.

And then a woosh sounded behind him. Saren took the seat beside him. Her blue leather crinkled in protest as she lowered to the piece of tree. She glanced at him, looked where he watched, and sighed in disgust.

"You humans are all the same," she snorted, rolling her eyes.

Lucas gave her a restrained look. "I am a vampire."

"You're still human."

"I eat humans."

"You drink blood. It is different. You still feel. You let those feelings overtake you. You're still human." She nodded across the fire. "As are they. They are worse."

"How so?"

"Vampires act like they're better than humans, but they know deep down they aren't. They're worse. You all are vain and weak, but werewolves feel their arrogance is fulfilled. They think they're the greatest creatures on earth, all because they are still human, they have mortal lives if they want them, and they think they're in control of everything." She snickered. "Davy always talked how wolves were the best to be around. They repressed everything; she didn't have to feel their emotions."

A grin teased over his face. "That sounds like her."

She mirrored his amusement, but looked over and it faded. She stared with an intensity now. It drew him to ask, "What?"

Her mouth tightened. "Why did you leave the witch with Mavic?"

His jaw slackened at her words and he whirled to her. It happened so fast, faster than in the blink of an eye, and his hand clasped onto her arm. "How did you know about him?"

She never blinked. "I've been watching you since Davy insisted she was in love with you. She was a fool," she spat out. "You're both fools."

His fingers loosened. Just a little. "What do you know about Mavic?"

"He is a traitor. He is the worst scum underneath the dirt on my shoes. I want to squash him into the earth until his loins burst and his body bleeds dry. I want to—"

He lifted his hand free. "Okay. I got it."

She drew upright. The embers in her eyes burst into flame. "What are your plans for the traitor sorcerer?"

Roane shot her an annoyed look. "I'd still like to know how you could stalk me without me knowing about it."

"I did not stalk." She squared her shoulders back. "I do not stalk."

One of his eyelids twitched.

She frowned. "I hunted you. I did not stalk you. Hunt. That's more . . ."

Bastion stuck his head around. "Less creepy?"

Her shoulders dropped. "Yes. I am not creepy."

The two vampires shared a look.

"What?" She looked from one to the other.

Bastion shrugged. "You're a bit creepy."

"I am not."

"Yeah. Yeah, you are. Sorry to break the news."

She took a deep breath. Her chin lifted and she sat to her fullest height. "I am the representative of my clan. I am here to help a fellow sister, the followers of my sister, and I—." She clamped her mouth shut.

Bastion raised an eyebrow. "Yes?"

Her shoulders sagged down again. "Nothing."

Roane grinned. "You're creepy, but in a good way."

"Thanks." She lifted her head again.

The two shared a slight smile, and Bastion groaned. "I'm getting the creeps now."

"What is the plan?" The question was almost thrown from the other side of the bonfire like a challenge. The small exchange between Saren and the two vampires was interrupted, and the small moment of a slight break in tension was sniffed away like it wasn't supposed to have been there in the first place.

Roan straightened, remembering how Christian Christane had once taken the woman he loved. A dark emotion took root inside of him. He wouldn't allow that to happen again. He didn't fear for the same repetition, but that he'd lose Davy because of the Alpha wolf. That would not happen, and the wolf sensed the deep determination. It was like an old rivalry, once buried was awoken again. His nostrils flared, knowing the near loathing was there. He couldn't do anything about it, and the two weren't on speaking terms. They couldn't speak about Talia, at least.

Pippa glanced up at him, picking up the undercurrents. She pressed her lips together and let out a small growl. She looked at both and said one word. "Davy."

Roane and her brother received the message. The small flare-up dampened immediately, but it was still there. It was a back burner turned to simmer. It was still hot and still dangerous if left ignored.

Saren narrowed her eyes. She harrumphed. "Foolish human emotions."

No one responded, but she stood, and as she stepped away from the fire, she vanished.

Roane continued to stare across the dancing flames at the werewolf. Neither looked away.

7

DAVY

I woke up on a bed and lifted my head, or I would've. My neck wouldn't move. Stabbing pain sliced through me, and I cried out. My body instantly locked up, and I started trembling, sending even more stabbing pain through me.

"Davy."

Gavin rushed inside, the sound of something was shoved aside, like a tarp. He added, "You're awake? Are you okay?"

"Yeah. I'm—" I couldn't talk. My teeth were grinding together.

He laid a hand on my arm and said, "You've been out for three days. Rest."

"Wha-a-at happened?"

"You."

Me? I frowned at him, trying to remember. The Immortal was with me, she told me to sleep, and I was watching from above. "Lucan was going to catch us."

"You teleported Tracey and yourself. We only just found you guys yesterday. Tracey was exhausted by the time we did. She'd been standing guard over you."

"Teleported?"

He nodded, grim. "You sent the both of you to the highest mountain. We're twenty miles from the Mori camp. Wren's the one that kept us going to find you. She said she could feel Tracey and used her scent. She tracked you guys."

He thought I did this. I didn't. The Immortal did it, and I tried to sense her right now, but I couldn't. It was like she wasn't even inside of me. All I felt was nothing. Exhaustion. Pain. That was it.

Gavin added, "It must've taken it out of you."

"Yeah." I looked away. "It must've."

He gestured around, but I could only see above. It was a dark wall of rock. Gavin said, "We brought you into this cave. We used a tarp we found by a riverbed not far from here. It's used to block out the cold for you."

For you. Those two words—they were all vampires. The cold didn't matter to them, but I was human. I was The Immortal, or I thought I still was.

"Is she awake?"

I tensed, hearing Wren outside. She was angry. I could feel it coming off her in waves.

Gavin studied me. "Are you up for her?"

No. I said, "I need answers."

He nodded, then left my side. The tarp was lifted and he spoke to them, "She's in pain. I don't think she can take too much."

"She's The Immortal. She can take more than any of us." She shoved at the tarp, coming inside. I didn't move my head over. My neck would've seized up again, but her anger became stronger. As she stood over me, glaring down, it was blanketing on top of me, and I struggled to push through it all.

This wasn't normal. This was my empathic side. This was how it had been when I still struggled to control my senses. Since becoming The Immortal, I hadn't had this problem. Everything was easily controlled, even kept at bay so I could pull it forth as I pleased.

Something was wrong.

"What happened back there?"

"Wren." Tracey came inside. "Don't berate her. She needs rest, not to be interrogated."

"I don't care." She twisted back to look at her. "She brought you both here. Why? How? Was it The Immortal power in her? Is Lucan coming for us? Does he know our location? Do we even know our location? We need answers."

"And we'll get them." Tracey touched her lover's arm. Her voice gentled. "But not now. I was carrying her body. Her body, Wren. Not her, but a body. Her heart stopped."

My eyes snapped to her, and I jerked upright.

Oh.

Shit.

I held my breath, knowing what was coming—and yep, there it was. A crest of new pain crashed onto me, and I stifled a scream. I bit down on my lip, but I was wailing on the inside.

"Davy?"

I shook my head, holding a hand up to Gavin. I'd be fine. Answers. Answers. I focused on that. Wren wanted answers, well, so did I. I waited out the pain, then lifted my gaze to Tracey's, and I asked one word. "Stopped?"

She nodded. "I thought you died. I was carrying you when you suddenly stopped breathing."

"And you continued to hold her?"

Tracey shot Wren a dark look. "I wasn't going to let him have her body. She wasn't slowing me down."

"But you said they were going to catch you," Wren spoke.

Tracey nodded. "They would've, but then," her hand lifted toward me, "we were on this mountain."

"I was dead?"

"You weren't alive."

I couldn't—I'd been dead. Had The Immortal left me? Was I only an empath now? A cold shiver of panic wound down my spine, but I shook it off. I wouldn't start thinking about that, not until I knew for certain. "How long?"

"A day."

"A day?" I was gutted. I was dead for an entire day? "She's The Immortal. How is that possible?"

Tracey looked at Wren. "I don't know. I didn't think it was, but she had no heartbeat. But she's alive again, so I guess it doesn't matter."

But she didn't sound so certain. Neither was I. I always had a heartbeat. Always. Not having one—I didn't want to not be a human. I'd completely become The Immortal then and I knew that wasn't right. I needed to hold onto my humanity as long as I could. A heartbeat was part of that.

"Davy," Gavin said.

I looked to him.

He said, "We need to decide our next move."

Wren snorted. "Leave. Get back to Roane as fast as possible."

Gavin didn't look at her. He was waiting for me, and I knew what the unspoken question was. Kates. We had left her behind.

Raw emotion rose up, threatening to choke me. Like the panic, I shoved it away. I needed a clear head. "Where is Gregory?"

Tracey answered, "He's on point, watching."

"We're twenty miles away. I think we're safe, for now." Wren threw both a disgusted look. Her anger melted into pure impatience.

I nodded. Okay. So this was the decision that had to be made. "We go back—"

"Go back?" Wren echoed me. "To die?"

I ignored her and finished, "—for Kates or we continue forward, hopefully toward Roane."

"Can you sense him?"

I couldn't even sense The Immortal, much less my lover. I

wasn't going to say that, though. I shook my head. "I'm too tired, I think."

"You need to rest," Tracey said.

"We need to move." Wren shook her head at both of them. "We move or die. Those are the options we have."

"Not if we have her at full strength." Gavin indicated me. "If we have an Immortal at full strength, we can fight back."

"We're in Mori territory. They're going to find us."

He shook his head. "It's Davy's call. We do what she wants."

"I want to go back." Tracey cut through any more argument. Wren's mouth hung open, and before she could say anything, Tracey added, "I wanted to stay behind. My niece is there. I want to know her."

"Your niece?"

Tracey looked at me and said, "If you go back for Kates, I'll go with you. I'll fight at your side."

"As will I." Gavin stepped beside her. The two were in solidarity and both turned to Wren.

She shook her head. "We'll die."

"Not if she can rest."

Wren clipped out, "We go to Roane. He's coming for us. He'll have an army with him. We can go back for the traitor and your niece, but with him. We'll have numbers on our side." Her voice rose. "We'll have a fighting chance. These are Mori vampires. You guys are forgetting that. They're not like us. We're lucky we got free at all. They're a force all at once. They fight as one being. We'll never win, with or without a rested Immortal on our side."

She was right. I looked to Gavin and Tracey. They both knew she was right, but they'd do what I said. They believed in me the way they believed in Roane. The same loyalty Wren felt for her leader hadn't transferred to me, but it didn't matter. Even though Gregory wasn't in the cave with us, he would do what I said. That was his way.

It was my call, and as Wren turned to me, reluctance written all over her face, I knew she knew it as well.

I said, "Let's rest. For now." That was all I could say.

8

ROANE

"Vampire."

Two days earlier, Roane would've been surprised at the sudden appearance of Davy's blue-clad mysterious friend, but as he was standing on the cliff, overlooking the camp, he was starting to recognize when she'd appear. A slight buzzing would fill the air and feeling the same sensations this time, he merely looked over as she was standing next to him. The wind was fierce where they stood, high above the others, so her blue-tipped black hair was immediately flowing behind her. She gazed out over the cliff's edge. "You take point up here because of the wind, not just because of the view."

It wasn't a statement, and Roane didn't respond. He was up there for other reasons. Yes, he could smell any enemy approaching better from there, and yes, he could see beyond their camp better, but he was also up there because it would've been a spot that Davy would've loved. It was the highest vantage point where he could see as far as possible, and if she was within range and if she happened to send him a signal, he wanted to be in the best possible spot to see it.

As it was, he gazed back over the horizon and it was only

mountains, trees, and a river's glimmer sparkling from the moon-
light's reflection. There was nothing in the distance, nothing that
he was hoping to see.

"Who are you looking for?"

He gazed back at her and still didn't answer.

Saren narrowed her eyes and folded her arms over her chest.
Her leather made a swooshing sound as her arms rubbed over
the material. "Answer, Vampire."

"Why?"

Her head cocked to the side. "What do you mean why? I
asked you a question."

Roane was growing tired of her impatience and condescension. Seeing her reaction, he hid a grin, but answered, "I don't
owe you answers to anything, so why would I start reporting to
you now?"

Her eyebrows furrowed together and the corners of her
mouth curved down. "I do not understand what is going on right
now. What is happening?"

He sighed. "I'm giving you 'attitude.'"

"Why?"

"Because you're not my boss." Roane shook his head, turning
back to continue searching the land beyond them. He hadn't
had a boss for a while. Going rogue from the Hunters' Line was
freeing, but nerve-wracking. He knew they would come for him,
along with Jacith's army. And, suddenly, as if feeling them hot
on his trail, he almost imagined seeing them moving along the
trees. They would've been moving silently, like ghosts,
approaching their camp with near perfection. He knew they
weren't out there, not yet, but they were coming. Their camp
had been traveling at a fierce speed, but they needed to rest.
One more night of rest, then another full week of going hard.
The vampires could handle it. They were letting the wolves
catch up.

And Saren must've felt the same because she said, "We

shouldn't stay long. Davy is in trouble. I sought you out to remind you of the importanc—"

Roane had a hand at her throat before she could finish that sentence. Her eyes widened from the quick turn of events, and she looked down at the arm. Before she could respond, Roane leaned forward and growled, "Do you think I don't know?"

"We must keep going." She spoke stiffly, her eyes lifting and holding Roane's gaze. A fire started in her eyes. It sparked, but it was pulled down to a simmer. It was there. It was burning. The flames were bright, but she was keeping it contained. "The Immortal thread is separating from Davy. The sooner we get there, the better."

Roane tilted his head to the side. The growl was still there, but he muted it. His hand dropped, releasing her suddenly. A normal being would've fallen from the abrupt departure, but Saren held still. He asked, "What do you mean? The thread is separating? I didn't think that was possible."

"It's the witches."

"The witches?"

"I was able to connect to Davy, and the last time was when *your brother*," she spat the last two words, "had a coven working to pull the thread out of Davy."

Roane wasn't surprised to hear that Lucan was trying to pull the thread out of Davy, but he was surprised about two other items. His nostrils flared. "You can connect to her?" His hand started to curve again. He wanted to grip her by the throat once more and squeeze until she gave him all the information she had. She was keeping this from him, keeping a part of Davy from him. He was close to becoming murderous, but he kept his arm next to his side. He had to, or he'd kill the other being, whatever Saren was.

She didn't answer. It was her turn to become silent.

He asked the second question. "Is that possible?" If the thread left Davy, she'd die. She told him that herself, but hearing that it could be ripped out of her—he couldn't think of the possibilities. If he did, he would leave this army and get to her on his own. Nothing and no one would get between them, even his own allies.

"No."

He relaxed. Slightly.

She added, "Not normally because Davy merged with the thread. She became The Immortal, but the witches are strong. They're powerful and they've been able to unbalance the merge."

Roane shook his head. "What does this mean?"

She hesitated.

For the first time since he met her, Saren looked uncertain. That sent a slice of panic through him. If she was nervous . . . No. Even before the thought entered his mind, he turned it off. He had to stay with his army. He couldn't arrive without them. Lucan had an army of Mori. He wouldn't be any help to Davy if he showed up alone.

"Speak!" he snapped.

"This means." She lifted her head back up, rolling her shoulders back to a ready position. "We don't know."

"We?" The more she talked, the more Roane was questioning why she was needed. "Who else are you connected to?"

"My sisters." She closed her eyes. The flame disappeared for a second, but when her eyelids lifted, Roane saw thousands of flames in them. It wasn't just hers. And they were all different colors. Blue. Pale green. Sunlight yellow. A pastel shade of pink. They were all there and they were waving back and forth as one unit. The longer he stared at them, the stronger they grew. They began to take over Saren, moving past her eyes and moving along the rest of her body. Within seconds, her entire body was lit up with all of the colors, then the flames began to sizzle and meet the air. When they stopped, she was standing in front of him, completely on fire.

She spoke, but it wasn't her voice. It was thousands of voices, all speaking as one. "We are one. The past, the present, and are awaiting our future sister."

"Roane shook his head. "What? What are you?"

"We are the last carriers. Each of us has had the thread inside of us."

That meant Talia was there.

And, as if reading his mind, Saren's body shifted. The blue leather changed into a shimmering white dress and her blue-tipped black hair transformed into deep auburn curls. The flame didn't lessen or change, but it was Talia's body in front of him.

"Are you—" His eyes roamed over her, taking in every aspect of her. The small dimple in her cheek, the curve of her waist where his hand used to rest so many times. "Talia?"

She nodded, a small and impish grin appearing. "It's me. Saren stepped back and is allowing me to come through, but it's not for long. We're all here, Lucas. All of us together. It's such a glorious event."

"Glorious?" The end of his mouth dipped down.

"It is. All of the thread-holders are united, and we've been waiting."

"For what?"

"For one purpose."

"And that is?"

"To help the last thread-holder. She will need us when she battles the only threat to The Immortal line."

"Jacith," Roane breathed out. His own flame of fury started inside. He knew the sorcerer was mounting allies against them. "Is he close?"

"He's close to Davy. He's talked with her."

His fury lit up, like gasoline had been thrown onto it. "He was close to her?"

"Only his spirit. Not in body. He can't do much to her, not unless he's in closer proximity. There are some limits to Jacith's power."

"But he's tried to hurt her?"

"Not yet. She was weakened from the witches. He's underestimating her right now."

His rage lessened, just a bit. "How do you know all of this?"

"Because we watch, Lucas. All of us together. We're everywhere, watching, listening, protecting. Saren is the one chosen to be here in body, but we've all connected as one."

Roane had been around enough in the world to know that every being, no matter how powerful, had limitations. The Immortal was no exception. While that was in the back of his mind, he asked, "Christian is here. Would you like to talk to him?"

"No." The impish smile returned. She lifted and pressed her hand to the side of his face. She cupped his cheek. "I came forth because of you. Thank you, Lucas. Thank you for loving me. Thank you for loving Davy as a separate entity. And thank you for taking in my sister."

"Tracey?" But as he said the name, he knew that was who Talia meant.

She nodded, a wistful sound coming from her. "She will find my child and raise her. When she does, and when you're reunited with Davy, I'd like to come forth again. I'd like to talk to Davy and my sister."

He nodded. The wolf would be pissed when he told him that Talia could've spoken to him and declined. Roane was looking forward to passing along the message.

"I must go now." Talia waved a hand at herself. "Saren is balking by how long this is taking. We wanted to show you that we're all together. We're here to help Davy and to be reassured. We will be victorious. You don't have to worry. I know you still will, but we, also, are watching out for your soul mate."

"Thank you, Talia."

She nodded, her eyes growing fond. As if she couldn't help herself, she leaned forward, then wavered. She paused, but her eyes grew determined and she closed the distance between them. Her hand fell from the side of his face to his chest and she leaned forward until her lips pressed against his cheek. She whispered, "Be assured, Lucas. Not all is as it seems. You will have more on your side than you realize."

Still standing there, he felt a tear fall from her eyes onto his cheek, but he felt her distancing. It was changing again. And as soon as Saren had taken over the body, her eyebrows arched high and she sucked in her breath, realizing the closeness Talia had been standing. Her eyebrows snapped down and a scowl formed, but before she could spew something out, Roane's hand was at her throat.

He did what he'd wanted to do since he met her.

He snapped her neck and let her body fall.

9

DAVY

I was up shit creek.

It had been three days since I woke from our escape and in those times, it was me, myself, and I. A.k.a. no Immortal. I hadn't tried to use any powers, just because I didn't know if I was ready to admit we were sans Immortal powers. I didn't want Wren to use that as an excuse to make us leave completely to find Roane. It wasn't that I didn't want to see Lucas. I did. Badly. It was Kates. No matter how she betrayed us, I could still hear her screams. They'd been bloodcurdling and I knew they'd haunt my nightmares. I needed to know what happened. If Lucan forced her to betray us or if she did the backstabbing all of her own free will.

Either way—I needed to know, and we weren't going anywhere till I did.

Gavin lifted up the tarp and peered inside. When he saw that I wasn't lying in bed, his eyes warmed and he came in, carrying some logs in his hands. "You're sitting up."

I nodded. "I am. I was considering doing some yoga planks even."

He stared at me and cocked his head to the side. A beat passed, then he nodded. "You're teasing me." He grinned. "Yes, Gavin." I wish I hadn't been. "I was joking. No. Sitting up is the best I can do right now."

"That's good." He put the logs in the corner before placing the last one in the fire pit. "Your body needs to rest as long as possible."

"Wren doesn't think so."

Gavin was somber. "Yeah." He sighed. "She fears the Mori will find us, and we can't defend ourselves properly against them."

Which was true, and I could be putting them in even more danger. I needed to tell Gavin, at least one person about my problem, but I didn't know how he'd react. As he turned and left again, I knew I needed to figure out what was going on with me. At least, to know my limitations, if I had any powers or if it was just my empathic self, like the old days.

I closed my eyes and tried to sense—well, anything.

I needed to know that the thread was still in me and that I hadn't let everyone down, but as I tried to feel outside of myself, I was picking up Gavin's restlessness. He was anxious, wary, and fearful. There was a small amount of concern emanating from him. I knew it was about me, and I tried to pick up his thoughts.

There was nothing.

I couldn't hear his thoughts, and holy crappola, that sucked.

Okay. Power from The Immortal was gone. What else was gone, and I kept sensing farther out until I hit Gregory. He was farther away like he was on point, and as I slipped inside of him, nothing. I was met with a cement-like wall. He was feeling stuff. I could pick it up, but it was slight like the tiniest of ripples on a smooth surface. That was when I realized that he was just waiting.

I pulled away from him, searching for the other two, but I couldn't find them.

Without realizing it, I was up and moving out of the cave. I lifted up the tarp and stepped outside. I could feel Gavin's surprise, but he didn't say anything. I kept going, past where I felt Gregory standing, guarding. I wasn't really seeing as I walked forward. I was fully focused on my empathic abilities. I trusted that extra sense to help guide me, and I was moving beyond the camp. I kept going until I felt a cold breeze against my face and heard the sounds of water rushing past me.

I was by a river, but there was still no Wren or Tracey. Gregory and Gavin were trailing behind me, but both kept quiet. They were letting me do my thing. It was later. I wasn't sure how far I walked, perhaps half a mile when I picked up the first traces of anger.

Wren.

I thought that immediately, but no—I was wrong. It was Tracey. Talia's daughter flashed in my mind, and two things happened at once. An overwhelming surge of relief crashed down on me. My knees buckled from how strong it was, but I caught myself. I needed to know what else I could still do. Tracey was thinking about her niece, then I felt how torn she was. She wanted to leave, and I heard her thought, *"I should leave tonight. Davy is too spent. It's not fair for the human child. She shouldn't tax herself—"* Her thought abruptly stopped, and I cried out.

Was it me? Had that brief power left me again? But no, I grew aware of another vampire. This one had even more rage, mixed with love, yearning, and misery that had me blinking back tears.

This was Wren.

The two began to converse, but when it turned personal, I left. Wren knew Tracey was planning to leave. She didn't want her to go. That was the last I heard before I returned back to myself and looked around for the first time.

I turned around. Gavin and Gregory were standing with their backs to each other. Both had a hand on the swords they wore, ready to pull them out for a fight if necessary. They had been guarding me.

"I'm sorry," I said to both.

Gavin's hand fell from his sword. He shook his head. "Don't be. It was good to see you out and about again. I was starting to worry."

I nodded to him. "I know you were."

He laughed.

I let the sound wash over me. It was refreshing to hear it because it was genuine. It wasn't forced or restrained. In that one brief moment, there wasn't the weight of the world on us. I heard all of that from Gavin, and I was envious. I wanted that brief respite, and I wanted to experience it in Lucas's arms, but that wasn't going to happen.

"Did you find Wren and Tracey?"

"I did. They aren't far." But I wasn't sure. I gazed around. I couldn't see any traces of our camp either. "Where are we?"

"A mile from camp." Gavin gestured to the other side of the river. "Those two are a mile farther. I'm surprised you didn't see them, though. You were only sensing them?"

I scratched my forehead. This was the opening I needed. I could reveal the truth about The Immortal, but even as quickly as I realized I should tell them, I knew I wasn't going to. The words died in my throat and instead, I said, "Yeah. I was using my empathic ability." I gave him a reassuring smile. "I'm still trying to let myself rest."

Gavin nodded, accepting my answer and started back up the trail. "We should get back. We're safer from a higher vantage point."

As he took the lead, I watched him, and my gaze went past Gregory's. I was going to keep watching Gavin, but I saw a knowing look in Gregory's eyes. Our gazes caught and held, and for the first time in a really long time, I felt exposed. I felt like he could see through me, like Roane used to be able to.

He knew.

I don't know how he knew, but he did.

He said, quietly so Gavin wouldn't hear, "Just keep resting." There was more unspoken to his statement, and I felt it. I needed to rest, but if my powers didn't come back fully—a decision would have to be made.

He added, looking down the river, "The Mori, when they come, will be coming from there."

A knot formed in my stomach.

He said, "They'll come so far, sensing outward with their sonar ways. Then, when they find that they're close to us, they'll fan out and come at us from all angles. They'll be on us before we'll know. That's how they are. They move as one being and they strike as one. No one has bested a Mori vampire. We got out because of you. I don't know if you realize you helped us, but you did. There was a whole group of them, and we strolled right past them, like we were invisible. Only one being that could do that." He nodded to me. "You." His eyes narrowed, inspecting me. "And judging by the shock on your face, you had no idea, did you? You helped us, and you helped you and Tracey. It'd make sense if you were taxed."

That knot doubled. Taxed, was that all it was? I hoped so. God, did I hope so.

"But they'll be coming."

I looked down. We didn't have long. That was what he was saying. "One more day."

"You think you can handle an entire Mori army in one day?"

I felt slapped by his disbelief, but it was because he was right. I wouldn't . . . I'd have to go alone. I couldn't take them with me into danger. I could cloak myself. If the Mori hadn't realized they were there, three very powerful vampires, maybe I could do the same for myself. I could wait one more day, work on being able to cloak myself, and once that happened—I'd leave on my own. That was what I would do.

I looked back up and said, letting the Goliath-sized vampire see the truth, "One more day, then we'll go."

"For what it's worth," he said quietly. "I'm rooting we won't have to leave."

The knot moved up to my throat, forming into a lump. I whispered back, "Me, too."

———

THE MEETING WAS SET in a back corner of a restaurant. As the wolves strode past them, in their human forms, the customers were clueless to the danger so close to them. They laughed, drank, ate, and conversed. They flirted. Others fought. All were clueless, except a few. As the wolves walked by, one after another, they surrounded the most important wolf, their Mother Wolf.

She was dressed in a white dress with a blue robe covering. It wasn't a robe that one would wear at home. It wasn't comfortable or made with the purpose not to be seen. This robe was extravagant. It was made of silk with gold trimmings lining the edges. As it draped over her head, a jewel hung from the tip and it dangled above her forehead. The other wolves kept their eyes forward. They weren't there to play with humans. The lesser ones, the human servants, were at the end of the line. Their heads were bent forward, and their shoulders were slumped down. One was right behind Mother Wolf, holding the end of her robe and dress so it didn't get dirty from the floor.

A hostess led them, but she didn't hold any menus. Her head was held high, and she walked with purpose. She wasn't in fear of the wolves, though she knew who they were. She had been told to stand at the front of the restaurant and wait for the other supernatural beings. And as the wolves came into the restaurant, the other human hostesses shrank back. They didn't know what beings the wolves were, but they knew they were something other than human. The power came off them in waves. The only reason the other customers were clueless was because a spell had been cast over the customers. They almost didn't even see the impressive parade except a couple that came in, after the spell was cast. They felt the power immediately, and while they were seated in the back, their eyes were huge by the time the wolves went past their table. Neither moved, reacting on a primal instinct inside of them. They knew they were the prey among predators, and as the wolves went past, they shrunk down in their seats. Their hands trembled, holding onto each other in their laps.

They were ignored. And as the last servant went past them, the couple got up and ran out of the restaurant.

The Mother Wolf turned at the doorway, right before entering the back room, and watched their departure. The corners of her eyes crinkled up and her lip twitched into a faint smile, but as quick as it appeared, it disappeared. A stoic expression settled back in place, but her insides were amused. She forgot how some humans were. It'd been so long since she was around these new humans, ones that knew nothing of their existence and only were aware of their own lives. They were self-absorbed and ignorant, thinking they were safe in their daily lives. They were not. The rest of her wolves had stopped and were waiting for her. She went into the back room, but she had a brief thought in the back of her mind. Perhaps it would do to send her wolves out to this new world, maybe every now and then. It would be good to remind humans how weak and powerless they were. They could do with the reminder.

Then, she turned and faced why they had arrived in this very busy city, and to a restaurant that the world thought was trendy. She saw the sorcerer. He stood in the back, still in the shadows, but she felt his power and it was equal to hers. He came from the oldest and most powerful vampire family, and normally, he would be her enemy.

Right now, on this day, he was her friend, and she smiled. "Hello, Jacith."

R oane felt her arriving, just like the last time on the cliff, but he felt her rage more than the slight buzzing in the air. When she did appear, he was scouting ahead of the group on a higher embankment, and he dodged the impending attack.

"Vampire!" Saren roared, flying through the air.

She regrouped and came at him again.

He ducked one more time. As her hand jabbed at him, he bent backwards so he was almost horizontal to the ground. Saren flew up in the air again and kicked out with her leg. This time, as he started to come back up, she clipped him in the head, but he was unfazed. He reached up and caught her ankle, twisting her body in the air again.

Saren gasped from the surprising speed of his reaction, but countered once again. She dipped backwards, jerking her foot out of his hand and she followed through, doing a backwards roundhouse. As she righted so she was standing on her feet, her second foot swiped out at Roane. He caught that one, too, but instead of trying to throw her, he shoved her away from him.

She landed on her feet, her knees buckled, her arms out in a ready stance. "You killed me."

"I snapped your neck. There's a difference."

The flame in her eyes sparked up. "Oh? Please unveil the difference to me."

"You're Immortal. Snapping your neck did nothing to you." He smirked at her. "But it did me a world of difference. Thank you. I had a whole day away from you."

The flame lit up, overtaking her entire eyes, and it burned the air. "And if you were attacked while I was gone?"

Roane drew back, startled. His eyes narrowed. "I would've slaughtered them like anyone else. You think you're that needed? Trust me. We did fine without you, and we'll do so again."

"You have no idea—" she started.

He cut her off, shaking his head. "Don't. You're here as a tag along. That's it. You need the army to rescue Davy. We don't need you. Let's get that straight."

She stared at him, and as she did, the flames doubled in size. But then, they stopped. They drew back and simmered so only a light smattering of smoke showed. She said, almost saddened now, "You're wrong, Vampire. I am more needed than you realize."

Grass was stepped on in the distance, and both went silent, looking toward where the sound came from. A second piece of grass was crushed, then a third. Both remained silent, now on high alert as predators, as they waited for the newcomer. Whoever it was, kept coming. They seemed unheeded by the sudden lull in voices. As one unit, without looking at the other, each drew to opposite sides of where the new arrival would appear. Both moved silent, as if touching air when they moved, and drew their weapons. Saren held a sword across her chest, her head dipped low, and her eyes downcast. Roane pulled out a knife, but kept it tucked against his arm. He waited with his arms down at his side.

The person continued toward them.

Roane lifted his head, filling his nose with as many smells as he could get. It was a werewolf, but he couldn't identify what family. If it were a Christane wolf, he'd only maim him. No wolf should be on his path, unless sent there because Christian didn't trust him. If it were an enemy line, he'd do the same. The wolf would be brought back to camp for interrogation, but when the person stepped forward, now between them, Roane held back. It was Christian himself. But Saren didn't hold back. She launched forward. Christian twisted and caught her. He fell back from her momentum, but tossed her over his head.

"Wolf," she snarled, her nostrils flaring, as she hurled toward a tree, caught it, and flung herself right back at him.

Christian wasn't ready for the quick counter-attack. She kicked him right in the chest, and he went down once again. This time, instead of being bucked off, she remained on his chest. Her feet were planted there and she knelt down, her sword immediately placed in position. The sharp edge of it pressed up against his carotid artery, and she knelt down, a warning hiss from her, "Move, Wolf. I dare you."

Christian started to retort, but the words caught and held in his throat. He looked to Roane instead and sighed. "This is my greeting by both of you?"

Roane had tucked his knife away during their scuffle, and he held his hands up now. A slight grin was on his face. "We needed to know the hierarchy. Now we know."

"Hierarchy?" Christian echoed, a scowl forming.

"I am above you." Saren pressed her sword against his throat before jumping off him. She sprung backwards in the air, looking as if invisible strings suddenly yanked her from him. She lowered herself to the ground a few feet away, sheathing her sword back in place, strung across her back. She gestured from herself to Roane. "And the vampire and I are equal for now."

Christian got up to his feet, dusting off his pants. "I held back, whatever you are. Get that right."

"Right." She smirked, folding her arms over her chest. "Let us get on with it. Our group approaches, and we're supposed to be scouting ahead." She sent that last statement to Roane, a flare of disapproval in her tone.

Roane narrowed his eyes at her. "You're making me want to snap your neck again. For a while there, I didn't want to. Funny how that emotion is never far for long."

Christian hid a grin.

The flames lit up again, but they were contained. They only filled half of her eyes, waving together in sync. "I'm sure we'll have another disagreement. You can try at that point, but until then, I suggest you remember the reason you're scouting ahead." She stepped toward him, dropping her voice. "For Davy, remember?"

He was scouting ahead to keep the group safe, but he got her meaning. This was all about Davy.

Christian sensed the new tension and cleared his throat. "That's why I'm here." He looked at Roane. "Another family of wolves is coming."

Roane frowned. "Who?"

"They come from Mother Wolf."

Roane had killed their Alpha, but the younger wolf was second in line to the female wolf. "She's allied with Jacith."

Christian nodded. "More than likely."

"How close?"

"Half a day behind us."

Roane said, "Then we keep going. I'm going to fall behind to watch them. I want to study my opponent first."

"I'll go with you."

"No." Roane shook his head, speaking to Christian. "You keep ahead. We'll switch our teams. You had your wolves trailing us, and my vampires were scouting ahead. I'll pull my team to trail behind. Your guys go ahead this time."

"They're wolves—" Christian started to argue.

"And they'll react to other wolves," Roane interrupted him.

His tone was firm. The decision was made. "They won't be expecting vampires."

"If they bite you—" Christian warned.

"Then nothing. A wolf bite doesn't kill us." Roane started back to the group.

Christian turned, watching him go. He called after him, "Since when?"

Roane threw over his shoulder, "Since ever. You need to rip us apart to kill us." He kicked forward with a sudden surge of speed. He was moving faster than the other two could see, and when he was gone from eyesight, and from within hearing distance, Christian looked at the blue-leather girl.

She was watching him back. She saw the questions forming and shook her head. "I still will not explain who I am to you. No one except one needs to know."

"Why do I get a feeling that Lucas is that one?"

"Because he was. He's the leader. You pretend you are, and may tell yourself that you are, but he's the true leader. Even myself, as I am a more evolved being than he is, must acknowledge that he has the power in this situation. Your men follow you. You follow him. His men follow him. He is the one who needed to know." Her top lip lifted in a sneer. "And even now, I am regretting revealing myself to him."

"Why did you?"

Christian was more than curious about the girl. She wasn't a witch. He thought that was all she was at first, but he was wrong. Witches didn't fight like she did, and if there was an impasse between herself and Roane, which he doubted there was, then that said more about her fighting abilities than he found from his own little skirmish with her. He held back, as he assumed Lucas had as well. They wouldn't really know who the better fighter was until there was a day, it was kill the other or die. Only that day would show the true winner, and as long as they were allies, Christian knew it wouldn't come.

Saren answered his question, "Because he needed to know. He needed to know who else was on his side before we arrive in the Mori territory." She waited, feeling the wolf's desire for more information. He was like the vampire. He didn't like not knowing, either if she was truly an ally or an enemy in sheep's clothing. He was also sensing the familiarity of Talia through her. His previous lover's essence lingered with her, since coming forth to talk with the vampire, but the wolf knew her on a carnal level. Saren said nothing, though. She wasn't lying. Only one needed to know. That was it if another knew that one past Immortal thread-holder was still on this plane, linked to all of the past thread-holders, she would become the hunted. Within her own self, she held the power of a complete army, and when she would be reunited with Davy, that power would be doubled. The true Immortal was an army on her own as well, but the wolf still didn't realize how powerful Davy could be. He, like so many others, was just becoming aware of an actual Immortal. Davy was a new entity. When she faced against Jacith, it would be realized the depths of her power, and that would change everything.

But Saren said none of this to the wolf. It wasn't her place to tell. She did ask, "Can I be of service of to you, Wolf?"

Christian held back a slight laugh. The girl was feisty, and he was starting to enjoy that. He shook his head. "No. I'm just curious about you. That is all."

"I know." And with those words, Saren stepped back by a tree and vanished from his eyesight. She was still there. She was still watching him, but he couldn't see her. He couldn't sense her or smell her either, and because of that advantage, Saren waited until he left. She followed him, because even though the vampire seemed to trust that the Christane Alpha would play along, she didn't. She sensed a darker turmoil inside him and wanted to find out the reason for it. Would he actually be the vampire's ally or would he turn on him at some point? If he turned, Saren would be there first. She would have to kill the wolf then, hopefully before the vampire realized he'd been betrayed. It was her gift to Davy. She knew she would want the vampire protected at any cost.

That was the other reason she was among them, to do Davy's bidding, as much as to help rescue The Immortal.

11

DAVY

It was time to go.

Wren and Tracey had returned to camp and acted normal. There'd been no sign of their earlier fight. Gavin and Gregory didn't say a word either. Everyone went on like normal, waiting for me. As for myself, I rested and spent the entire night trying to cloak myself. I prayed. I wept. I tried talking to myself. Nothing worked, or so I thought. It wasn't until around three in the morning when I found out that I had been cloaked the entire time. Gavin brought wood inside for the fire, couldn't find me, and raised the alarm. As everyone was leaving camp to look for me, I ran outside of the cave and started flailing my arms around. I yelled at them. I was there, but nothing worked until I was following Gavin down a wooded path and he abruptly turned around. He barreled into me, but once he hit me, he froze.

"Davy?" he whispered out.

"It's me." I jumped in front of him again.

Nothing. No reaction.

I poked him in the side. This was when I realized I was cloaked, and I scrunched up my forehead, summoning the strength to now uncloak myself.

"Look." Gregory turned a cautious eye around him, skimming the woods. "If that's you, poke me again."

I did, right in the fleshy stomach his giant size had. I was expecting something like the Pillsbury doughboy, but I got The Rock instead. He was solid muscle, and I said, "Ouch."

"Ouch?" His eyebrows shot up.

My head jerked up to his. "You can hear me?"

His eyes were trained on where I was, but he still wasn't looking at me. He was looking through me. I gritted my teeth. This was becoming annoying. I had convinced myself that I could control my powers. I don't know if that was true or not, but here I was. I was a fledgling newbie once again, not even able to let my friends see me when I wanted them to.

Suddenly, I had enough. I yelled in my head, *"REVEAL!"* And poof! I felt something snap in the air, and in me.

Gregory's eyes snapped to attention. "I can see you." His hand came to rest on my shoulder. "You're here. Thank God. I thought I was going nuts."

I shook my head. I was glad I could be seen again, but still frustrated. Was that what it took? I had to scream it in my head? I bit down on my lip.

Wait.

"LET ME SEE ROANE!"

Another burst of energy in the air, and Gregory was gone.

"Vampire!" I heard Saren's scream in the air, and my heart lurched to the bottom of my throat. I twisted around. I thought Gregory had disappeared, but it was me. I wasn't on a wooded path. I was high up. I could feel the cool draft of a breeze and closing my eyes, I sensed from where I was. There was a sudden drop in elevation ten yards from me. I was high up on a cliff somewhere.

Then I felt him.

I started to take a step out, to find Saren, but I felt Roane's laugh. He hadn't laughed aloud, but it was inside of him. It washed over me and for a moment, I soaked it in. It was like a warm blanket on a cold night. I wanted to grab him, pull him over me, and hold on forever.

"Lucas," I whispered, starting forward. Getting over the shock, I felt Saren's fury right after. It was overwhelming the rest. I was starting to lose my connection to Roane, but then a hand clamped on me, and I was jerked backwards.

I looked up to Gregory's furrowed eyebrows. He asked, "Where'd you go?"

"What?"

No, no, no. Rising panic was threatening to choke me. I looked around. My head was whipping back and forth. Roane— he'd been close. Saren was angry with him—I had to find both of them. I started forward, but Gregory held me back.

He said, "Oh no. Were you practicing some invisibility spell or something? You were here, then you weren't."

"Oh my God," I muttered. My knees started to tremble. I'd been so close.

"Try again."

I stilled. That was The Immortal. She was still with me. Relief like I had never experienced coursed through me, and I did fall.

"Where were you?"

"I was here. You silenced me."

"I did?"

"Davy." Gregory broke through the conversation.

I shot a hand up. "Stop." Then, I closed my eyes and concentrated on The Immortal. She was here, and she was talking to me. I was slowly gathering my strength and abilities. That was what this meant. Had to be.

"You always had them."

"I did?" I cocked my head to the side, but the words never left my lips. I asked The Immortal this.

She answered, *"You were angry with me. I was becoming too much for you, so you silenced me. It was just recently that you allowed me to talk again. I'm not happy with you."*

I laughed. *"You're not happy with me? You were trying to take over."*

I felt her shrug. *"You weren't doing anything. Something had to be done."*

"I wasn't doing anything? Me?"

"Yes. You."

My teeth were still grinding against each other. She was self-righteous, looking down on me for being a captive. I said back to her, I couldn't do a thing. *"The witches—"*

"Could've been killed," she interrupted me.

"What? How?"

"Next time they try, because they will try again. Let them have me. I will go to them, but I will infect them. One by one, I'll move through all of them. I'll soak up all their power, and I'll return to you. Don't fight it next time."

"Fight it?" She was delusional. How was I supposed to know to do that?

"You should trust me." A calming and reassuring wave passed from her to myself. *"You are The Immortal, Davy. I am merely a part of you. I will never be taken from you, and I will always return to you. It's as if you would be loaning me to them,* but a darker and sinister feeling came from her next, *remember that any that I go to, I will poison. All will fall beneath me. All will fall beneath you."*

I gulped. That sounded ominous.

I felt her withdrawing, but she whispered again, *"Remember. All will fall."*

"All will fall?" I echoed her.

"Good." Gregory clapped me on the shoulder. "Let's use that, whatever it was, and go with it. Come on. Let's return to the others. You can let them know you're one with your Immortal self again."

He started back, but I couldn't move. I was rooted in place, gazing around. I'd been so close to Roane. I heard his laugh. He'd been amused by Saren. I wanted to go back there, and I realized now that I had been there. It was a brief instant, and I could go back. The Immortal powers were awakening in me again, but as soon as I thought that, I knew I couldn't.

My original plan to leave on my own was here now.

"Davy?" Gregory called from farther down the path. "Are you coming?"

"Yes." I coughed, clearing my throat. "Coming." My legs moved on automatic pilot. My body was with them, as we went back to camp, and as I explained that I had accidentally cloaked myself, but my mind was ahead. I was planning my route back to the Mori village, and a few hours later, as the vampires fell asleep, it was time to go.

I packed a bag of food, pulled on a coat that Tracey gave me, and cast a sleeping spell. They were already asleep, but this ensured that they wouldn't wake when I left. Even though my powers were coming back to me, I was learning I needed not to assert them. I would tire, and I wouldn't have them when I needed them. Because of this, as the others snored, I walked out and left them behind.

KATES DOUBLED OVER, coughing up blood. She gazed down at it. A good solid pool of it had formed beneath her hands. She wanted to disappear in it. She wanted the torture done and over with, so her body could fall in the blood and become one with it.

"Come now," Lucan taunted her, coming to stand over her and gazing down. He lifted an eyebrow and shook his head, an ugly smirk appearing. "You wish to leave me? That's not the Kates I know." His eyes darkened, turning lustful, as he ran a hand down her arm. She recoiled, feeling even more disgust rising up as his laugh grew louder. He said, "We used to have such fun, Kates. Where'd that girl go? I miss that girl."

Her teeth were clattering together, but she tried to seethe out, "That girl left when you compelled me to betray all my friends."

"Oh yeah." He withdrew his hand from her and shook his head, still laughing. "I figured that would be a wrench in our relationship."

"You're an asshole."

Her insult came out with less heat than she wanted, but she couldn't muster up the extra oomph. He had taken her life in his hands, ending it, having the witches give it back, then torturing it out of her again so many times that she was almost a shell. Any fire she still had in her had been reduced to one small coal. Even that, she didn't know if she could light it up. She didn't have the strength anymore.

"Okay. Come on." He flipped her back up and slammed her onto a table so she was face first, lying on her stomach.

Her eyes almost bulged out. Renewed panic had her fighting against his hold, but it didn't matter. Lucan was stronger than her. Always had been, and always would be. He swatted her hands away and restrained her again, pulling each one tight into leather binding that was almost cutting off her blood flow. It never mattered to Lucan. He didn't need her alive or the blood flowing in her body. He pulled the restraints to the side of the table so her arms and legs had her spread eagle on it. Then he squatted down so he was at eye level with her.

He grinned at her, almost leering. "How's that feel?" Without waiting for a response, he stood up and ran a hand up the back of her arm, across her shoulder, and down her back. It was left exposed to him. He had ripped the shirt from her so it hung over her in rags. He took a moment to enjoy the whipped marks on her back. He enjoyed having her in this position. She tried to fight him before. She hadn't wanted to lead Davy and the rest into his trap, making them powerless to him. She even tried to break free from him, running to jump off the cliff near his brother's house. That had shaken him. Knowing that Kates tried to take her own life, rather than help deliver her best friend and new friends to his hands, but he would've rather known it then and not later. Because of it, that sealed her fate.

Since arriving back to the Mori, Kates had become his favorite toy to play with. When he wanted a drink, she was here for him. When he wanted something else, far more sinister, she was still there, and thinking about that now, his hand drew down to her naked waist. She wore her jeans. He had allowed that, but his hand caressed over her ass. He grew hard, remembering the times they had in the bedroom and when he would take her from behind.

He hadn't done that again, not since she made her loyalties known, but he was tempted. Taking her against her will had been a game they had liked to play before. His nostrils flared, feeling his body's blood pumping through him, remembering the feel of his dick inside of her. His hand curved around one of her ass cheeks, and she whimpered.

He chuckled. He smelled her fear in the air, but he chided softly, "Even now, even after all I've done to you, you still want me." His hand squeezed the other cheek.

"No." She tried to shake her head, but couldn't because of the restraints.

"Yes." His hand moved lower, falling to the curve of her ass, and he kept going. He was about to touch the core of her when the door opened. His head whipped up, then he jumped back as if burned. "Jiyama," he rasped out.

The Mori vampiress stood there, showing no emotion, but her eyes darkened. He felt her instant anger, and she moved into the room. "You would touch her against her will?"

He didn't respond.

"The human told me you were torturing this one." Her eyes glanced down to Kates on the table.

Lucan narrowed his eyes. He didn't like what he was seeing or what he was hearing. "You're a vampire."

"So?"

She was challenging him. Lucan frowned. Jiyama had never challenged him before. He scratched his forehead. "What are you doing here?"

"She told me you were doing this." Jiyama pointed to Kates and the table. "She said you had a lover here, and you were torturing her."

"She's for me to play with. Why are you judging me for this?"

"Because it's wrong."

Lucan's frown deepened. This wasn't the Jiyama he knew. "You're a vampire. You drink from humans. This," he pointed to Kates, "is nothing out of the ordinary. I've seen you out there, Jiyama. You enjoy playing with your meals."

"She's not a meal for you." Jiyama continued to gaze at him. "Anymore."

His jaw clenched. "This is The Immortal's power over you. You gave her your power, and she infected you because of it."

"No." Jiyama shook her head. "You have this human here because you still feel for her. You're going to turn her."

That last sentence came out like an accusation. Lucan tilted his head to the side. His hand came up to rest against his cheek. He needed a moment to realize what was happening here. Jiyama was jealous. He thought it was disapproval, but it wasn't. She had loved him since finding him at an early age. It was assumed among her family and the rest of the Mori clan that he would wed her, but she never pushed him. Lucan had enjoyed his freedom. Going where he wanted. Being with who he wanted, and she was right. As she said the words, he realized that was the real reason he kept Kates around.

He was going to turn her, but not till he was done having fun with her.

His eyes closed to slits, watching Jiyama carefully. She was the predator to Kates in that moment. He could see the words forming in her mind. She was going to kill Kates. He saw the intention on her face, and he forced himself to speak casually. She couldn't know the extent of his wishes, not for Kates. He said, "She is still of use to me."

"Why?" Jiyama still looked down at Kates. "The Immortal is gone. She will not come back."

He shook his head, softening his tone. "She will." His hand lifted.

Jiyama's eyes snapped to it.

He caught himself, but still lowered it to touch the back of Kates's calf. He had been about to caress it, but instead he touched the tip of his finger to her skin. His nail cut into it, filling the air with fresh blood. Jiyama's gaze was focused on that now, floating toward him and the blood. Her nostrils flared and he knew Kates's blood had done exactly what he wanted. She wanted to feed now, not to kill his ex-girlfriend.

As Jiyama stood next to him, pressing into his side, he added, "The Immortal will return for her."

"Why?" But the Mori vampiress wasn't listening. She was too distracted by the blood. Lucan pressed harder into Kates's leg and more blood spilled out. He knew the power it had over Jiyama. This was slayer blood. It was the best kind to a vampire. The slayers used to use their own blood to entrap vampires and in a way, maybe that was still happening. Lucan remembered being ensnared by Kates. Perhaps that was why he still wanted to keep her.

If he didn't obtain The Immortal thread, he would become a vampire again. That was when he would turn Kates, but he wanted to be the one to do it. He wanted to be her sire, to have that connection with her for eternity. And part of that was keeping her alive—for now. If Jiyama killed her, she might take Kates's body away. He needed her body to have the witches bring her back to life, and if Jiyama turned Kates herself, he didn't know if she could be turned back to human without Davy's assistance. Too many variables had entered the room when Jiyama found Kates. Lucan wanted to control everything, so he needed to distract Jiyama and then remove her as soon as possible.

He ran a hand up Jiyama's arm, feeling the shudder that he created in her, and his hand cupped the back of her neck. Jiyama started to tremble against him, her small breasts rubbing against his chest. He lowered his head, his mouth right next to her ear, and he whispered, "Drink, Jiyama. Taste what vampires have thirsted over for centuries. Taste a slayer's blood."

He smelled her wanton desire in the air. He knew she was close. One taste and Jiyama would forget everything she saw in this room. The feeding would overpower her. He pressed her head down, pushing her close to Kates's blood. His finger cut more into Kates's skin. The slayer didn't move, and he looked up —she had passed out.

Probably for the best, he thought as he grinned, his mouth still so close to Jiyama. He pressed a kiss to her ear and whispered to her, "Quench yourself, Jiyama. It's like nothing you've tasted before."

Her body kept trembling against his, but he felt the instant she gave in. Her fangs came out, and she drew in a deep breath, before lunging for Kates's leg. He pulled his finger away just as her teeth sank in, and she drank. As she kept drinking, Lucan ran a hand down Jiyama's back, enjoying this moment. His vampire lover was feasting on his human lover, and as she kept going, he moved to the back of Jiyama.

She groaned, moving against him. He knew what she wanted. It was what he wanted as well, and as she kept drinking, he lifted up her dress and lowered his pants. He slipped inside of her, thrusting deep as she arched her back from the pleasure.

Grabbing ahold of her slim hips, Lucan pulled out, only to thrust back in. He fucked her hard, and once Kates would be willing, he couldn't wait to do the same to her again.

12

DAVY

I was hurrying.

The farther I could get away from the others, before they realized my disappearance, the better. The spell I cast should keep them asleep for an additional few hours. Long enough so they couldn't catch up if they dared to try. Every hour, I gave myself some Immortal speed, zooming through the woods, but I stopped almost as soon as I started. I didn't want to wear myself out. I was still hoping to keep regrouping The Immortal powers, but once I got to another mountain and came to a cliff's edge, I knew I needed to use a bit more than I planned.

Mustering up an extra amount of energy, I felt the world falling away. I looked down. It wasn't the world. It was me. I was lifting myself in the air and over the deep ravine until I landed on the other side. Once landing on my feet, I let out the breath I'd been holding and tried to stop any powers that I might've still been using, any leftover. Once I was sure I had completely stopped, I looked up. I needed to head over this mountain, but I knew there was so many more to go. I felt the Mori and Kates. It was low in my gut, but it was like an anchor deep inside of me. It was pulling me toward them.

I was going for Kates, but I was going to kill Lucan. He couldn't be allowed to remain alive. He'd keep coming. He'd keep trying to hurt me, hurt Lucas, hurt anyone else that I loved.

There was another battle coming. I felt Jacith's presence. He was over my shoulder, watching me, studying me, and I knew that he would arrive soon. But first, head ducked down, I started up the embankment. I needed to kill Lucan first.

"SHE'S GONE!"

Wren ripped down the tarp and raced outside. She repeated, "Davy's gone."

The rest of the vampires were awake and on their feet instantly. Gavin reached for his sword, but there were no enemies to fight. He forced his hand to release the weapon as he gazed around. "What are you talking about?"

"No." Tracey shook her head. "Wren is right. Davy is gone. I can't hear her heartbeat anywhere."

Gavin stifled a curse. Lucas would be furious about this. Davy wasn't helpless, but she still didn't know the full force of her powers, and she had struggled. She used too much of her powers helping them escape. They shouldn't have been able to get away from the Mori, but they had. They all knew it had been because of Davy, and she'd been exhausted since.

His anger started to mount. They had to find her. They had to stop her, or at least slow her down. She couldn't go back unassisted.

Gregory began picking up his weapons and the rest of what little they had around the camp.

Gavin asked, "What are you doing?"

The giant vampire stopped and gave him a hard look. "What do you think? We have to go after her."

"No." Wren drew both of their gazes.

Gavin took a step toward her. "What did you say?"

She raised her chin up. "I'm not going." Her eyes cooled. "She made her choice, to go without us. I'm going to find Lucas. It's time we returned to our leader's side."

"He would want us to aid Davy."

"Then I'll get that order from him." Wren reached down and grabbed the bow and her satchel of arrows. She fitted both over her back, pulling her arm through the strap. "I'm going this way."

"Davy went that way." Gavin pointed the opposite direction.

"I'm going, Gavin." Wren's tone was final. "I'm sorry, but I have to go where I feel I'm supposed to be. Lucas needs us. He'll move at a faster rate if we are at his side."

A low and primal growl came from deep in Gavin's throat, and he started forward. If he had to force her to go with them, he would. His hands were in the air, ready to battle his sister vampire when Tracey stepped between them. "I'll go with you."

Everyone paused.

Gavin realized she meant him at the same time Wren did. His eyes widened in surprise, but Wren let out her own growl. "Are you kidding me?" she snapped at her. "I thought you had come to your senses."

Tracey held Gavin's gaze for a moment longer. She thought in her head to him, *"Give me a moment. I need to say my goodbyes to her."*

With Tracey's decision, Gavin looked to Gregory. He asked, "And you?"

"The Immortal promised me she'd help my daughter." He had picked up his sword, but he sheathed it now. "I'll go to be at her side."

It was decided then.

All three of them, Tracey, Gavin, and Gregory all turned as one and regarded Wren. Her mouth fell open, and she looked to all of them slowly. She gutted out, "Are you kidding me?"

"We've made our choice, Wren."

She shook her head. "You all are wrong. You're abandoning our leader."

"Lucas would want us to help The Immortal." Tracey reached out to touch her arm.

Wren twisted away, her eyes flashing in anger, and she hissed back, "Do not lie to me. You're not going to help the human. They are." The last two words were spat out as she pointed to the other two. "They go for her, but not you. At least, give me that consideration. You're going for a whole other reason."

"Wren—" Tracey stopped. Wren wouldn't listen to reason, Tracey saw that now. There was nothing else to be discussed. The goodbye would be pointless. Wren would leave in anger. She wouldn't be able to hear anything else. She had reached out for her, but her hand fell back to her side now. She couldn't shake the forbidding feeling that was the summation of their relationship. They could've been together again. They could've been a force to be reckoned with, but it was only Wren's way. If she didn't go to be at her side, there would be no going together. Tracey's head hung down. She said quietly, "I have to go for my niece. I have to try."

"Your niece is a Mori. She will only hate you. She will never love you."

Her words stabbed at Tracey, and she sucked in her breath. Closing her eyes a moment, the blonde vampiress choked out, "That is something I hope does not come to fruition. I have to try, Arwena."

"Stop," Wren hissed out, her hand clenched around the end of her own sword. She didn't pull it out. Her hand fell to it out of habit. It was what she held when she was in battle. And right now, as her lover was leaving her, she felt very much in battle. She shook her head. They were being foolish. The human didn't want them. She always thought she was better than the rest, that her powers made her more valuable, and perhaps they did. But, Wren knew her place was beside her leader. Her place had always been there, no matter whom he might've sent her to protect.

It was done. The three she considered family remained in one line, and she took a step backwards. She rasped out, "So be it."

"Wren—"

She'd been about to turn and leave, but she stopped at Gavin's words. She looked back. He added, his eyes looking bleak, "Be safe. Fast travels."

Her entire body was tense, but she forced her head to nod. "To you, too." She hesitated, then added, "Brother." She looked to Tracey, who had a tear in her eye. Wren bowed her head to her, saying, "Sister, too."

Sister.

Tracey closed her eyes, feeling the acknowledgement for what it was. Their relationship was done. Sister. Not lover. She murmured back, "To you, too. Sister."

But it didn't matter. Wren was gone.

13

ROANE

The wolves moved underneath them.

There was a path in the valley where they walked two by two in a line. They were in their human form, but there were others that panned out to the side. They melted among the trees and mountainside. Those were in their wolf form and as they moved past the trees where they were perched, their bows and arrows already readied and aimed, they weren't sniffing for vampires above them. They were sniffing for the Christane wolves.

Lucas glanced over to Bastion, who was in the tree next to him. They'd been in position for two days now. His army and Christian's were ahead of them. They were still trekking toward the Mori territories. Lucas and Bastion would catch up. They'd have to, and Roane had started to worry. He wasn't sure if they dared stay any longer, hoping for a glimpse of their enemy from behind. It was the last morning they held back. He'd been about to suggest covering the fire and catching up to their group, when they heard the first scout behind them.

They turned, and a wolf was there.

The wolf hadn't expected to find vampires. He recoiled immediately. He started to dash back to his allies, but Bastion and Roane moved as if one unit. Both leapt for the wolf. Bastion came from the left side. Roane was on the right and as the wolf turned back, prepared to meet their onslaught head-on, Roane didn't let a battle ensue. He grabbed both sides of the head, rooted his feet in the ground and ripped it right off. As it came clear off, Bastion grabbed the body and threw it into the fire.

They had to move fast after that.

The body and head were both destroyed in the flames, but they needed to cover up the smell so Bastion gathered sage and dumped it on the fire. When it wasn't enough, he dumped more. Roane knew they needed to leave if they were going to get in position before the rest of their enemy showed, so they lit the entire camp on fire. It would spread far and wide and leave no trace of a wolf at all.

A day later, as they were still moving to meet the oncoming army, the skies split open and down-poured. The fire would be doused. Lucas hoped there'd be no remnant of the wolf at all, and now, watching as the enemy wolves passed them, he knew they hadn't found any body. Word would spread once they did.

He waited, frozen in place against the tree, as the last of the wolves passed by. Once they moved along, he and Bastion still waited half a day. It was nearing the time when they needed to jump back to the ground and start following behind, but Lucas didn't move from his position. There was no reason to wait. They had sentries trailing behind, just like their own group, and those had already gone beneath them, but Lucas didn't emerge from his hidden spot.

He knew Bastion was waiting. He would follow his leader's movement.

Roane still waited.

Then, he shook his head. He was wasting time. His hand relaxed around the bow's string where his arrow was notched and ready, but he sensed their presence. He didn't hear them, see them, or smell them. They were like him, almost invisible to the senses, but he felt them.

Looking down, moving as if they were ghosts, was another army. They were vampires, like him, but they were dressed in black ninja-style robes. Some had their hoods pulled low over their heads with a gold lining around them. Others had their hoods back and their ears were adorned with gold chains. Roane knew of only one army that had worn similar gold colors like these—the Romah Family.

He looked over and met Bastion's gaze.

They were severely outnumbered, and this army was the oldest and therefore the strongest there was. He hadn't realized how many wolves Mother Wolf would send, but as the Romah Army kept going past them, and they had to wait up there another entire day, he knew his army with Christian's would be overpowered. They didn't have enough. They'd only be able to contend against them if they had Davy at her fullest strength.

"Roane."

He whipped his gaze to Bastion's. The silent thought sent to him could've been picked up by another, but he saw Bastion's gaze was trained on the ground.

A foreboding sense began to fill him and it increased as his gaze turned to see what Bastion was riveted by.

There, in the middle of five Goliath-sized wolves and four Romah guards in full armor, was a woman.

He knew who she was.

This was Mother Wolf, the one that Christian told him about. She was stunning. Black hair fell free and loose past her shoulders. She wore a blue and silver robe. The colors were striking, matching the air of strength she was emanating. Her eyes were dark. Her lips were bright red, curved into a half smile, and her head was raised in a confident and authoritative manner, but that wasn't all that clung to her—magic. He felt it in the air. Older magic that he never felt was in the air, and as they progressed below them without sensing their presence, Roane was surprised.

If anyone would've felt him, it would've been her, but it hadn't happened. They waited another half day before dropping back down to the ground. Once they did, both vampires groaned from the impact. Their legs had hardened into stone from the lack of movement. Both had gone without blood for days. There was no point to talk. Both needed sustenance if they were going to get around the army and back to theirs. Christian would need to know Mother Wolf was with the army, and she was protected by Romah vampires, but hearing a leaf stepped on in the distance, Roane lifted his head up and smelled the air. It was deer—that meant blood for them.

Both vampires took off and were on the deer within moments. Both fed because both knew their days ahead would be grim.

————

DAVY

ALL RIGHT.

I had to admit to myself that the idea of going alone was ambitious and honorable. It also sucked. I was hungry. My feet were bleeding. My back was sore, and my hands were almost frozen. The first leg of the trip had been glorious. I used my Immortal speed and zipped over any cliff that needed an extra boost to cover. My head had been high and my shoulders were firm. That lasted a day. I was on day four and because I was doing all this the 'human' way, I had an entire mountain still to cover. I didn't know why I'd been so eager to blast us so far away with my Immortal powers before, but like Gavin said—we'd been safe.

Oh yes.

We were safe. We'd been four mountains over safe. I was cursing myself, just like I'd been the last day, when I heard a sound that I didn't think I'd hear again.

"You doofus! We need that to burn the Mary Jane."

Humans.

Glorious, doofus-saying, Mary-Jane smoking, humans.

I almost doubled over in relief. The mere sound of that voice slammed an old sense of reality back into me, one where I had been human, somewhat normal, and I hadn't been interrogated, tortured, wounded, or hunted by a supernatural being, or an entire army of supernatural beings.

I was so overwhelmed that I was frozen in place as two guys stumbled past the clearing and onto the same path that I was on.

I was there, standing with my hand wrapped around a walking stick, and my eyes so damn wide a flying saucer could've entered them. I knew I must've been a sight. I'd alternated between shivering and sweating over the last day and a half. I still didn't want to use any more of The Immortal powers than necessary, and because I wasn't expecting to find anyone so close to me, I hadn't resurrected the cloaking spell. I was still stunned. I hadn't even thought about making myself invisible.

These two guys, one was tall and lanky, with a bright green rain jacket and glasses on his face, and the other was an inch shorter and pudgier, wearing a matching jacket, stared at me. They both had hiking boots and had large hiking bags strapped to their backs. They were dumbfounded.

Then, one broke out, a wide smile appearing, "Hey! Are you a hallucination?"

The taller one frowned and smacked the shorter on the back of his head. "If we're both seeing her, I doubt it." He paused, his frown deepened, and he took his glasses off. After cleaning them, he put them back on and leaned forward. "Nope. She's still there."

"Hey!" The shorter one pumped his hand in the air. "What's your name? Do you speak English? I'm Spencer."

"Of course she speaks English," the taller one muttered, but stopped and scratched behind his ear. "Wait. She might not."

At the same time, Spencer twisted around and muttered to him, without moving his lips, "You don't know that. This place has some strange folks in it. She could be from some native tribe or something."

"She's wearing jeans."

"Oh yeah." Spencer nodded to himself, his smile brightening even more. "What's your name?" He jerked a thumb over his shoulder. "This is Cal. We're here on holiday. We're hiking through these parts before heading back to the States. Figured this was a trip of a lifetime. We were nearby in Brunsby on a semester visa, but that's done for in a week. You on holiday, too? Wait." He glanced around, narrowing his eyes and pursing his lips in concentration. "Where's your group? You're not alone, are you?"

This was absurd. Both were from America, and both were high. A laugh started deep in my throat and before long, it doubled in volume. I couldn't contain it. They were hiking. They were on holiday. They thought I was a student.

I was so very far from just a student.

Drifting closer, warming to me from my laughter, the taller one chuckled, too. "I know we're a sight. We got separated from our group yesterday. We haven't washed or eaten anything except a little marijuana that Spencer had left over. And side note, if that's all you have to eat, don't do it. The munchies are making me go crazy. Spencer won't let me eat any of our food. Rainforest tree bark started to look a lot more appetizing than the pine trees back home. Say," his eyes focused on me again, "You haven't seen any other U.S. students, have you?"

No, no. Just vampires. That was all.

My shoulders were still shaking, and I shook my head back

and forth. I was trying to form a coherent word, but the hilarity of the situation was still hitting me. A few tears leaked from my eyes, and my cheeks were starting to ache from the laughter.

"What's your name?" Spencer's lips were still curved up, but any slight chuckle he might've let out had dwindled. The bright smile he had was no longer. It lessened and a look of alarm was starting to enter his gaze. "You haven't said yet."

"Da—" I was Davy. The nickname of Davy didn't pertain to me anymore. It hadn't for so long, since my first torture session, but I heard myself saying, "Davy," to these two strangers. I wanted to be Davy again, even if it was for a brief moment in time. I could be that girl with no big responsibilities, where I only had to worry about being empathic. I suddenly missed that girl a whole ton.

"Davy." Spencer pumped his head up and down, his lips tugging into a smile again. "That's an awesome name."

The taller one glanced up to the darkening sky. "Well. I hate to admit it, but I think we're going to be lost for another day. It's going to be nighttime soon."

Spencer looked pained. He repeated the earlier question again. "You haven't seen any other Americans, have you?"

I shook my head, growing somber. They were lost and I had one last mountain to cross before being back in Mori territory. I could feel their magic. It was growing more and more the closer I got. I also knew that I didn't have long before the others caught up to me, whoever it was that was coming after me. Gavin. Gregory. Tracey. Any of those three or none of them. I didn't figure Wren would come. Seeing that these guys were looking around to put their bags down, I spoke up, "Uh."

They stopped and looked at me.

I gulped suddenly. What was I doing? I should send them on their way, but I said instead, "There's still some light, and it was a full moon last night. It'll be one again tonight. We can keep going."

"You know where you're going?"

The taller one asked that. I forgot his name.

"Cal," the shorter one said, "I don't know."

Cal was the tall one. Spencer was the shorter guy. C and S. I nodded to myself. That was how I'd remember their names.

Cal was saying, gesturing to me, ". . . I think we should. She knows where she's going, or she looks like she knows. Let's go with her, and maybe we'll find our group."

I cleared my throat, drawing their attention. "I'm headed over that mountain behind you. I-uh—I have a friend over there. I need to get to her."

Spencer frowned at where I pointed and he scratched behind his ear. "I'm pretty sure that's where we came from over the last two days."

Cal's head bobbed up and down. "Hey, yeah. I think you're right. Wait." He twisted around to the mountain I just came from. "Fuck. I have no clue. They all look the same."

"Well." Spencer grimaced, his hand falling back to his side. "Let's just go with her."

"You can't." I corrected, "I mean, not all the way. My friend—there's dangerous people where I'm going. You can come with me part of the way, but not all the way."

"Oh." Both gave me alarming looks.

I didn't want to go alone anymore, but they couldn't go all the way with me. The Mori would kill them, if they hadn't already killed their group. But if they went alone—I didn't know if that was safe either. My allies and I were the only ones I knew that wouldn't harm them. Whoever these guys were, whatever fucked-up kind of karma that put them in the middle of this war, I needed to protect them. Or I had to try, at least.

The decision was made then.

I nodded at them. "You should come with me, at least as far as its safe. If you find your group, I'll keep going it alone."

Cal cocked his head to the side. "What are you doing out here?"

Saving my potential ex-best friend.

Saving the world.

Saving myself.

None of those answers sufficed. I only said, "Just looking for a friend."

The small surprise both had when they first saw me was wearing off. I didn't know if it was my doom and gloom attitude that I couldn't seem to shake, or if the Mary Jane was wearing off. Either way, both seemed more wary of me than they had been in the beginning.

Or maybe they were just realizing the absolutely fucked-up situation they were in.

I was going with the latter, and with that cheerful thought, I started up the trail, and after a few moments of hesitation, they did as well.

14

My two new besties and I hiked most of the night. The full moon gave us enough light until we got to a large canopy of trees. No light got through so we were forced to camp out. Cal and Spencer had large hiking bags, and they came in handy. They had an extra blanket, and when they pulled out a tarp, and after securing it between two trees, I snuggled into their makeshift hammock. It was blissful.

Sleeping in the cave had been—well, I'd been out of it. I don't know if it was restful, but this was. I almost professed my love for these two lost hikers, but sleep overtook me, and it wasn't till morning when I woke again.

Once my eyelids opened, I felt The Immortal again.

It was amazing. It was fabulous. It was about-freaking-time!

I jerked to a sitting position. The blanket fell to my lap and I could feel everything. We were half a mile away from a river. I could sense the fish in there, all the berries on the way that we could eat. Beyond the river, was Mori territory. I thought it didn't start till after the mountain, but we were just on the precipice of it. The steep incline for the mountain started right behind the river, and as I realized that, alarm bells started ringing in my head. My brief moment of euphoria was snatched away.

I couldn't go over that river with these guys. We must've gone farther than I expected last night, and we discussed our plans before sleeping last night. We were supposed to trek around the last mountain, then they were going to head north where they thought their group was, and I was going to keep going east to where the Mori were.

"Morning!" Spencer held a hand up, bent over by the fire. He was stirring a pot over it. His hair was wet and he had a changed his clothing. Seeing my lingering gaze on his hair, he grinned and pointed to the top of his head. "I took a quick dip. There's a river half a mile thatta way." Twisting around, he pointed in the direction I hoped he wouldn't have. I'd been hoping he said there was a different river. I could've led them that way instead, but nope. He'd been closer to the Mori than I ever wanted him to be.

I took a beat and pushed the small panic aside, then I smelled coffee.

Wait—coffee? I sniffed the air, and scrambled out of the tarp. "Oh my God." I started for him.

Spencer's grin spread. There was an extra pan sitting at the bottom of his feet and he moved back. "Yep. Instant coffee." He lifted a spoon of it and poured it into a thermos he'd taken out of his bag. I couldn't even let him fill it. I grabbed it after the first scoop and guzzled it. "Oh hey." He laughed, taken aback by my quickness. He blinked a couple times. "You must've been out here longer than you thought, huh?"

I closed my eyes, savoring the taste of the coffee grounds. I stuck my nose into the cup and inhaled the aroma of it. My euphoria was back, and I held the thermos back to him, a dreamy smile on my face. "I declare it here and now. I love you."

"You love me?" he teased back, taking the cup from me.

"And I'll worship you forever if you have more in there I can drink."

"Ha!" He was already reaching for the pan. "I'll take you up on that. I got my heart crushed before going on this trip. Knowing one girl worships me does wonders for my ego." He poured three more scoops into the thermos before the spoon scraped the bottom of the pan. "Oh." He peered inside, and grimaced. "It's half full. Sorry about that."

He held it out to me, and I took it, sinking down to the ground beside him. Good God. Being The Immortal should've allowed me to make coffee out of nothing. I needed to work on that magic. Screw protecting vampires or Kates. I needed to look out for my caffeine needs first.

"Hey," he called out, turned behind us. "Did you bring more water? Davy loves coffee, apparently."

I glanced over my shoulder at the same time I heard shoes breaking a twig. Cal was coming back from the river. His hair was wet as well, and he had changed his clothes, too. Both guys were up and ready to go.

Fuck.

"Oh yeah?" Cal ran a hand through his hair, shaking some of the water out. A towel was thrown over his shoulder and he flipped up the end to dry his face. He lifted up his other hand, holding a bucket. "Good thing I brought extra. I figured we'd need it for the pans, too."

"Sweet ass." Spencer shifted around, still bent down, and took the water from him once he got to the fire. He pointed to the other pan he'd been stirring. "I splurged this morning. I made the grits."

"You did?" Cal grabbed his bag and sank down on the other side of the fire. He glanced at me. "Spencer is pulling out all the stops if he made the grits. We were saving it for a celebration day."

Spencer snorted. "Yeah, when we weren't lost anymore." He pointed to me with a wooden spoon. "And thanks to her, we won't be. Since she came from the west, and knows what's east of us, we're pretty sure where our group is. We won't be lost for long."

Aaaaand that was my cue. They couldn't go past the river.

"Hey, um." I lowered the coffee cup. "You know. We could wander north from here. We don't need to go over the river just yet."

"The fuck?"

Cal shared in Spencer's sentiment, frowning instantly. "Why?"

"I mean, we might've overshot our destination a bit. I mean," Fucking A. I was horrible at lying. I felt my cheeks growing red. "Well, I mean, I recognize that river."

The two guys shared a look. Both furrowed their eyebrows forward.

Spencer echoed my words, "You 'recognize' the river—"

"—that you haven't seen yet?" Cal finished for him.

I couldn't squirm under their gazes. "Yeah." I shrugged, glancing down at the cup on the ground. "How many rivers are there? And I recognize this area, too." I gestured to the trees around us. "We're closer than we realized. I think you guys need to head straight north." I paused a beat, swallowing over a knot in my throat. "And, you know, maybe steer clear of the river if possible?"

Shit. Shit. Shit.

I used to be so good at being evasive. Who would've known I'd be wishing for the days when I had kept so much secret?

The guys glanced at each other again before Cal cleared his throat. "We've not run across another river as large as that one, and I know we crossed a river the same size before, so I think we should stick to the original plan. Cross the river, go around the mountain, and split up on the other side."

"No," I cried out before clamping a hand over my mouth. Seriously. I would've sucked at espionage. "I mean." I scratched behind my ear. "I really don't think it's safe, you guys."

"But you're going over it, aren't you?" Spencer narrowed his eyes.

"Um." I averted mine.

Cal stood slowly, grabbing his bag. "I think we should stick to the original plan, like I just said."

"No." Spencer shook his head.

"Spencer," Cal started.

Spencer held a hand out to him, stopping him. His gaze was still firmly pinned on me. "What were you going to do?" Spencer asked me. "Were you going to double-back and cross then? Were you going to lead us somewhere else?"

Cal's frown deepened. His hand wrapped tighter around his bag. "You mean, like into a trap?"

Oh fuck.

At the *T* word, I knew I was done for. Suspicion jumped to both of them. Spencer stood and as he did, Cal moved back a step. Spencer went right with him. They were both regarding me like I'd stolen their pot.

"Come on, guys." I jumped to my feet, too.

"Yeah," Spencer shot back. "Come on, yourself."

"Tell the truth."

I was caught. I'd backed myself into a corner, and both weren't backing down.

"Use me."

Of course, The Immortal would pop up here. Nope. Not going to do it. I shoved that thought away.

"You're wasting time. Let me take over. I can get in their heads and make them do what you want."

"Nope." I shook my head.

Spencer and Cal saw the motion, and both of their eyebrows lifted.

Cal asked, "No what? What was that for?"

"Uh."

"Use me, Davy. This is ridiculous. You're being foolish. They're both humans."

"I'm human!" I shot back at her.

"No." She said it so calmly, so—I gulped—final. *"You're not and you know it. You're clinging to a past that's not with you anymore. You need to let go of your humanity."*

I scoffed in outrage. Let go of my humanity? She was being ridiculous.

Cal and Spencer heard the sound I made and the suspicion was turning toward doubt, like I'd grown two heads and they didn't know what to make of me. Spencer checked his pocket and pulled out a baggie. He was checking if the pot was still there. Reassured it was, he put it back, and his eyebrows bunched together even more.

"Davy. You're indulging these two humans. You don't have time to be kind. Let me take over. They'll go to safety, and we can be back in the Mori camp."

"Why do you even want to go back there?"

She was silent.

I almost laughed out loud. Of course, she was silent now. The witches had separated us enough where I couldn't read her thoughts, but she knew my every wish, thought, and feeling. It wasn't fair.

But then I felt a growl coming from inside of me. It was from the farthest part of me, deeper than my consciousness had ever been in touch with. It was her. I angered her.

"Witch," I thought.

Her anger doubled. It grew in volume and strength.

That was why she wanted to go back. *"You want vengeance?"* I asked her.

"No. You want vengeance. I am you. You are me. We are as one. Don't fool yourself into pretending you're the 'good' one. You want to taste their blood every bit as I do. That's why we're going back, Davy. We're not going for your traitorous friend. It's time you were honest with yourself, just like how these two hikers came to be in the first place."

"*What?*" I snarled at her, whipping my head to the side as if I could see her.

I sensed Cal and Spencer's growing caution, but for once I was in sync with The Immortal. They were human. Lying to them could be easily done. I had a more important fight to deal with now.

"*Tell me!*" I yelled at her.

There was nothing. Just silence. She was there. I felt her, but she was pouting. No—that wasn't right. She was waiting.

"*What are you waiting for? Tell me the truth.*"

Fury and impatience ebbed into resignation. The first two emotions slid away like a wall inside of me, opening up to the back room where she was. I felt her honesty then, and she said, "*It was you, Davy.*"

"*Me what?*"

"*You brought them here.*"

I didn't respond. I couldn't. That was preposterous. But I couldn't argue with her, because as soon as she said those words, I felt it inside of myself. She was right. I backtracked in my memory, looping back over the last two days. I was walking through the woods. I was tired, hungry, alone—there. I felt the instant I did it. I had stepped the wrong way on a rock and my foot went one way while my ankle went the other. I cried out, grabbed onto my ankle, and I wished for someone else in that split second to come. I wanted to be normal, not in that place where I was traipsing back to vampire territories.

I wanted someone that reminded me of my humanity, where I was normal again.

The Immortal reached out for me. As I mended my own ankle, she found a group of hikers. She picked up two and brought them so they were right in my path. They didn't even know it themselves, but I made them get lost. Their group wasn't even in this same area. They'd been in another country.

I had done that.

The Immortal did it on a whim.

I gaped at them now, feeling the guilt coursing through me. I choked out, "I am so sorry."

"You're sorry?" Spencer echoed me again. "For what?"

"I did this."

They shared another look, and both edged back one more step. Spencer asked, "Did what?"

"I brought you here." And I had to take them back, but I didn't know how.

"What do you mean, you brought us here?" Cal spoke this time.

I couldn't explain. I shook my head. "Come on." I grabbed my bag, turning toward the river. "When we get there, I'll fix it. I'll have to, somehow."

"Not to be mean, but you're sounding like a nutcase."

Cal nodded in agreement. "I second that. You're not making any sense."

"Let's go." I pointed ahead. "When we get to the river, I'll explain everything." Regret flared up. "I owe you that much, at least."

"You owe us?"

I wasn't listening anymore. I started for the river, and the other two scrambled to get all their stuff together. I should've helped, but I used the extra time to try to send them back. Once they were ready and walking behind me, I knew it was going to be harder than I imagined. The entire trek to the river was in silence. I kept trying to send them back, but once I heard the sounds of the water rushing ahead of us, I had to admit the truth. I had little to no control over my powers again. Getting both of them back to their group, an entire country over, was beyond my capabilities. The only way I could do it was if it was on a whim, just how I brought them here in the first place. I needed to wish both of them back there, and the closer we drew to the water, I kept trying. Nothing happened. They were still with me.

I was frustrated, and I had no idea what to do now. They couldn't go into Mori territory with me. I never looked at the river. I knew we were there. I'd have to cross it and they couldn't, and I was gearing myself up for a fight when I turned around and looked up at them.

They weren't looking at me.

Both of them were frozen in place, their eyes wide and fixed on a spot behind me.

"Whoa," Spencer said under his breath.

Cal closed his mouth, but a vein bulged out in his neck. Fear that I hadn't experienced since before Lucan took me blasted from him. I gasped, falling back from the intensity of it, and I felt Spencer's fear mixing with Cal's before I whirled around.

And, right there, standing on the other side of the river, was the reason.

Three Mori vampires stared back at me.

15

Three things happened at the same time.

The Mori lunged for us, leaping the river in one bound. Cal and Spencer wet their pants. And I flung my arms out at the same time a scream ripped from my throat. With it and the motion of my arms, two spells burst from me at once. One swept behind, picking up Cal and Spencer and carrying them far back to where it was safe. The other came from the scream, and it slammed the three vampires backwards. They fell the same distance that I threw Cal and Spencer, and both groups landed at the same time.

Cal and Spencer had to scramble back to their feet, but they stayed back.

The vampires did neither. As soon as they touched down on ground, their feet firmly planted in place, all three launched at me once again.

I was ready.

My arms swept forward, pulling the same power I cast Cal and Spencer backwards, I propelled it forward. It hit the vampires back once again, but they fought this time. They were prepared for my onslaught and magic sparked from one of them, breaking my spell in half. It still moved them back, but not far enough.

They were too quick and too powerful.

They were on me within seconds, and I could only stare at them as they leapt over the river. They were in the air, and their fangs were out. Their mouths were open, and they'd be on me—then they were shoved back once more, but not by me. I didn't have a spell ready to throw back.

I had a second's warning as a deep roar sounded from behind me, before three bodies leapt over me, meeting the Mori vampires in the air.

Gregory, Gavin, and Tracey each grabbed a Mori, and all three pairs crashed to the ground in a wrestling fervor.

"Whoa," one of the guys muttered behind me.

I didn't glance back. I couldn't look away from the others. If there was an opening, I had to help. And, as if reading my mind, Gavin flipped his Mori over his head. The other vampire fell to the ground, not far from me. I ran over, my hand in the air and a spell ready to cast when the Mori was back on his feet. He was back in the air, hitting at Gavin. The punch was blocked, but the Mori was back in the air, his knees bent toward his chest and his feet ready. He slammed into Gavin, this time on the top as the two were on the ground. After that, everything began to blur. The vampires were too fast.

I recognized Tracey's growl and whipped to where they were. She and her opponent were close to Cal and Spencer, too close. Any second, they would be hit or used as a hostage.

I ran for them and yelled at the same time, "Get back."

They both jerked backwards, eyes wide, faces pale, and beads of sweat on both of their foreheads. Spencer pointed to Tracey, who heard my voice and kicked her Mori in the opposite direction. She stopped once and looked to me. Our gazes caught, and I nodded at her. Her eyes narrowed, and her fangs showed, then she turned and leapt in the air, landing on her Mori.

"Who are they?" Spencer grabbed my arm.

Cal surged to my other side. "Yeah. Were those fangs on that chick?"

I couldn't answer. I didn't know what to say, not yet anyway.

"Davy."

I shrugged off Spencer's hold and said to him, "When this is done. I'll tell you everything when this is done."

"When the crazy, freakish fighters are done fighting?" he shot back.

Cal frowned at Spencer, but didn't say anything against him. His Adam's apple bobbed up and down as he surveyed the battles once again.

"Davy!" Spencer's hand wasn't on my arm anymore, but he stepped close. His presence was demanding answers.

"When it's safe," I hissed at him.

"We should be running for our lives, not waiting to see who wins."

Cal added, "Let's go. They're all freaks."

"Sounds good to me."

Before they could leave, I grabbed both of their arms, and because I knew there'd be no words to explain everything, I showed them. Using The Immortal's power, I slipped into their minds. Okay. When I say that I slipped, it was more like I burst through their door and charged my way in. I showed them everything using my memories, of when I first became an empath, of when I lit a vampire on fire, how I enjoyed watching him burn, when I went to college and tried to be normal. They were there when I first met Roane, my first college date that Roane ended coming along with, how I kissed him to distract him, later when we kissed more in a professor's office, and the first time I realized I was The Immortal. After that, the memories were coming in quick spurts and all at once. I introduced them to Brown, to Kates, to the werewolf, to who Jacith is supposed to be, to Pippa, and lastly they were shown my time in the cage. They were there when I was tortured by the witches, and again when we escaped. The last memory they were shown was when I stumbled upon them in the forest.

I released their arms before anything else could slip through. I didn't want them to hear the conversation I had with The Immortal and how I learned it was my fault they were pulled from their group.

"Whoa. Holy—" That was all Spencer got out before he ran a few feet away and bent over, throwing up.

Cal didn't look too far from the same. He raised his arm and pressed it over his mouth, but his face turned a slight shade of green.

"You going to throw up, too?"

He started to shake his head, but as he did, his eyes bulged out, his cheeks puffed up, and his entire top half of his body lurched upward. He sprinted next to Spencer, and the two were throwing up in sync.

I sighed. Maybe I shouldn't have done that.

"Friends of yours?" Gavin was behind me. He was sweating, bloody, and his chest was heaving up and down.

I grinned, though I didn't feel it. "Apparently, I'm not so in control of my powers as I used to be."

He frowned at me. "Were you ever?"

I shrugged. "I thought I was better."

A deep and ferocious roar came from behind us and we looked over, just in time, as Gregory stopped, grabbed the wounded Mori in front of him on both sides of his head, and he twisted the head completely off. The body fell back to the ground with a thud, but Gregory wasn't done. Tracey yelled at him as she lit her Mori on fire. She tossed the lighter to the Goliath-sized vampire, and Gregory lit the head on fire instantly. He dropped it on the ground as he lit the rest of the body on fire, too.

Both of them, Gregory and Tracey, looked at where Gavin had left his Mori on the ground.

He hadn't burned the body, but it wasn't needed. The body had been pulled apart, literally. Arms, fingers, legs, parts of its stomach and chest were scattered all around the beach.

Gavin remarked, "I was mad."

Gregory grunted. "Got that."

Tracey didn't reply, but she began to gather the body parts. Gregory did the same until every part of the Mori were thrown in one burning pile. By that time, Cal and Spencer were done throwing up and we gathered around the fire. It wasn't enough. The flame should've been higher, and without thinking, I held my hands out and began to mutter a spell. The fire began to grow.

"Who-a," someone muttered.

I didn't care. Every last part of them had to become ash and even then, the pile of ashes would need to be spread all over. I didn't know the Mori lore and how to kill them, but I wasn't taking a chance. I kept chanting and the flames doubled in size. A white twinge started to grow on the outskirts of the fire, but that was from The Immortal. I couldn't see myself, but I knew my eyes had changed to The Immortal white. I kept them lowered so no one could see them until the Mori were completely gone. Then, as the last piece of ash fell to the pile, I raised my hands and made a motion to the left. A strong gust of wind swept through the clearing where we were and picked up the ashes. I sent them off, directing where I wanted them spread, and once I was content, knowing they would never return and never come back to life, I stopped.

I could still feel The Immortal in my blood. She was on an adrenaline high, like she was intoxicated. I was buzzing, but I still waited until an ounce of calmness settled over me. Cal and Spencer had come up behind us, and I turned to look at Tracey, so my back was to the hikers.

I asked in my head, "Are my eyes still white?"

She answered back, "You're fine."

Reassured, I looked back over the group.

All of them were staring at me with mixed emotions. Cal and Spencer looked like they were crapping their pants, while Gavin was closed off. I felt his anger. It was just underneath the surface. He was keeping it contained until the humans were dealt with. Gregory and Tracey had similar reactions. I felt the awe in both, but they were also resigned. They were waiting for Gavin and me to fight, then to keep on with whatever we decided.

I grinned slightly, but felt regret, too. "I shouldn't have left."

That was all Gavin needed. He erupted, "YOU THINK?"

"AGH!"

Cal and Spencer fell back again, their fear spiking once again.

I took a breath and held a hand out to Gavin. "You didn't need to come."

He bristled back. "You had three Mori about to rip your spine out, and you're telling me we didn't have to come?"

Tracey said quietly, "You knew we would."

"You cast a sleeping spell over us."

I stiffened, hearing the accusation coming from Gregory. I started, "I'm sorry—"

"Wren is alone," Gavin interrupted. His eyes were narrowed to slits, and his jaw clenched. "She continued to Roane."

"I didn't ask you to come with me," I argued back. My blood started to pump again. "I came here on my own."

"To do what?"

His words felt like a slap in the face. I winced. "To save Kates."

"You're lying to them."

I closed my eyes. This is not the time.

"Too bad," The Immortal snarled at me. *"You're going to have let me talk. You have to stop lying to them."*

"Davy?"

I shook my head at Gavin, turning half away from them.

"They can smell your lies."

I grew still, hearing her answer. It was simple and given to me so calmly. I asked, *"What?"*

"If you want to be rid of them, stop lying. Believe your truth. They'll smell that instead and will do what you want."

"I want them to be safe."

"So send them to safety."

I frowned. *"What are you talking about?"*

"It'll cost you, but it'll be worth it. Send them back to Roane. They'll be safe with him. They won't be with you."

"I don't have enough strength."

She laughed at me. *"You do. You've been restoring it since you woke. You just have to tap into it."*

"What have I been using since I woke?"

"You have a back channel of power. It's all stored up. It's where I'm speaking to you from. You are me. I am you. I am this back section of power. Open up your mind and let me in."

"I . . . can't . . ." I was going to say I didn't know how to do that, but it wasn't true. I did. It was the same way I had gotten into Cal and Spencer's minds. I had my own door closed off to myself. I just needed to find it and burst through it, but thinking about it, I hesitated.

"Come on, Davy," she started to chide.

"Stop it!" I screamed back, the words coming from my throat as well. My heart was pounding. I could feel her wanting to get in. That was when I realized it—that door wasn't keeping me out, it was keeping her in. It was keeping The Immortal from completely taking over me.

"Davy?"

I didn't know who said my name, but I looked to Gavin. Seeing concern and his anger lessening, I almost whimpered. "It's The Immortal. She's trying to take over."

A wave of alarm swept over all of them.

Gavin froze in place and asked, his voice dipping low, *"What did you say?"*

ROANE

ROANE AND BASTION had been tailing the Romah army for three days. They were trying to go around them, moving higher on the mountains to give the entire army a wide berth and their progress was painstakingly slow. More than once they were almost discovered and each time, Roane worried about what they'd have to do if that happened. No matter the consequences, whoever discovered them would have to be murdered. If the body was found, that could start a war before he was ready for it. The only plan he had was one he didn't want to do. It put them at risk as well, but so far, he hadn't needed to put it into play.

So far.

They were high up, at the highest line of trees on the mountainside. If they broke free from their cover, they'd be seen from below and every time there was a clearing, both had to drop to the ground and crawl across, going as fast as possible.

They weren't moving as fast as Roane wanted. They needed to get ahead, but the break hadn't come for them. The Romah army didn't rest. They slept in shifts. While some would walk, the others would sleep on some makeshift carts. The awake ones would pull them ahead, then switch places and progress even further. The weight of their comrades slowed them down, but not enough.

They were being assisted with magic. Roane felt it in the air. It was covering all of them and it was a problem. It'd be a problem in the future as well. He wasn't sure where the magic came from, but he knew it was there and he knew it was protecting and helping them to go at an unnaturally faster pace.

He and Bastion were running, sprinting from tree to tree, when suddenly they felt a shift in the air. Both vampires froze as one, looking like statues now.

"*Do you see anything?*" he asked Bastion in his head.

Bastion leaned forward and his nostrils flared. He closed his eyes and smelled the air, like a wolf would do. Roane knew the answer was nothing before Bastion thought to him, "*No. Whoever it is, is beyond the next ridge.*"

He edged farther. Instead of their break-neck speed, he and Bastion snuck ahead, keeping to the trees for camouflage. They were going at a snail's pace now. He wanted to see whoever or whatever it was before they saw them, and as they cleared the hill, both froze in place. A wolf scout was thirty feet in front of them, resting against a tree. Its head was down with closed eyes, and the wolf panted for a moment. In and out. It sounded like it was struggling for breath, but that was from the speed the group was traveling at. Even the wolves were tired.

Roane thought to Bastion, "*Hold. The wolf will move forward.*"

Bastion didn't move an inch. "*The wolf will keep moving ahead of us. We're stuck behind him.*"

Roane grimaced. There was no way around it. If the wolf didn't move down, but kept going straight ahead of them, he knew Bastion was right. A confrontation was imminent. He was about to signal Bastion to move around when a wolf's howl filled the air. The wolf in front of them immediately responded. His eyes opened and his head fell back. A long howl ripped from deep in its throat and the two vampires shared a look. From the intensity of closeness of this howl, both knew they wouldn't forget the sound. It was haunting, sounding from a deep sorrow.

As the wolf finished, he lumbered forward. His head went back down, and he took two quick breaths before bounding ahead.

"*He's keeping to the same path.*"

Roane nodded, knowing what Bastion meant. They had to kill the wolf. Giving him the signal, Bastion took off to the left as Roane sprinted forward. Instead of going upward, Bastion would circle around the wolf, coming from below. The wolf would sense

Roane's presence and prepare for an attack, assuming a second opponent, if there were one, would circle up and out of the army's territory.

That would be his death then.

But before Bastion could go far, the wolf ripped through the foliage, coming straight at them. Roane felt the wolf's surprise. He had doubled back, not knowing what he'd find, and before he could call for help, both of them were on the wolf.

As Roane impaled the wolf, drawing his sword and shoving it deep into his enemy's chest, a sadness filled him. He had come to know that creatures such as this one followed orders. That was their only reason for its death. If he had been born or turned by the Christane bloodline, his blood wouldn't have been spilled on the ground that morning. But this wolf hadn't been and because of that one fact, Roane reached in and yanked out its heart.

The sword harmed him, but it wouldn't kill him. His own touch delivered that fatal blow and as he stood there, with the heart still beating in his grasp, he said a small prayer honoring its death. Bastion was beside him, and without saying a word, both knew what had to be done. One by one, they took the heart and spread its blood all over them. It would aid in their travels and they could move at a faster rate. They would smell as one of their enemy's own, which would turn an invisible eye to them. The wolves wouldn't be looking at their own.

Once they were done, both completely covered in its blood, Roane put the heart back. It was his way of paying homage to the wolf, giving back its heart. After that, knowing they only had limited time before they realized one of their own was dead, Roane and Bastion sprinted ahead. This time, they could move farther down the hill. They didn't need to travel along the highest tip of the ridge. The wolves were scouting the mountains, and their noses would allow them camouflage.

It was time they made up their lost time.

As they ran forward, weaving around trees and giving every

wolf ahead of them a wide berth, Roane glanced down. The army had changed their positioning. The Mother Wolf was in the middle of her men, along with Romah guards behind her.

They were nearing his army. They wouldn't risk leaving their leader in the back. It was too vulnerable of a position. She was more guarded this way and for a brief second, Roane knew he could fly down and rip her heart out, as he had one of her brethren just now. It would be a suicide killing, but for the briefest of moments, he considered it. It would be a harsh blow to this army, one that could assist in their victory, but Bastion reached back and grabbed Roane. He pulled him forward with him, and as he did, the moment was gone.

Roane knew he'd have to find an opening later. He couldn't regret that moment.

16

R oane and Bastion were nearing their camp. Roane could sense his own men and knowing it was safer, they began killing the wolves and any Romah guards they came upon as they made their way out of enemy territory, closing the gap into their own. They still needed to cover twenty miles, but once they came upon the last of the Romah scouts, and let their bodies fall to the ground behind them, they slowed their pace. They still kept to a brisk speed, but this was their resting time. Once they hit their encampment, he knew their army would have to pick up its own speed to stay ahead of their enemy.

They cleared a tree line, and he sensed an attack from behind. Roane twisted around, his sword drawn before he realized the body hurdling at him was a Christane wolf.

"Halt!" a voice cried out in a commanding tone.

The wolf couldn't, but Roane tucked his sword down and ducked, evading the wolf's attack. It hit the ground where he had been standing, but rolled once and was immediately on its feet and rounding to attack again.

"Stop." Roane held a hand out, showing his Hunter hand symbol. "I'm one of yours."

"It's the Hunter." The same voice from before materialized out of a foliage. It was Christian. He lifted his head, sniffing the air, and he frowned at Roane. "You reek."

"Your rival's blood." As he spoke, Roane signaled to Bastion to keep ahead. Once the other vampire took off, with instructions to ready the rest of their men to move forward at a faster rate, Roane fell in step with Christian. The other wolf moved back to its hidden post, ready to attack anyone else that followed them. Roane said, "It camouflaged us the last few miles. I sent Bastion ahead. The group needs to go faster."

"Roane—"

"They're moving faster than us. Your Mother Wolf is in the middle of their group. She's protected by her wolves and Romah vampires. We need to get ahead and get Davy on our side if we're going to stand a chance. Or—"

"Roane—"

He ignored Christian, continuing to talk as they grew closer to the main camp. "And I couldn't find Jacith. He's not traveling with his family, but he's a sorcerer. I'm sure he'll be with them at the battle line."

"Lucas!"

"What?"

He twisted around, a fierce frown on his face. They had just cleared the last opening, leading to where the others had all congregated. Christian wanted to say something, and he stopped to listen, finally, but he felt one of his own coming toward him. He paused, distracted from whatever Christian was saying when he looked. It was one of his that shouldn't be there. He hadn't felt her for so long, since she was taken, and as he searched for her, or whoever it was, Christian's words broke through his concentration the same time he spotted her.

"—Wren is here."

She paused on her path. Vampires had stepped aside to let her pass, but she stopped, and her chest lifted. She took in a breath before she tucked her hands behind her, but he saw how they trembled. The usual defiance wasn't there. Instead, she was hesitant, and he sensed the guilt through their blood connection.

He asked her in his head, *"Why are you fearful of me?"*

Her eyes widened at his question and she swallowed, her eyes glancing to the side for a moment. Her head lowered, but then her shoulders rolled back and she lifted her eyes once more. As they found his, they were strong once again. Her normal flare was back, and she replied, *"Because I left them behind."*

Roane started for her. The relief at seeing her faded into alarm. She braced herself for him and as he drew abreast, he grabbed her arm and propelled her with him. There were no tents assembled, but Roane didn't say a word until he pulled her far enough from the group so no wolf could overhear. As soon as they moved out of earshot, he released her and asked in his head so no nearby vampire could eavesdrop on their thoughts as well, *"You left them? What do you mean you left them?"*

"She's safe. Davy is safe."

"You guys got free?"

"Yes." She didn't answer for a split second, then, *"Davy got us all free. I don't know how because she didn't have her magic, but then she did. She carried us twenty miles away."*

"Why aren't they with you?" But he knew, as soon as he asked. He answered for her, *"Because Davy went back, didn't she?"*

"She didn't get Kates out. Davy went back for her."

No. Roane knew that wasn't the truth. She wouldn't have gone for her traitorous best friend. That would be an added benefit, perhaps, but he knew the real reason Davy was going back. For Lucan. She wanted to kill his brother so he wouldn't have to. He looked to Wren. He kept his thoughts barred from her before he asked her now, *"How far?"*

"Five miles away. I can take you to her."

He nodded, though he knew the chances of catching up to Davy before she got to the Mori was low. Still. They had to try. He spoke out loud, "You'll show me on a map where you were and we'll go from there. We won't return to the same spot. Davy will be ahead of us. We have to try to intercept them."

"I will."

He started to return, but glanced back. He frowned. "Was there more?"

"I wanted to return to my leader's side."

He sensed her fear come back, and the guilt made sense then. She left Davy's side to return to his. Reaching out, he gave her arm a slight squeeze. "The others remained with her?"

Wren nodded, feeling her first wave of relief since they escaped the Mori. "Yes. Gavin, Gregory, and Tracey went to find her. Davy left us behind. She didn't want to endanger anyone."

For the first time in a long time, Roane allowed a half-grin to show on his face. "Of course she did." His hand squeezed her arm once again before dropping back to his side. "You came back. That will help us figure out where to intercept her. You did good, Wren, but rest as quick as you can. We need to proceed as soon as possible."

She nodded, and he left her behind to find Saren. He needed to know where Jacith was, and he had a hunch Davy's Immortal sister could help him with that information.

DAVY

THEIR GROUP VENTURED across the river and into Mori territory. If Davy hadn't seen the Mori vampires before, she would've known the instant she stepped from the water and onto land. She felt the magic all over. It was in the ground, the trees, even the rocks. The air had a shimmer of it even and she breathed it in, but got another shock. It was her magic. It bonded to her and she realized it must've been left from when she carried her group from Lucan's captivity. Enough magic must've burst out of her, that it was only now moving to the outskirts of their land.

Gavin noticed her reaction. "What is it?"

"I feel my magic."

"What do you mean?"

"It's like a rock that's thrown in water. It causes waves to emanate from it. My magic, what I used to get us out of here before, it was like that. Instead of a rock, though, it was like I dropped an entire mountain in the ocean."

Gavin turned back to look at the river. "And you didn't sense it on the other side?"

"Their lands are protected. They use magic anyway, and they want to keep what is theirs already. They have a barrier. It's why my magic won't extend over the river, and it's why I didn't sense the Mori vampires. Their essence was blocked because of the barrier."

"Oh whoa."

Davy glanced to the side, farther down the river where Cal and Spencer were crossing. Tracey was with them. She had a sturdy arm around both of them and carried them so the river's current didn't sweep them away. Spencer had just stepped down on the ground, and those words had been his reaction. He was human, but even he felt the magic, too.

A knot formed in her throat. They were going to be changed because of their presence among the Mori. She didn't know how, but she knew it wouldn't be for the better. They were humans and she had brought them into this war. After reuniting with Gavin, Gregory, and Tracey, they hadn't moved into the Mori land for a few days. They stayed, camping on their side of the river, while they decided their next move. After hearing that Wren went back to Lucas, Davy knew what would happen. He would use Wren's information about where they had been and he would try to intercept them before they got back to Lucan. She didn't want that to happen. Davy wanted to infiltrate the Mori, cloak herself, so she could kill Lucan herself. She wanted to save Lucas this demon. If he had to murder his own brother, she knew it would haunt him for the rest of his life. The closer she got to Lucan, the more her real desire grew. It wasn't just to retrieve Kates. It was more about enacting vengeance. Kates was fast becoming an after-thought, but it was one she needed to cling to. It would save her humanity, or that was how she was feeling. When she thought about Lucan, The Immortal grew in strength inside of her. When she remembered her best friend, the human side of her sparked alive again.

But she hadn't shared any of this with Gavin or the others. She just let them know there was a battle inside of her. The Immortal wanted to take over, but she was holding it at bay. They had been reassured it wouldn't happen, that she had a handle on it, but the longer they camped near the Mori, the more her blood lust for Lucan grew and the stronger The Immortal was becoming.

Finally, after waiting a few days where Davy wasn't able to send the two humans back to their group, they decided to keep going. She hoped at some point she could send them back, but now they were on Mori lands, she knew their death was imminent. Even if they stayed behind, they were smack in the middle of a vampire and werewolf war. They'd be dead by someone's hand, so it was voted on by everyone, and it was unanimous. Cal and Spencer were to be brought with them, and they'd remain protected by their group of three vampires and one Immortal that wasn't in control of anything anymore.

"Davy?"

She tore her gaze from Cal and Spencer. Gavin had been trying to talk to her. She blinked a few times, as if waking up. "What?"

He gave her a half-grin, seeing where her attention had been. "They'll be fine. We'll protect them. Don't worry."

He had no idea. A doomed feeling was in her stomach, and it was growing, but she only replied back, "Yeah. You're right."

But he wasn't right. She felt their death in her already. In fact, she felt all of their deaths. The only one who wouldn't die was her, but she wished for it because what was going to happen was much worse than death.

"Are we going?" He gestured ahead to a walking path that led through the trees.

"Yeah." She started forward, falling in line behind Gregory who had taken the lead. "Let's go."

Her head went back down, and she began chanting in her head. She was connecting to the magic she had left in the Mori land. It had been waiting for her return and it gathered inside of her now. As they progressed into the forest, she cast a cloaking spell over all of them.

She didn't need to worry about tiring out. It was the opposite here. The Immortal was so much stronger. She needed to use her energy, to try to keep *her* at bay. They wouldn't realize it, but as they made their way farther into the Mori lands, they were completely invisible to the magical breed of supernatural vampires. It wouldn't be until later, much later, that they would realize the cost of returning to enemy territory would have on them.

17

BROWN

The Bright witch chewed on her lip and wrung her hands together. Mavic had been helping her 'become one' with her inside magic. He explained, many times, if she could burrow deep inside of herself, she could release her family's power within herself. It sounded easy enough. Get one with thyself and pop that lock except it still hadn't happened. Every time he cast a spell that would help her become in tune with herself, something went awry. The first couple of times, his magic bounced off her and spread throughout the room. Objects that weren't supposed to be alive came alive. A couch began singing a One Direction song once. Mavic zapped the couch a.s.a.p., quicker than Brown wanted. She enjoyed the song, but when a lamp started doing the Whip and Nae song, complete with dancing, he cut off all those efforts.

The next few weeks were spent where he blasted her with magic. Instead of having her awaken inside, he was trying to do the deed himself. All that ended horribly too. His own magic cut back inside of himself and he ended with a nosebleed that could've filled a small pond. Brown felt bad after seeing that side effect. She could live with the dancing couches and lamps, but seeing her trainer in physical pain, she had to keep reminding herself of the end goal to stop from calling it quits.

Help Davy.

That was her reason to keep going. She had to help her friend, no matter how many nosebleeds Mavic endured. It wasn't until the last week where they finally made progress. He had her drink a concoction. When she asked what it was, he wouldn't tell her. He pushed the cup against her lips and growled, "Drink."

She did.

Davy's vampire boyfriend brought this guy to help her so she had to trust him. She closed her eyes and drank the bitter tasting liquid. It churned her stomach, making her feel nauseous, but Mavic clamped his hand over her mouth and began uttering words under his breath. He was spelling the liquid and she began to sputter, feeling it spark to life inside of her. Her body seized, wanting it out of her. Her stomach began to spasm, trying to push it all back up, but even when it hit her mouth again, ready to spew outwards, her lips wouldn't open. They'd been spelled shut. The liquid kept trying to break free, but nothing. Her mouth wouldn't open and a scream built up inside of her. It was like cement hitting cement. Pain sliced through her, then backed up and rammed through her over and over again. She was bleeding inside. She tasted it among the bile, but Mavic was undisturbed. His hand remained over her mouth, and his head went down. He kept the same chant until her body surrendered.

The liquid began to seep inside of her, merging with her body's organs and down to the cellular level. It was becoming one with her, and casting one last chant, Mavic backed up. He held his hand still in the air, but it wavered. He was ready to slam it against her mouth again if need be, but as he watched, he saw the transformation begin.

The spell was working how it should've. It was moving throughout the witch. It was a physical structure, therefore it couldn't be spelled from her like all the other magic he cast, but it could root out wherever her magic was locked up. It was supposed to find the location inside of her and it would help unlock it. He knew The Immortal had been able to do the same, but with The Immortal's power. His wasn't as strong, but if anything would help, this would, or he hoped. His choices of getting her magic unlocked were fast depleting.

Brown watched him as he watched her, but she was held immobile. She couldn't move, not during whatever was going on with her body still happening. She felt the change inside of her. The liquid found her core, and it settled there. It was her spiritual core, where her magic was, and she closed her eyes, suddenly knowing what was going to happen.

The magic he forced inside of her was going to do a full-on assault where her magic was, to open it up. She knew it was going to be painful, and she had a second to brace herself.

Then it began, and a scream erupted from deep inside of her, lifting her body in the air.

THE
BATTLES

18

LUCAN

He stared down at Kates's bloodied body. He had broken her so many times, mended her, and then broke her again. As it was now, she was done. He saw that she was at the edge. She had no will, no fight, nothing more.

He withdrew from the table that he tossed her onto it and grabbed a washcloth. Wiping at the blood left on his hands, he washed himself clean and glanced over when the door opened to the room.

Jiyama stood there, her eyes going to Kates's broken body first. An emotion akin to sympathy flashed in her gaze before she said, "Three of our men never returned from their mission. They're believed to be dead."

Davy...

His jaw hardened. "Did the Healers go out?"

She nodded, her head bowed to the ground. "Their essence was last sensed at the river. It is believed they died there."

He frowned, distracted for a moment by Jiyama's actions. She was acting like a demure little girl. He ground his teeth against each other before asking, "Why are you acting like this?"

She stiffened and her hands tucked under her long sleeves. "I feel remorse. I think."

"You think?"

She lifted her head then, and a pained expression was there. Her gaze trailed to Kates before she said, softly, "I've only felt wonder. I've wondered about life, about who Davy was, about the magic inside of her, about the world beyond these lands, about life as a human, but I have never felt this sensation inside of me." Her hand, fisted around her sleeve, lifted and pressed between her breasts. She kept it clutched tight to herself. "I have never wondered about the side of life, about right versus wrong, but this—" her hand left her chest and indicated Kates, who hadn't moved or made a sound. "I feel almost like crying. I've never experienced that emotion." She lifted haunted eyes to Lucan, her bottom lip falling open. "Why is that?"

Anger filled him, but he bit back a curse and moved to the vampiress. Cupping the side of her face, he made sure his tone was soft as well. "That just means you are evolving. That is all."

Her eyes traced back to Kates. "I feel a pit in my stomach. I have only felt the fullness of blood in there." Her eyebrows pinched together. "I do not like this emotion."

"It's because you've spent too much time near humans."

A brightness filled her eyes. She asked him, "It's because of them?"

He nodded, leaning forward to brush his lips over her forehead. "Yes. Right and wrong, guilt and sadness, those are all human emotions. You've spent too much time near them with Davy before and now this one." He moved, adjusting her so his back was to Kates. He was blocking Jiyama from looking at her, and he pressed another gentle kiss to the Mori vampire. "They are a unique species, wracked with silly emotions. It's like a cancer to them, one that they don't realize is something to be expunged. They almost worship these sensations."

Her hand lifted up and grabbed onto his arms. "They do?"

She was pressing her forehead tight to his lips. Her entire body was against his.

"They do. I didn't realize their 'humanity' could infect you."

"Humanity?"

"Hmm mmm." He nodded, clasping her to him still. "It's their sickness. I'm plagued with it too, but once I have The Immortal thread in me, I won't suffer from it anymore."

"You think Davy suffers this same sickness?" She pulled back, leaving enough space to look up at him.

Lucan paused, sensing there was more to her question other than curiosity. He frowned slightly, still holding her head in his hands. After a few beats, he asked, almost gruffly, "Why do you ask?"

Her hand fell to his chest, and she stepped to the side to see Kates again. "Davy said they were friends. If she is sick as well, I can't imagine what she would feel knowing what we have done to this human."

His frown deepened. "Why are you saying this, Jiyama?"

She stepped completely away from him. Her hands fell from his chest and balled into fists around her long sleeves once more. "The Immortal was good. I knew that as soon as I touched her. I don't know what this 'sickness' is that you're talking about, but it was different for Davy. I remember that. She was like honeyed blood. She was alluring to me. I had to go back and experience her again, but it wasn't her blood I wanted." A stricken wonder entered her gaze. "I wanted to give her my magic. I wanted to help her, and I haven't been able to get that out of my head. I keep thinking about our time with this one." She stepped forward and touched the table near Kates's leg. "I don't think she would be happy with what we did. She cared about this one. I knew that when I touched her. Lucan," she looked back to him. "I don't think we should have done what we did."

"No, Jiyama." He shook his head and moved once more so he

was between her and the table. His hands lifted to her head again and he cupped her cheeks. "You're sick. That's all this is."

"I don't understand the sickness, but I remember how I felt when I helped The Immortal—"

He cut her off, saying, "And that will be me soon. I will become The Immortal. Remember? You will be helping me again. You can experience the same feeling with me, too."

"You want to become a vampire once again."

"No. I'll have to stay as a human if I become The Immortal."

She shook her head. "The Immortal will only go to a female. That's what they said—" She broke off, her eyes wide and startled. She jerked backwards from his touch. "I—"

A deathly stillness came over Lucan. He cocked his head to the side and narrowed his eyes. "They said? Who is they?"

She took another step backwards.

He took the same step toward her. "Who have you been talking to, Jiyama?" His tone was so soft, eerily soft.

"The child."

"The child?" He stepped back, his thoughts whirling, but then it clicked. He took Talia's child with him. She had been given to a Mori family to be raised. It was decided that he would not raise her and he had forgotten about the child till then. Then, it began to click with what else Jiyama had said. "You've been to the child's home?"

She nodded. "I was curious, Lucan. I wanted to know more about The Immortal and about Davy. I was not used to this feeling, wanting to know but not having the answers given to me. The child is still human. I thought she could explain more to me."

A human child within close proximity and a female one at that. No. He had completely forgotten about the girl. She came from an Immortal thread-holder already. Once the thread would leave Davy, it wouldn't bounce to him. There hadn't been a male thread-holder, but he had been determined to become the first. No other human within close distance, it would have to go to him, but now he realized his mistake. He had planned to turn Kates when the witches told him Davy was close to losing the thread, but the child—it would've gone to the child then.

The family.

He was trying to remember whom the child had been given to. They were going to let her grow as a normal human until she got to the age she wanted to be at for eternity. He was recalling all of the meetings now. She hadn't been born a Mori. If she were turned, she wouldn't continue to grow as the Mori vampires did. There'd been so much debate about the child, they had been furious he brought the human into their lands in the first place, but then a woman fell in love with the girl. She volunteered to raise her, and the husband . . .

"Who took her in?" he muttered under his breath. His hand turned into a fist, and he rapped it against the table. "Who was that?"

His questions were spoken out loud before he realized how they sounded, and he felt Jiyama's withdrawal immediately. The air grew cold as she stepped away, a scowl instantly on her face.

"Jiyama." He reached for her. "It's not how it sounds—"

She clipped her head from side to side. "No." Her eyebrows bunched together again. The corners of her mouth dipped down even more. "I felt your intentions just now. You want to murder the child. That goes against the Mori. You must not touch a child. Ever."

His anger rolled into fury, but he kept it contained. He knew he was broadcasting his emotions. Jiyama was in tune with the earth and all sensations rolled together. She could feel his rage even though he was trying to keep it blanketed. She just hadn't sensed how much rage he had. He was still trying to keep it locked inside of him. As her eyes became hard and accusing, he knew he was failing.

He knew what he had to do then, but he wouldn't think about

it. If he did, she would know. He couldn't let himself experience that sadness, because he really did love her.

"Jiyama," he said quietly. "I need to thank you."

She paused, thrown from his change in demeanor. "Thank me?"

He nodded, tucking all his hostility aside. He reminded himself that he would become The Immortal. Davy was close. She had to be. No one else would be able to kill three Mori vampires, unless they came upon an army. All would happen as it should. He would find Davy, because she was coming for her friend. She would try to rescue Kates, and he would grab her then. He would use the child to distract her. Everything would work wonderfully, and as he let himself believe his thoughts, a peace settled inside of him.

Jiyama felt the peace, and she started to look more reassured.

He went to her, closing the distance between them. They were lovers and he held her face for the third time that day. He leaned down until his forehead rested against hers and he breathed out, "I would've completely forgotten about Talia's child, if you hadn't reminded me."

Her eyes widened, but before she could recoil—he snapped her neck.

He let her body fall to the floor, and he murmured, "And then all would've been in vain. So thank you, Jiyama, for you saved my plans after all." And then, knowing he would have to burn her body to kill her completely, he reached down and hoisted her up. He carried her to where he had kept Davy imprisoned and tossed her body onto the fire in the corner. No one would think to check this room. It was considered forbidden because it was used to hold captives, and they would never consider checking the ashes for any Mori essence.

Lighting the fire, he waited until Jiyama was burned beyond recognition, and then he left, knowing the fire would die down on its own.

He had an Immortal child to hunt down now, but once he stepped into the hallway, a Mori guard came rushing toward him. "Lucan." The guard stopped, his chest heaving. "There are two armies approaching our lands."

Lucas.

Lucan narrowed his eyes. "Who are they?"

"One is your brother, but the other army have their own magic." He stepped back and gestured down the hallway. "The Archon requests your presence."

The Archon was the Mori leader and Jiyama's father.

Lucan nodded and proceeded ahead of the guard, but this wasn't good.

This wasn't good at all.

19

"This is ridiculous."

Saren appeared next to Roane, who was perched in a tree and watching as five Benshire wolves were combing the trees a mile away. They were doing what he and the Christane wolves had already done. They arrived at the river three days earlier. On the other side were the Mori lands, but a protection spell was cast as soon as they tried to cross the water. Two wolves exploded in thin air and since then, no one ventured across. Because they couldn't move forward, Roane and the Christane wolves set up their camp and scouted their perimeter. They arrived three days ahead of the Benshire wolves and the Romah vampires. It was why Roane was in place and was disguised when the Benshire wolves would move underneath him.

He shot Saren a dirty look. "I'm trying to hide here."

She waved a hand and snapped her fingers. Immediately, Roane felt the difference. They were blanketed in place. It was like being on the inside of an invisible plastic bubble, but the plastic was rock solid. He asked, "What is this?"

"I shielded us. We can talk. They won't hear us, smell us, or see us."

"It's like a cloaking spell?"

"Cloaking is harder. This one was easier, takes less of my strength to keep it up, but if the wolves try to climb this tree, they'll know we're here."

"The plan is to sneak behind and kill them, one by one."

She nodded. "I'll wait until they move far enough ahead. We can both slip behind them."

His eyes narrowed. "You're going to help?"

She'd been absent for the last week of their trip. Once Wren arrived, Saren disappeared. Roane didn't know why and he wasn't the only one who realized it. Christian asked one night as well, but Roane couldn't tell him the reason. He had a feeling it had something to do with Davy, but he wasn't sure, and he didn't know if he even wanted to ask.

"Are you asking me why I've been gone?"

"I guess I am, yeah."

Two Benshire wolves were almost directly underneath them. Roane's instincts quieted him, but he knew the spell would protect them. Davy's magic was strong, and he knew Saren was connected to the same power. The other three wolves spread farther down. They were all in one line, a hundred yards between each of them. The other three wouldn't react fast enough. He could jump down and take care of both wolves before they'd be on him, but he still waited. One paused to sniff the tree where he sat.

He met Saren's gaze. She had quieted as well and was watching alongside him. He asked in his head, *"Does that spell protect my trail as well?"*

When there was no answer, he had the answer.

Roane nodded to himself. It was time. He reached and pulled out one of his daggers. It would do better in such close quarters against an enemy.

Then, Saren held up her fingers. She counted down, from three . . . two . . . on one, the air exploded. The spell was lifted and both leapt down from their spots. The wolf reacted too late. He'd been too startled.

As soon as he realized they were there, Roane was already in front of him. Saren landed behind him, and as the wolf glanced back, taking note of his surroundings, Roane plunged his dagger into his heart.

It was an instant death, but as quick as they were on this wolf, the second was on them. Roane had enough time to pull the dagger out and turn around. The second wolf was in the air and leaping onto him. Before its claws and teeth could pierce him, Saren slammed into it from the side. The two fell onto the ground and rolled once, then twice before coming to a stop, but Roane didn't wait. He wasn't watching as a bystander. He leapt in the air with them and as soon as they came to a stop, he waited long enough for Saren to roll free from the wolf before he was on the wolf's back. It reared up, trying to pull him off, but it couldn't. Roane was too fast. His hand went back as he plunged the dagger into another wolf. This time he was coming from the back so he used his entire body strength and weight to drive the dagger all the way into the body, ripping through skin, cartilage, and organs.

Roane held on, pushing it into the wolf, who was wriggling around. The wolf was trying to dislodge Roane, but he held on. He was vulnerable, though, and seeing his situation, Saren readied on her feet.

She drew her sword and braced because the other three wolves were coming. They were moving at a faster speed than normal, and they were on them before she could blink a couple times.

A silver-maned one leapt right at her. His mouth was open and his fangs ready. The other two, an all black-haired one and another black with a white strip running from under his head and down his torso, went for Roane, but as she swung the sword up and sliced across the wolf's nose, one of them turned to help.

There were now two against Saren and one trying to bite into Roane, to pull him off.

Saren couldn't help him.

She swung the sword, but it only grazed across the silver wolf. He pulled his head back in time, but recoiled in pain.

Roane had been watching and he saw the smoke that rose from the silver wolf's gaping hole.

The sword was spelled as well. He didn't know with what, but he didn't care. Then, he was brought back to attention when the white-striped wolf bit into his back—or tried. Roane saw the teeth coming and yanked out his dagger. He couldn't keep pushing for the heart. Pulling his weapon free, he swung it at the striped wolf. It did the same as Saren's sword. It only grazed the wolf, who pulled back in time.

Roane fell to his feet and rounded.

The two wolves held back, regarding him. The first one was hurt badly and was panting for breath. He was falling down, even as Roane surveyed the scene. There was no element of surprise anymore. It would be a head-on confrontation. Hearing a sudden roar from behind him, he knew Saren was holding her own.

Then, he saw his opening.

The hurt wolf looked at his comrade and in that split second, Roane shot forward, kicking off the tree behind him for an extra burst of speed. He slid to the ground, coming up underneath the hurt one, but he didn't stop. He slid all the way under the wolf and as he did, he plunged the dagger into the heart, releasing it as he kept going. Coming to a stop, he watched as the wolf fell to the ground, impaling the dagger further into the body. Roane had a split moment where he grimaced before he realized a worse danger.

The striped wolf stopped, lifted its head, and howled. The bellow sent chills down Roane's spine. It was haunting, but there was more to this howl. He heard other wolf howls, but this one held more power.

"It's Jacith." Saren stepped next to him, wiping her sword against the grass to clean the blood from her sword. "The wolf's call traveled farther and imprinted its urgency on the rest of the Benshire wolves. They'll be here faster than normal."

And that left them with one option.

As the striped wolf ended the call, he lowered his head and regarded both of them.

It was a standoff between them now. The wolf couldn't kill both of them, but when he didn't leave, Roane knew the wolf was willing to die. He wasn't running.

Respect for this one wolf grew in him, but as he shared a look with Saren, he knew what had to be done.

She nodded, swinging her sword up, and both of them launched ahead.

The wolf met them, but it was a similar exchange as the first wolf. Saren jumped higher than Roane, landing behind the wolf. He twisted his neck to try to nip at her legs, but that was his mistake. As he did, Roane pushed ahead with an extra boost of speed and used that momentum to ram his dagger into its heart.

But, unlike the other two, this wolf didn't fall to the ground.

He didn't lunge for Roane either. He stood there, panting for breath, as both Saren and Roane waited.

The wolf did nothing.

Roane looked, but no blood fell from the wound.

"He's been protected," Saren gasped, her eyes widening.

"What does that mean?"

"That means we run." She rushed forward. The wolf tried to bite her, but she evaded him and as soon as her hand touched Roane's arm—he felt them coming.

He was pulled backwards into what felt like an invisible vacuum and Saren gritted her teeth, still pushing forward into whatever she had woven for them. Roane watched from where they had left. The wolf started after them, and behind him, more wolves appeared suddenly.

Saren waved behind her. As she did, the hole vanished.

They stumbled to the ground. There were no wolves around.

"What just happened?"

Saren stopped and took a breath. She reached for him again.

Roane caught her hand and held it in place, an inch above his arm. He asked again, "What just happened?"

"It was Jacith." Saren pulled her hand free and reattached it to his arm. "I only pulled you a mile away. He was aiding them. They'll be on us again if I don't get us farther away."

Alarm spiked in him as she grabbed his arm, and the same invisible vacuum effect happened. They landed again. Saren took a breath, then grabbed his arm again. They kept doing this until they landed outside their own encampment. She was doing it to save her power, only using it in short bursts. Once they were done, she closed her eyes and bent forward, resting her hands on her legs. She was the one panting for breath now, much how the wolves had before.

Roane knew they were safe so he started, "Was Jacith there with them?"

She nodded and opened her eyes. They were strained as she answered, "Yes. I watched their army before and his body wasn't with them, but he was there. Or he was in close proximity."

"I don't understand what you mean."

"He's powerful enough to project his magic, but he can only go so far. And it's only so powerful. The closer his body is to where he is projecting, the more power he has, and back there, his magic was very, very powerful. It was too much. The magic alone would've killed me. I knew he had spelled the wolves so they were unnaturally strong and faster, but that was him. That wasn't the power he had already given them."

Roane was reeling. Jacith was here. He had come for Davy.

Saren felt his urgency and panic rise and she held a hand up, stopping him. "Davy will have enough power to beat him. That is why I'm here after all."

"But if he can get to her—"

"He can't. The protection spell the Mori put up isn't for us or the other army. It's against Jacith. They feel his magic, too. They don't want him within their lands either."

"Can they defeat him?"

Saren lifted up a shoulder. "I don't know. The Mori have ancient magic, but I'm unsure about how powerful they are or if they even want to war against him. They're already with Lucan."

Roane stifled a groan. He clipped out. "My brother is with them, not the other way around."

"What do you mean?"

"The Mori are relatively peaceful. They don't leave their lands, but they did with him. I can't help to wonder if they've been told the full truth of why they held Davy in captivity."

She narrowed her eyes at him. "You think they don't know?"

"I don't know. Talia said not everything is as it seems. I'm wondering if that's what she meant."

"Maybe."

"Roane!"

Wren was coming down the path toward them.

Roane said under his breath, before the other vampire could reach them, "Don't tell the others about Jacith. They don't think he's here."

Saren glanced at him, a question lurking deep in her depths, but she didn't respond.

SAREN

As THE FEMALE vampire got to their side, Saren stepped back and tucked her head down. The Christane wolves should be aware of what they are going against, but this vampire that Davy loved had proven his intelligence. He must have a reason for her silence. However, she was uneasy. She needed to move ahead and find her Immortal sister. The sooner she could merge her power to Davy, the better for her sister, but as the days had been progressing Saren found herself more and more reluctant to leave these group of warriors.

They were simpletons. They were weak, but spending time in their presence was like a sickness. An infatuation grew for them. She found herself wanting to protect them, to aid in their survival. It was because of Davy. Her sister would want her to make sure this vampire lived. Saren tried to reassure herself it was because of the true Immortal—that was why she hadn't left them to enter the Mori land.

Roane and his comrades weren't aware, but the protection spell wasn't cast to keep Saren out. She had already crossed the water and explored a day's trek inwards before she realized the others were kept outside.

As Roane moved forward to intercept the female vampire, Saren felt it was time to pull herself away from this group and so, as she thought it, she vanished from their sight.

Sireenia felt her presence and greeted her. "I have missed you, sister."

They were on their plane, though Saren kept a window open. She could watch Davy's vampire and materialize if her presence was needed. She said to her other sister now, "Jacith is near them."

"Yes. He didn't travel with his army. He went somewhere first."

Saren heard the fear in her voice. "We aren't aware where he went?"

"He cloaked himself, even to us."

"How is that possible?"

Sireenia didn't respond, not at first. It was a beat later when she said, "We don't know."

20

DAVY

Davy realized she had cloaked their entire group the first time they ran into a Mori. It was unexpected, and none of them realized the other vampire was there until they stepped around a tree. The Mori was right there, in the middle of a path. Davy froze while the others drew their weapons. The humans were behind them so they didn't know what was going on, but as soon as Davy thought about casting a spell, it didn't matter.

The Mori never reacted.

Wearing a dark brown robe, the hood was pulled over its head. Davy couldn't sense if it was female or male. Its back was to them, but they bent down and picked up a flower. It turned halfway to them, and they watched as she sniffed the yellow flower.

There was still no reaction.

"We're cloaked." Tracey put her sword away and turned to Davy. "Have we been cloaked the whole time?"

"Um."

Gavin twisted to her, too. He raised an eyebrow. "You don't know?"

"I remember wanting to protect all of us and I thought as we left the river that I wanted us to be invisible, but I didn't know I actually cast a spell."

Tracey moved closer. "There's five of us. My sister had a hard time cloaking one individual and she could only keep it up for a few moments." Fear, wonder, and another emotion, one that Davy didn't like seeing and one she didn't want to identify, flashed in the vampiress's eyes. "We've been traveling for days."

"Are you going to wear yourself out?"

Davy stepped back. The question was almost hurled at her from Gavin. She shook her head and held up her hands. "I didn't even realize I was doing it." She couldn't keep them in the dark anymore. They had to know what danger they were walking into with her. "I'm not in control of my powers."

"I thought they were coming back just fine."

That was what she had told Gavin earlier when she relayed The Immortal's wish to take over. Once that slipped out, Davy instantly regretted revealing that truth. They looked at her like she was an atomic bomb waiting go to go off, one she couldn't diffuse herself. She lied after that. She made it sound like she was in control, that she could hold off The Immortal, that there was nothing to be worried about.

"Did you lie to us?"

Davy nodded, waiting for Gavin's response.

What she got was instant anger. It slammed to his surface and she felt it, stepping back from reflex. But, balling her hands into fists, she stopped herself from taking another step. He had reason to be upset. They all did. She hung her head. "I'm sorry. I—"

"So what."

The three looked over. Gregory had joined the conversation. His plump lips pressed together, and he was putting his own sword away, too. He added, swinging his head to look at both vampires, "There's nothing you can do about it. The only choice you have is not to travel with her."

"You've known?" Gavin's tone was accusing.

Gregory didn't answer, not at first. A beat of silence passed before he nodded. "I did."

"When?"

"Since a day after she woke up in the cave."

Tracey went rigid. She resembled a warrior statue, made in stone while Gavin's nostrils flared. He hissed, "Are you kidding me?"

Gregory was unmoving. "She didn't even have powers at that time."

Davy gulped as the others looked at her. She turned away. She didn't want to see the shock and outrage. She didn't want to see the disappointment.

Gregory said further, "She's got her powers back, but we can't act surprised. We all heard her screaming. Who knows what Lucan's witches did to her."

Davy still couldn't bring herself to turn to them. She cared, more than she should've—perhaps, but they would be the first affirmation that she was different. She couldn't see that look in their eyes, like she was less than human, like she wasn't human at all.

"Uh." *Cough.* "Dudes."

Hearing Spencer's voice, a rush of relief went through her. These were the humans she had pulled to her, because she wished for them, because she needed a reminder of how to be a human. Spencer just fulfilled that desire for her and her lips twitched, forming a grin.

He went on to say, "So we don't hear you guys, but there's a monk smelling a flower dead ahead of us. Should we, be like, doing something about the dude?"

"I think that's a girl." Cal shuffled forward and craned his head, looking around them. "Yep. She's a girl."

"Yeah?" Spencer's excitement was obvious. "Is she hot?"

"I can't tell. She's got a robe on." Cal started to edge out from behind them.

"Stop." Tracey pushed him back. "You're back there for safety."

He pointed around her. "Either the chick nun is deaf and blind or there's something funky going on for her not to see us. I think we're safe."

"Cal." Spencer pulled him back. His voice dipped low. "We gotta do what they say. They're not human."

Cal said back, his voice dipping just as low, "I don't think that chick is either."

"Great."

"Why do I have a feeling we're not going to get out of this alive?"

The more the two humans conversed, the more guilt Davy was feeling.

"Get off your high horse."

The Immortal was laughing at her. *"They're lucky to be brought on this path with you."*

"Stop," Davy said to her.

"No. I mean it. Their lives were useless. Humans are weak and pathetic. They'll probably be turned into vampires. If you don't send them back to safety, the others will change them. They'll do it to save their lives and when that happens, the two humans will get the best thing possible. They'll have power and immortality."

"Losing one's humanity is not a gift. It's a curse."

"Having humanity is a curse. Look at you. Once you give in, you won't feel any pain. There'll be no more guilt, no more shame, self-loathing. None of that. You'll be free. We'll be free and we can do anything we want."

"Stop . . ." But as she tried to muster the strength to shut The Immortal up, Davy found there was none. Her strength was depleting, at least against her own inner demon.

"That's what you think of me?"

Davy shot back, *"Aren't you? You're not human."*

"I'm not weak. There's a difference."

"Humans are weak."

The Immortal snorted. *"Right."*

"They aren't."

"Yeah. Sure."

Davy growled, her hands back into fists, and she lashed back, *"Being human is strong. It's courage. It's strength. It's moral."*

The Immortal interrupted, saying, *"It's pain. It's misery. It's heartache. It's loneliness. It's suffering. It's being selfish. It's opening up your heart and only getting hurt in response. It's helping others and having them turn their back on you. It's loving and being cheated on. It's giving, then getting betrayed. It's foolish. You're not human anymore, Davy."*

"Shut up."

"Admit it. The sooner you do, the freer you'll become. The stronger you'll become."

"Shut up."

"You've already started to turn your humanity off. I don't understand why you won't admit it. You don't feel pain. You don't feel misery. You don't feel fatigue. In fact, you're impatient. The others are slowing you down. You can go faster, farther, beyond any of them. They're an anchor to your abilities, but you won't leave them—

"SHUT UP!"

A surge of power and magic burst inside of her, and as it happened, Davy knew instantly it was a mistake. She wanted to silence The Immortal—she silenced her magic instead . . .

She looked up, and the Mori was staring right at her.

"Oops."

"What?" Tracey whipped around, her hand grabbing onto her sword.

Davy couldn't look away from the Mori. She didn't move. In a normal situation, she should've fled or at least attacked with a spell. She did neither. Something was holding her in place, and she continued to hold the Mori's gaze.

She was drawing the vampire into her mind.

Tracey and the others knew they could be seen by now and had their weapons drawn. Davy flung her hands out and barked, "No! Don't move."

"Who are you?" the Mori asked in her mind. She had beautiful doe eyes, high cheekbones, a heart-shaped jawline that curved to petite pink lips. She didn't stand in Davy's mind with the robe. The Mori female was in a white dress and nothing else. No makeup. No shoes. No socks. She was barefoot, and her long black hair swung freely as she gazed around her surroundings. A small line appeared in her forehead. *"Where am I?"*

"My mind."

"Your mind?"

This Mori wasn't the enemy. Davy felt goodness from her. She wasn't a warrior that would instantly kill. That was why Davy was drawn to her, pulling her into her mind. It was a safe place, for both of them.

Davy asked, taking a step toward the vampiress, *"Do you know who I am?"*

She gazed around once more, the corners of her mouth pressing in. *"You're The Immortal thread-holder. No one else would have the power to pull one, such as myself, into your mind. I'm a priestess for my people. My own powers have not been challenged by more than a handful."*

She was a big deal. Davy nodded. She got it. *"What's your name?"*

"Yaeyn." The vampiress added, *"Jiyama spoke about you. She said your magic was addicting. She yearned to touch it again."*

"Jiyama helped us. My friends and I could escape because of her. I'd like to thank her someday."

"She's missing."

Davy frowned. *"What?"*

"She's gone. No one can sense her essence anywhere. That's why I'm out here. I thought perhaps she went in search for you." Yaeyn

turned around and regarded the others. *"I am not seeing her with you."*

The one Mori that Davy hoped could help them was gone. She—there was nothing she could do about that. *"Lucan loved her."*

Yaeyn nodded. *"She loved him as well. It is troubling. No one can find where my sister went, even Lucan himself. He was the last to have spoken to her."*

A dark cloud of suspicion lined the bottom of her stomach. Davy wondered, but that didn't make sense. Lucan loved her. She witnessed their exchange herself. If he did something, then that would be on him. It would be another reason to make him suffer.

Yaeyn said, *"I hear rumbling."* She focused on Davy. *"That is you. That's your anger."* She inclined her head, a soft question coming from her, *"Lucan was to wed my sister. Why would he harm her?"*

"I don't know, but the Lucan you know isn't the Lucan I know." The rumbling in Davy grew, shaking, sending Yaeyn from side to side. She held her hands out, trying to steady herself, but the beautiful landscape that Davy had sculpted for the Mori turned to the inside of a volcano. The heat was rising, more and more, and Davy was ready to explode.

"Kill her," The Immortal hissed.

Yaeyn's head whipped around. *"Who was that?"*

Davy was standing in front of the Mori, but another presence stepped beside her. She knew, before looking, that it was The Immortal. It was herself.

Yaeyn's eyes widened, and she took a step backwards. *"They unhinged the thread. You are no longer merged."*

"Kill her," The Immortal said again, ignoring the Mori. *"Take her power for yours. We can use it instead of using the power you're restoring for Jacith. Take her power, Davy."*

"No." Davy shook her head, but her voice was quiet.

Yaeyn started looking around. *"Release me, Thread-Holder. Release me now."*

It was too late, though. The Mori sensed what Davy already knew, it was why she released The Immortal to stand next to her. Her power was still locked up, but Davy knew what she would do. She needed the extra encouragement or she didn't think she could go through with it.

She was going to kill the Mori.

They were all attached. It was why they called each other sister and brother. If she took this Mori's essence, it was a gateway into their community. She would be connected to all of them and she could yield that connection as she pleased. She could slip into their minds. She could tell them what to think, feel, do, and so much more.

Yaeyn whispered, shaking her head, *"Don't do this, Davy of the Thread-Holder. Jiyama said you had good in you. She longed to assist you. She wanted to be your friend."*

Davy snorted. *"She loved Lucan. Her judgment's off."*

"I can feel it in you, too." Yaeyn's eyes were piercing, pleading with her. *"It's why I didn't attack or flee. My reflexes are faster than yours are. I feel what she felt. You are good. You are pure. Do not listen to the evil in you."* She gazed with scorn at The Immortal. *"This one is power hungry. She wants to take control over you, and she'll swallow your soul whole to do that. She won't hesitate. Don't let the darkness win."*

But as the Mori was talking, The Immortal reached over. She clasped her hand onto Davy's, who turned her palm around. They were now palm to palm, and their fingers intertwined. They were the most connected in a long time, before Davy merged with her back at Roane's restaurant.

"This is good. This is the right thing to do." The Immortal spoke quietly to her, clasping her hand tight.

"No, Davy." Yaeyn thrust a hand out, as if to grab ahold of Davy.

Davy closed her eyes and hung her head.

"Block her out. Don't listen to her. You need her essence. It will help you against the Mori and Jacith. You'll be able to find Kates."

Davy still hesitated.

"The Mori captured you. They assisted Lucan with taking the others and torturing you. You can use her essence and her power. When we're done, you can let her essence go. It can rest with her family." The Immortal squeezed her hands. *"We have to, Davy. It's no longer you and me. It's us. We have to do this."* She paused a beat, then added, *"This will save Lucas, too."*

The last sentence was enough. Davy was wavering, but her mind was made up. She shut her emotions off and started to chant.

She concentrated on the words. Magic hadn't been an effort for her before. The effort had been in trying to control her power, but since Lucan's witches, it was like she was learning everything new. And this spell, drawing the Mori's essence, was beyond anything she had done knowingly.

"Davy!"

The Immortal moved so she was directly in front of Davy. Her back was to the Mori, and she tucked her head next to Davy's. She took Davy's other hand, and she began to chant with her. They both spoke at the same time, in the same breath, with the same focus and attention.

"Davy," Yaeyn yelled once again. *"I know there is good in you. Please don't do this. I'm one of my people's leaders. They will be devastated by my death—"*

Enough!" The Immortal slammed a hand behind her, and in a moment, she snapped Yaeyn's neck. Her hand returned to Davy's, and she squeezed it hard. *"Hurry. We can still take her essence. It hasn't depleted to the earth yet."*

They worked together, as one mind, one mouth, and when it was done, a peace settled over Davy. She opened her eyes, but she was back in her own body once again. She wasn't in her mind and she looked down.

The Mori was at her feet. Her eyes were wide open with death in them, and her mouth was open, like she had been gasping for breath.

"I can feel them." Davy didn't turn to the others. She said, "I can feel all of them. I know where they are."

Gavin gestured to the Mori. "What about her?"

Davy didn't look. She only said, "She would've killed us. I was protecting us." And with that, she stepped over the body.

21

ROANE

As soon as Roane walked into the encampment, the Christane wolves knew. He still wore Benshire blood on him, and it wasn't long after that before Christian issued the order. They were marching on their enemy.

"You'll lose."

Christian was leaving his tent, his sword ready. Pippa was next to him, and as Roane said those words, she stood next to her brother. Both regarded him with resolved faces. They were going to war. The order had been issued. They were ready.

Christian snapped, "You brought us here. This is why we're here."

"They're being helped by Jacith—"

"And we're supposed to have The Immortal on our side," Christian's voice bellowed. "Where is she?"

"Brother," Pippa said. Her head turned up, regarding him.

He ignored her, glaring at Roane. "You're the leader, but you come in here wearing our enemy's blood." He gestured around them. "Look at my men. If you wanted a battle cry, you got one. The smell worked them into a frenzy. They must have blood of their own now. They have to spill their enemy's blood for themselves."

"We have to wait." But as Roane said it, he knew they wouldn't.

He smelled the wolves' blood thirst. It was intoxicating, even to himself. It was bringing the Hunter in him alive again, the Hunter that he thought was long gone. Even now, as Christian started to speak, Roane wasn't paying attention. The Hunter mark on him started to burn. It was awakening and he closed his eyes. He needed to allow it to return. He had been stripped of his Hunter privilege, but for a reason unknown to him, it was being returned to him. He was no longer only powerful because of Davy's blood, but because of his ancestry.

"... We have no choice," Christian was saying.

Pippa added, "We have to go."

Roane didn't look at her. He hadn't paid attention to the wolf that was Davy's friend. It hurt too much, remembering the times when Davy fought for this one, proclaimed she was friend and not foe. That had been when Davy was safe, not like now. She'd been gone for so long.

Wren stepped next to him. "The witch is gone, but we'll fight with you." She glanced to Roane, then back to Christian. "It's why we all came here."

"It's not time." Roane shook his head, but he knew it was pointless. They were going. They had waited too long.

"It's time, Lucas Roane, Hunter of the Hunters' bloodline." Christian spoke to him, but he wasn't paying attention anymore. His gaze was directed beyond Roane's shoulder and he turned to see all of the wolves there. They were waiting. Then, one by one, they began to change into their wolf form. When they were all done, they turned as one and formed a line. Two by two, they began to leave. Roane stepped back with Bastion and Wren. As they watched, Christian and Pippa transformed as well and followed their bloodline.

They were going to war.

Wren said, when they left, "It's not enough. They'll all die."

Roane asked Bastion, "You sent your man?"

Bastion nodded. "I did."

"Would he have had time?"

"I don't know." Bastion took a breath, hesitation on his face, but it cleared. He was the fastest of Roane's men. "I could go, if you want me to."

"What?" Wren's head whipped around. "You are not thinking what I think you're thinking. You are not leaving. Are you?"

"I can go. He would be there by now, but coming back—"

They needed help. Roane realized that as soon as he saw how many Benshire wolves and Romah vampires there were. He had his own men, and he sensed them now. They heard the exchange. They knew the wolves were heading out, but they were waiting for their own leader. Roane didn't want to send his men to fight. They would die. There were too many Romah vampires. They were older, and they had magic. Davy was their ace in the sleeve, but they couldn't get to her.

"Roane."

He glanced down to the ground. Wren spoke his name, standing beside him, and he knew why. He felt his men. They had come, standing not far, and he knew why they were there. It was the same reason they came on this journey with him. It was time to fight. It was that simple. The wolves, who had come to be their ally, were going. They would go to their deaths. They didn't have Davy, but he couldn't put it off any longer.

It was time.

He turned around. Wren turned with him. Bastion was on his other side. It was too late. If he sent Bastion, he wouldn't get back in time. No matter what, the war was here and it had already started.

He spoke quietly, but every vampire heard him as he said, "We came to fight."

The excitement and adrenaline filled the air. Each vampire was on high alert.

Wren said, "We're ready."

Roane nodded. "Then we fight."

He turned and led his men to join the Christane wolves. So be it who fell and who lived at the end.

———

DAVY

SHE COULD FEEL THE MORI. She knew exactly where they were, even the little babies in the mothers' wombs, and she walked toward them. Her feet glided soundlessly over the forest as she kept moving forward. Davy walked and walked. She wasn't aware of the time, the weather, even where she was. She could've been walking on a cliff's edge and she would've kept going.

Everything was tuned out, except for the Mori.

The Mori meant more magic, more power. And as she kept going, she moved with a serene and ethereal quality to her. Gavin, Gregory, and Tracey followed behind. They were no longer guarding her. They were merely trailing now. It was as if they didn't exist, and more than once the three vampires shared a worried look. This was a Davy that they didn't know, and while the humans didn't know the old carefree Davy, they reacted on a primal level to this new Davy as well. They were silent and had grown pale. Their bodies started to tremble from the exertion they were being put through. Showers erupted in the sky and drenched their group. The two humans shivered. They accepted blankets that the vampires offered, but when Cal's teeth's chattering overpowered the sound of his own heartbeat, Gavin knew they had to stop.

"Davy." He reached for her. "We have to stop."

A part of him felt she wouldn't, but when she did, he was surprised. Some hope sparked in him. His senses were telling him she wasn't human anymore, had slowly been transitioning in that direction, but since killing the Mori, he could see The Immortal's power over her. As he stared at her, he could only see small traces of the old Davy.

Her chocolate almond eyes, that usually danced and laughed, were dead. There was no life in them anymore. Her cheeks, that would pink and plump up whenever she would grin at something Lucas said or if she was caught staring at Gavin's best friend, they barely moved. The color was gone. A white, almost tranquil, glimmer had formed over her skin.

"Why?"

She asked that one word, but instead of the impatience or even understanding that the old Davy would have, she sounded careless. It was like she was curious, as if the idea of exhaustion was a new concept to her.

He gritted his teeth and tried to quell his anger.

Davy's eyes sharpened. Her head tilted to the side and the age-old hierarchy was switched. He was no longer the predator that every vampire was to a human. He was her prey. Gavin knew it, and Davy knew it. A faint grin teased at the corner of her mouth, but it only remained a faint glimmer. Her eyes remained cold and soulless.

He shifted to the back of his heel. "The humans need to rest."

Davy stepped aside so she could see Cal and Spencer. As her dead gaze left him, Gavin could breathe. He'd been under her attention, which was a spell in itself now. He had to do something. This couldn't continue. She would be gone and the allegiance he owed his best friend, to watch over his lover wouldn't be upheld. He would be letting Lucas down. He couldn't do that. As Davy continued to study the humans, Gavin cast a quick look at Tracey and Gregory. He saw similar unsettled looks in their faces.

"You are too tired?" Davy asked Cal and Spencer.

Neither answered. They glanced behind them, tucking their hands against their sides. Their shoulders hunched down, like they were trying to make themselves seem smaller. They wanted to run from her.

Davy's eyes narrowed. "You are not too tired? Why are you not answering me?"

Gavin cleared his throat. His hand went to his sword, but he only gripped the handle. He didn't pull it out. "Davy, this is enough."

She looked back. He braced himself, knowing how her gaze now felt, and as it settled on him, he felt all his breath being stolen. It was being drawn out of him, slowly, and at a torturous rate. Her eyes fell to his sword and though there was no reaction on her face, he felt her attention sharpen.

She asked, "You would use that on me?"

"You're different. You're almost unrecognizable."

He searched her face, but nothing. There was no response. There wasn't even anger.

Her face remained flat as she asked, "How so?"

"Come on," Tracey burst out. She surged forward, throwing her hands out. "Look at you. You're not even like us anymore. We have emotions and with you—there's nothing. You're cut off. You're empty. You're—"

"Bat shit crazy," Spencer supplied, moving forward.

Cal snorted behind him. "Ditto on that. I used to think she was hot."

"Yeah." Spencer said over his shoulder to him, "If you're into Terminator Dominatrix."

Davy was quiet, but she asked, "I'm like a robot?"

"No." Cal and Spencer started to talk at the same time. Gavin threw both a look. "Shut up."

They did.

He turned back to Davy and held a hand out toward her. "Davy, this isn't you. This is The Immortal taking over you. It's happening. What you didn't want to happen, losing yourself to her, it's happening. You're losing your humanity."

He waited, almost hoping for a murderous reaction from her.

"My humanity?"

He closed his eyes. She was gone. That one question was spoken as if she'd been asked the weather. There was nothing left. He saw that now. His anger buried deep in him, but alongside it was an anchor, pulling it low and helping to drive it further inside of him. She was gone. He had let Lucas down.

He cast a sideways look to Tracey and Gregory. A deep sadness clung to both.

She was gone.

"Davy—" Gavin cleared his throat.

"The humans are tired. That's what you're saying."

She didn't get it. So much more happened here than just those few words, but he nodded. He felt a heavy weight on his shoulder, heavier than he ever remembered experiencing before. He murmured, so softly, "Yes, Davy. They're tired. They can't keep up with you."

"Then stay here with them." She angled her head to the side again. "Or kill them."

"Dude!" Spencer cried out. "What the fuck?"

Cal groaned. "Why do I get the feeling this isn't going to end well?"

Davy started toward them. "If you cannot keep up, you're no longer useful. I can relieve your pain right now." Her hand stretched out, a single finger pointing toward them.

Both jumped back. Their hands came up, and they were shaking their heads. Their arms began waving back and forth in front of them.

"No, no."

"That's okay. Thanks, though."

Spencer added, "We're good." He coughed, hitting his chest. "We can keep going. No problem here."

"Pretend we're not human."

The anchor stopped. It was all the way to the bottom of his feet, but Gavin knew what had to be done. He let go of the sword. He couldn't plunge it into Davy. He couldn't do that, not yet anyway, but she had to be handled. She stepped toward the humans and he moved behind her.

Spencer gave her a thumbs-up sign. "Really. We're good. We'll march all night."

Cal nodded, his eyes gleaming from fear. "Yep. Me, too. All night."

Davy shook her head. She said quietly, "No. I can help you. You're human. I remember what that feels like. So much pain. So much misery. You feel worthless half the time and then struggle to even feel that much the other half. It's a disease."

"Oh God." Spencer gulped. He backed away as Davy advanced. Cal was right with him. "Really. I like my humanity."

Cal jerked his head up and down. "Me, too. Lots of pain. I live for that shit."

"No, you don't." Davy let out a sigh. Sympathy laced it. "You were high when I met you. Both of you. You sought other planes of consciousness. No one does that if they're happy. They seek to escape life. They seek to distract themselves. It's why you went on your study abroad in the first place. I felt your reasons, in both of you. You wanted to get out of your home. You wanted to travel, seek new and exciting places to be. You were searching for yourself. That's what you were doing. No, no." She stopped in front of them. As they cowered, she seemed to grow in size. She didn't move, but she was suddenly looming over them.

Gavin kept with her, moving as she did. She couldn't know he was right behind her. He moved as silent as she did.

She paused, gazing at the humans for another second. "I used to want what you have. I wanted to cling to my humanity desperately, but I was wrong. It's so much more freeing this way. There's no sadness, no regret. You'll see what I'm talking about. The others know. They understand."

Spencer and Cal shrunk down. "Come on, Davy. Can we —please no."

Spencer didn't say a word. He saw what was coming and clasped his eyes shut. Sucking in a breath, he started to envision somewhere else, somewhere safe. He hoped to be there whenever this psycho bitch did whatever she was going to do.

Davy lifted her arms up. She closed her eyes, too, and started to say the words.

And Gavin moved.

His hands grasped both sides of her face, and as she stiffened in reflex, he snapped her neck. He let her fall. He didn't catch her. This wasn't a normal being. Another vampire and he knew they would have a few hours before they woke. This was Davy. She was something entirely else, and he had no idea how long she'd be out.

He turned to Tracey and Gregory, saying, "We have to go. Now."

They both nodded, and in the blink of an eye, the vampires were gone. They snatched the humans with them.

Davy's body was left on the ground.

———

DAVY'S EYES SNAPPED OPEN, but she didn't move from the ground. She remained there, staring at the sky, as she realized what happened.

"Well." The Immortal sat next to her, her legs crisscrossed. "I can't say that I didn't think this was going to happen."

Davy turned her head to the side. She knew only she could see The Immortal, dressed just as herself, but she didn't care. In fact, as she remembered Gavin snapping her neck and the others were gone now, she didn't care about that either.

In fact, she didn't care to comment back to The Immortal so she remained there and looked back to the sky.

She used to care.

Why had she cared?

What had she cared about?

It was nagging her, in the back of her mind, but she couldn't remember. Humanity. That was what she had been talking to the humans about when Gavin broke her neck. Was that what it was? Was that what was missing from her now?

"I'm dead," she spoke out loud, as much to herself as to The Immortal.

"Yep." The Immortal sighed, sounding impatient. "You are. Welcome to the official world of Immortality."

"My human body is dead."

"And you're still here. Still talking. Still breathing, well—" The Immortal leaned over and pressed her ear to Davy's chest. She paused, then straightened back up. "—you don't need breath anymore, but you're still breathing because that's what is natural to your body."

"Like vampires."

"I guess." The Immortal let out another sharp sigh, glancing around. "I think we should get going. The Mori aren't far now. We can get there before nightfall."

Yes. That was what Davy had been thinking about—the Mori. She needed to get there. She needed to take their magic. She wanted their power too. That was all she'd been focused on before, but now, she had a moment to rethink. Her neck being snapped wasn't something to be taken lightly. This was important. It meant something important. Or it should.

Davy moved her head, her eyes finding The Immortal again.

She was just like herself. Her brown hair was longer. Her dark eyes were watching her back, but while Davy felt shut off inside,

The Immortal's eyes had a glimmer of rage, impatience, and thirst. She wanted more. She needed more. She was going to demand more. Davy was separate from The Immortal right now. Before they had been walking side by side. Their hands had grazed each other's. Davy knew the others couldn't see The Immortal, but she was among them as much as they were. But there was distance between herself and The Immortal right now. Davy could think for herself, or so she thought.

She mused to herself, "What if I stayed here?"

"That's a joke, right?"

Davy shook her head. The sky was clear, but some stars were starting to show. It'd be dark in a few hours. She could do it. She could stay there. She could watch the rest of the stars appear and she could wait, do whatever she wanted. The Mori weren't leaving. No one was going anywhere. She could do as Gavin had requested for the humans. She could rest—that was what she would've done before.

She had been human before.

She would've needed to sleep as well, just like Cal and Spencer.

Davy frowned, marring the lines on her forehead. She brought them to her for the very reason she just tried to kill them for. Humanity. Weakness. Emotions. She had been trying to hold onto it, but it was gone.

She knew that now.

Inside was nothing. She felt nothing. She knew that when she would stand and resume her journey for the Mori, The Immortal would walk with her. She would become infected with The Immortal's wishes once again. Hunger. Need. Thirst. That was all The Immortal wanted, but Davy needed to remember what had guided her before all of this.

She was losing herself, and she was in a place right now where she needed to remember who she used to be. Who she used to be was vital. Davy knew that and she closed her eyes, trying to dig deep into herself. She needed to find that girl once more.

"We need to go."

"No." Davy kept searching. Somehow she had switched places with The Immortal. The human she used to be was locked away. Where had she gone? "I think I'll rest."

"Why? You don't need to rest. You're not a weakling anymore. You're not controlled by the same needs as them."

The Immortal was getting riled up. Davy almost smiled, but she masked her amusement.

"Davy!"

"No." Davy shook her head. "I'm going to stay a moment. I'd like to pretend I'm normal again."

"Why?"

"I don't know." She was honest. "But I feel it's important, so that's what I'm going to do." She rolled her head to the side. If steam could've left The Immortal's head, an entire cloud of it would've exploded from her. Her cheeks puffed out and her lips pursed together, she was about to argue, but Davy held up a hand. She motioned it to the side and because she willed it, The Immortal's neck was snapped.

The invisible being didn't drop to the ground next to her. No. She disappeared, that was it, but Davy closed her eyes and did as she said she would. She was going to rest and she was going to try to remember why she started this journey in the first place.

The Immortal would be back, but for now, it was nice to have silence.

22

"What just happened back there?"

Gavin ignored the human's question. They were still rushing back. He growled, holding onto whichever human he had grabbed. "We have to keep moving."

Tracey was sprinting next to him, holding onto the second human. "The Immortal is no longer our ally. We have to return to our leader."

"What?"

Spencer was held within Gavin's grasp and he looked over, able to meet Cal's gaze even though they were traveling faster than a race car. He shrugged in response to his friend's question. The vampires knew where they were going. All he cared about was that he hadn't died, because he was pretty sure that was what psycho chick had been about to do. Taking their humanity was code for, I want to kill you, bitches. As long as they were away from her, he was golden pie.

Until they got to the river.

When they stopped and saw what was happening, Spencer squeaked, "Can we go back to the psycho chick?"

Cal's hand shot in the air. "I second that."

Before them, right on the river's bank, was the battleground. Wolves were running at each other, tearing each other apart. Gavin leapt out of the path of two wrestling each other. They careened past him, right into the water, and both scrambled back to the bank, but the one on top ripped into the other's throat. Landing on his feet, in a crouching position, Gavin threw his head back. His vampire senses were on full alert. They didn't have time to stand there and take in the bloody and violent scene. They needed to identify allies from enemies and they needed to do it fast.

He yelled out to Tracey and Gregory, "Guard the humans. Roane is here."

Both vampires already had their weapons drawn. A wolf turned on them, leaping in the air. Tracey evaded it and sliced the sword through the wolf's throat. He fell to the ground, right at Spencer and Cal's feet.

"Holy—" Spencer started, his mouth gaping wide open.

Cal let out a harrowing groan and clenched his teeth together. "I suddenly feel warm. " He asked Spencer, "Why would I feel warm right now?"

Spencer shook his head. "Did you piss yourself? Because I think I just did."

Gregory grabbed the wolf's feet and threw it in the air. It landed clear across the embankment, and as it did, it drew the attention from a large group of feuding wolves. Those that were fighting, stopped, sniffed the air, and turned their heads until they were staring at the newcomers.

"Yep," Cal muttered. "Definitely soiled myself there."

A wolf was in mid-air sailing right past them when Gregory grabbed it. He held it up by its throat and leaned in close to growl, "What bloodline are you from?"

The wolf had a silver mane with a black streak around the eyes. It tried to bite him. Gregory adjusted his hold, bracing his arm on the other side of the wolf's neck when Gavin yelled out,

"Stop. That's a Christane wolf." His eyes were almost beaming as he looked at Tracey. "Christian Christane was Davy's friend's brother. Right?"

Tracey frowned. She shared it with Gregory, who asked, "So I shouldn't kill the wolf?"

As he held him, another wolf bounded up and pulled the wolf free. Gregory turned to reach for it again, but the rescuing wolf was there. It snarled at Gregory, but it was a soft snarl. There wasn't enough heat behind it to warrant that it was a threat.

The two wolves backed away and then ran to their allies.

Tracey stood close to Cal and Spencer, her sword in front of her. She kept her back to them, shielding them. Gregory and Gavin did the same.

She threw over her shoulder, "We need to identify who are allies and quick."

Gavin clipped his head in a nod. "I agree." He was scanning the battleground. Dead wolves were all over the ground, but as quickly as they arrived, the battle on their bank was already ending. The last wolves that were alive dashed off, going around a bend, and sounds from another battle were heard. Howls. Screeches. Whimpers. Shouts. Screams. They heard all of that, but there was a low rumbling in the distance, too. It sounded like thunder from far away, but it wasn't. As Gavin gripped his sword tighter, he took a step forward. He could feel the rumbling. It was coming from beneath them. It was in the ground, and he felt its magic.

It was strong, maybe too strong for them.

"There are vampires over there." Tracey was moving forward. "I can feel them."

Gavin hurried ahead, but didn't try to draw her back. They went together, hurrying at the same pace. Cal and Spencer jogged behind and Gregory brought up the rear. Right before turning the corner, Tracey melted into the foliage. Gavin was right behind her. The rest fell in line.

"Where are we going?" Spencer asked the group.

None of the vampires answered. All were tense, silent, and scanning their surroundings.

Spencer glanced at Cal, who shrugged and replied, "I dunno. Looking for friends?"

"Shut up," Tracey clipped out. "Both of you."

They kept moving into the forest. There were vampires hidden within the forest. Gavin, Tracey, and Gregory could feel them, but they couldn't identify if they were friend or foe. As they kept moving forward, each was waiting for an enemy to attack, but none happened until they were deep into the forest. The battle sounds lessened behind them, and each vampire started to loosen their hold on their weapons, just a bit.

Suddenly, all three whipped around until they were facing east.

Cal and Spencer were shoved behind them.

Gavin lowered his head, focusing every sense he had on who was coming. "A vampire."

Tracey and Gregory didn't reply. They both knew. All three were trying to identify who it was, but they were coming fast and they weren't being cautious. Whoever it was wasn't trying to hide their approach. Sounds of them whipping past trees, leaves, grass, leaping over logs, they all heard those tiny sounds. It was deafening to a vampire and then the assailant crashed through the last foliage.

They leapt over the entire group and kept going. They never stopped.

"Who—" Gavin's head snapped, watching the vampire. He had two seconds to decide and he did. He yelled over his shoulder, "I'm going after him." He sheathed his sword across his back and before anyone could argue, he was gone. The same sounds came in his wake as he sped after the vampire.

Gregory growled, "He shouldn't have done that."

Tracey threw him a dark look. "What do you expect? We have to find our allies. We need to find Roane."

There was another crashing sound from the forest. It was coming from where the battle was, and both vampires turned once again. It was the same as before. A vampire was coming at them. They knew it. They couldn't hide. They had humans with them. It would've been useless. Any vampire could smell a human. There was no point in hiding.

"We're like sitting ducks."

Tracey gave Gregory another annoyed look, but pressed her lips together. She couldn't argue with him. All she could do was get ready and she was.

Twenty yards.

Eighteen.

Twelve.

Eight.

The vampire was moving faster than the other one.

Five.

One—she leapt as the new vampire soared through the air. The first knew they were there and jumped over them already, but this one landed before them. The new vampire was going to stop, land where they stood, and push off against the ground for more speed. As he came through the last of the trees and brush, his eyes went wide at seeing them, but Tracey was attacking before he saw her, too.

She thrust out her arm, hit him across the chest with it, and rotated swiftly so her other arm was wrapped around the vampire's head. She snapped the neck before she stopped to see who it was, and when the body fell to the ground, her knee was going to his chest. Then, she saw his face.

Horror filled her and she leapt backwards. "Oh no."

Gregory looked and grunted. "Good one, Tracey."

It was Bastion.

23

DAVY

Davy knew there was something wrong with her.

The Immortal was still silent. Davy had shut her off with an extra boost of power. She was surprised for how long the mute spell was working, but she wasn't complaining. It was nice to be walking with only herself. No vampires among her. No judgments. No disapproval. No quiet condescension. And no voice in her head. When The Immortal was awake, Davy felt her persuasion. She knew she was being pulled in one way, but she wasn't sure of the direction now. All she knew, as she paused with only one more hill to go before she would arrive at the Mori community, was that she wasn't the old Davy anymore.

She tried to remember who that girl had been. There'd been a reason why she was taken captive. She only remembered the torture. The witches had pulled the thread so it was separated from her. And Lucan—it was Lucan who had taken her. He wanted the thread, but there was more.

She frowned, dipping her head down. She couldn't remember the other reason anymore. A faint stirring began in her. She didn't like this feeling, of being turned off to the real soul inside of her. A solid plastic wall had been erected in her and she was shut off from everything that made her *her*.

Davy. She didn't know who that person was anymore.

She closed her eyes and commanded, *"Remind me."*

A memory stirred. *"He'll come after you, you know."*

Lucan shot to his feet, but he didn't go anywhere. He didn't leave. He didn't threaten. He just stood there and waited.

She remembered that conversation—there'd been a guy. No, he was more than just a guy.

"He loves me. Do you think he won't come for me now?" I saw how he stood there. "Do you think he won't go against you for me?"

Lucas Roane.

She remembered him now. He was Lucan's twin brother. Lucas turned on his brother to save her. He protected her, and then Lucan came into his brother's house and took her. He took her and all of her friends too.

But no.

Davy needed to remember. She had a purpose before. It hadn't been about power.

It was about friendship, love, trust, making her loved ones safe.

Pippa, the wolf. Brown, the witch. Kates, the best friend. There were others, but those three were her human friends.

Gavin, Gregory, Wren, and Tracey—they were Roane's vampires. They followed him.

She remembered their first kiss.

As if I had no control over my actions, I watched my own hands grasp the front of his shirt roughly. Roane didn't have time to react before I pushed against him and slammed my lips over his. After that I felt like something unlocked inside of me. My eyes snapped shut, and I pressed harder against Roane. As kisses went, it was forced and impersonal.

And another time, when they were together. Then I felt Roane's hand slide around to the back of my neck, and he took a breath before he took over the kiss.

He moved his hand from my leg and slowly reached to untangle my hands from my hair. I gasped as the last finger was detangled, and then my fingers desperately sought his shoulders. He slid in, and I surged forward to wrap my arms tighter around him.

"You have to bear something that you didn't choose. I understand, Davy. I understand it more than you think." Roane tucked his head against mine. His lips brushed the tip of my ear. "I know what it's like to have your life suddenly change, and it's not what you decided. I do understand that."

I frowned.

His hand curved around my neck, and I felt the cool touch of his lips when he pressed a kiss to my ear. "You can do this, Davy. We'll figure everything else out." She remembered the last time she saw him.

Roane pulled me into his chest for a hug. After we kissed again, he thought, "I will be back soon or I'll call for you. Stay with Gavin or Wren. They are to protect you from now on."

"Be safe."

He nodded and kissed me a last time. His lips lingered over mine as I clung to him. Every instinct in my body told me not to let him go. Something bad was going to happen. I knew it. I felt it, but so did Roane.

He was the reason she was fighting. He preceded the need for power, before The Immortal became her own entity.

Davy faltered, stopping on the very top ridge of the hill. The Mori were spread before her. There were five hidden in trees a few yards away. They would see her, but she wasn't ready. She didn't want to go in there being detached from herself so she cloaked herself. She needed more time, just a bit more, and she needed to remember this vampire that the human inside of her loved so much.

She ordered in her head, "Take me to him."

The air popped, and she was there.

He was standing in front of her, peering out over a cliff as a war waged on beneath his feet. She didn't care about who was fighting. There was blood, sweat, and death all over. Many already died and many more would succumb to the afterlife. She wasn't there for any of them. She moved forward, still cloaked, as she stood beside him.

This man, this vampire, was the reason the girl inside of her lived. She felt her yelling, trying to break free. Even the sight of him, so close and within reach, had her humanity fighting like she had never fought before.

She wanted him.

The rage was whipping through her. It wasn't rage at him or where they were. It was rage at herself. The human was raging to take control once again, but no, that didn't make sense. She wasn't The Immortal. She wasn't the human. She was the in between. Davy cocked her head to the side and lifted a hand. The in-between was curious about this vampire. She wanted to touch him, and as she lifted a hand and extended it to him, the human grew silent. This was what the real Davy yearned for, to be complete with him once again.

Her fingers touched his cheekbone and held there.

He was beautiful.

His eyes were fierce. He had high cheekbones, a strong jaw, lips that Davy wanted to touch, and a warrior's body. Broad shoulders. A trim waist. Fresh blood was all over him, coating of dried blood underneath, but as she looked over him, she saw it wasn't his blood. She found herself wanting to make sure. She wanted to clean him, double-checking that none seeped from a wound on his perfect body.

As she had that thought, she realized that she thirsted for his body. She wanted to touch him, press against him, feel his arms wrap around her. Those lips—her gaze went back to them. She couldn't look away, and she stepped toward him. Her heart began beating, faster and faster. Her mouth was suddenly parched.

She wanted to touch her lips to his.

As if she had cast a spell onto herself, the battle melted away. It was only this vampire and herself.

She drew closer.

Her hand slid down to the side of his mouth, and she was directly in front of him. She stood on tiptoes—her breath held—she needed to feel this man again. Then, with her heart pounding to be freed from her chest, she touched her lips to his. It was soft. This was foreign to her, but the human inside wanted more. She demanded a harder touch, and Davy found herself answering. She pressed closer to him, and as she did, he felt her.

Her eyes widened, as she knew the instant he grew aware of her.

His hands grasped her arms. He stiffened in shock, and just as she feared he would pull away, he took control of the kiss. He caught the sides of her face and moved for a better angle to meet her. He breathed against her mouth, "Davina."

She didn't reply. She closed her eyes and sighed inwardly as he grasped her in his arms. Lifting her, her legs wound around his waist, and he stepped away from the fight. "Davina," he gasped again, but then he pressed her against a tree. "My God—I don't care." His mouth opened, demanding hers to do the same and his tongue slid inside. The brush of him against her was a caress and Davy wound her arms around his neck. She arched her back into the tree, pushing her breasts toward him. She hungered for more. She wanted his touch in the center of her. The human was clambering to get closer and Davy answered.

Her hands went to the side of his face and held him.

He kept kissing her. He was claiming her.

Me. He was claiming *me*.

"*No!*" The Immortal rose up. "*You cannot have her!*"

The Immortal slammed her backwards.

"Davy!" Roane roared, moving with her. He didn't know how she came to him. He didn't care to question it, but he had her. He wanted her back. He had to have her. Whatever was going on inside of her, he needed to grasp her. He had to be her anchor. He could tell that she was losing herself. He reached out for her and Davy tried to grasp his hand, but The Immortal growled, and broke through the barrier inside of Davy.

She gasped.

The power was immense. It spilled out inside of her, coating her insides with its power. It was a burst of cold air. It felt alien, but refreshing, and then it was over. As soon the floodgates opened, she was drowning. There was no chance of a fight inside of her. The power overwhelmed her, instantly suffocating her. Davy was gone. She had lost. The Immortal was free inside of her —her body bent in half. Her back arched upward, and as it did, her body flew in the air.

She flew.

Her entire body transformed. Her body was going up in the air, flying, and her hair billowed out, turning into a black color. A white dress covered her now, and her hands flung backwards. She pushed up into the sky, going higher and higher until she was above the entire foray below.

All of them stopped. The woman in white had taken over the battle, but as Roane watched, she stopped in mid-air and looked down.

A rumbling started in the distance.

Everyone stopped.

24

THE IMMORTAL

This was her world.

The Immortal relished this sudden experience. She was free. She was alive. She was in control and she gazed down upon the war beneath her. Simpletons. The lot of them. All of them were weak. She wrinkled her nose. Here she was in the air and looking down on them. She was above them.

She was a god to them.

She couldn't believe this was the world Davy honored above everything else. She wanted to be one of those weaklings. No. It was worse. These creatures were more powerful than humans. Davy wanted to be the lowest of the beings.

Never.

Determination coursed through her and as she gazed beneath her, The Immortal's hands formed into fists. She would never be replaced. The human in her would never become human again. Davy's destiny was linked with hers. She would not allow it. She would never go back into the shell, contained as a thread, jumping from one less than worthy human to another. All of them. They were all *stupid*. Everything they believed was wrong.

"Davy?"

She looked over to the cliff. Lucas Roane, the vampire that Davy loved. He was the vampire Talia loved as well, but he had no idea where their love for him was created. He would need to understand. Even now, while she was still acclimating to her new freedom, her body felt a stirring in her core. Her body wanted this vampire, but that was no surprise to her.

Everyone had stopped to gaze upon her, like the goddess she was. They felt her power. There were pockets among them, places where one person had more power than the other, but none matched her. She could feel her superiority over them, so they were ignored. For now.

She lowered herself so she was a few feet from the vampire Davy loved, and she cocked her head to the side. A small grin formed. He didn't move. He didn't dare. She sensed the horror in him. It was recoiling inside, pulling him from her. It was the body's instinct for survival.

She did not come in peace, and his body was trying to pull him as far from her as possible, but still, he didn't go.

Her eyes narrowed. "I can feel what is going on inside of you."

Roane remained frozen in place. This couldn't be. No, no. This couldn't—he choked out, "Davy?"

She shook her head, slowly, and almost gently. "You know I am no longer her." She took a step toward him. Her feet were bare, but she felt no pain. The ground was covered in blood, dirt, rocks, and she felt none of it. She only felt her power. Her dress glided over her body as she walked another step forward.

He jerked backwards. His eyes were piercing. A nerve bulged out from his neck. "Stop right there."

"Now, Lucas," she chided, wagging a finger from side to side. "You know I am not a being you can command. If anyone should know how powerful I am, it must be you." She sent him visions of their past. The first memory was when he realized the thread had jumped to Talia. The second when he watched her bring their dead mother back to life. The third, when Talia stood behind her sister. Her hand was up and she was going to attempt the same event. Tracey was turned into a vampire and Talia wanted to make her human. Lucas stopped her, but The Immortal remembered that moment. She wanted Talia to try. She wanted to test the boundaries of her power, see how far she could go. He stopped her, though, and the two made love. The Immortal made him remember that night. When he slipped inside the thread-holder, held her, and cupped her face. He gazed down into Talia's eyes, but it wasn't Talia he was looking at. It was her.

He loved The Immortal, just as he fell in love with the next thread-holder.

She relished that feeling now. When she slipped into Davy. It was right. The body was right. There was power already in the human, more than she could've imagined, and as soon as the thread was inside of the empath, The Immortal knew she found the right body. At last.

She pushed that memory into Roane's head, too. She wanted him to experience the moment he lost the next thread-holder, because he had. As soon as the thread was inside of Davy, it was over.

Davy was hers.

He fell in love with her vessel once again, and still, even as she pushed more memories into his mind, she knew he wouldn't realize it.

He was in love with her, not the vessel.

Memory after memory, she shoved them all into his mind. Every time she was there. Every time he was feeling her power, not the thread-holder. Her. The last vision was when he drank from Davy's blood. He was drinking her, not Davy. It was her, mixed in the vessel's blood, that filled him and gave him power.

She stood just before him now, her hand still in the air. "Do you feel me?"

His eyes rolled inside and he bent over, falling to his knees. She pulled at her power that was still in his blood. The Roane

Hunter-line had turned off his connection to the Hunters. He could no longer sense them, but she felt a faint stirring of them. She felt his Hunter tattoo. It sparked alive and that meant one thing, the Hunters were near. He was still not connected to them. They feared he was too powerful, but his tattoo was burning. It only burned when other Hunters were nearby.

"No," she murmured. She was lost in thought.

Lucas was reliving that moment when he drank from Davy. It was on a loop, repeating over and over again. As he was blind to everything else, she cupped the side of his face. He looked up at her, but he still couldn't see her. She pressed her wrist to his mouth and urged, "Drink."

The other Roane was turned into a human, but that was because Davy wanted it.

Lucas didn't fight her. He gripped her arm and his fangs sank deep into her skin. He was drinking her blood and more of her power went into him. It mixed with the other remnants of her power and everything became more inside of him. He was more. He was more of a vampire. He was more of a Hunter. He was more of her lover. He loved her more. His strength was more.

His power was more, and he was her creature now.

She traced the side of his face as he kept drinking. Her own love for him filled her. She could feel Davy protesting in her. She didn't want this to happen, not while The Immortal was in control, but the human was the one contained now.

The Immortal smiled. Still holding her lover's head to her wrist, she gazed out over the battleground.

She felt Jacith's magic. It was underneath the warring vampires and werewolves. He was there, but he was hiding. He had sensed she was near and he was cloaking himself from her. Even now, she searched each and every being below. Some of them were connected to him. She felt his magic in them. He had given his magic to them. He was aiding one side to win against the other. As she thought this, Roane sank his teeth deeper into her. She looked down, confused.

"Can you hear my thoughts?"

He drank harder, faster.

He could. She had taken over his mind, but that was his response to her.

He wanted her to help his side. She felt him imploring her. He wasn't thinking it, but somewhere his consciousness was reaching out to her. She felt his desires as if they were hers, and for his friends and loved ones to win was one of the most important.

She needed to consider it. If one side won over the other, how would it benefit her? Or would it not? It was Jacith's side versus Roane's. If Jacith won, her eyes narrowed—she had to locate him. She needed to understand what he wanted from her.

She focused on the battle again, waving a hand so she and Roane were cloaked. A group of vampires broke away from the rest. They were racing to find Roane, but they weren't of too much concern. She would stop them once they arrived. The rest resumed their fighting, and she used this distraction to go from one creature to the other.

Jacith had covered his tracks. His magic was disguised inside of his creatures. She had to go from one to another, one at a time, and sink deep into each of them to find the amount of power he had given to each.

Vampires. Werewolves—she found that the wolves were given new power. The vampires held his power, but it was buried deep. Their power and magic had been with them for centuries. Each had been weaned off. It was their own power now, there was no line back to him and that was what she needed to find him.

She focused on the wolves. She went from one to the other, until she had searched the last of the wolves. They were all linked, but there had to be a line back to him. She needed to find the one that held Jacith's power.

Wait.

She stopped and lifted her head. The answer was in herself. Davy would know. Closing her eyes, she began to shift through her own memories. Lucas was still drinking from her and she continued to hold his head in the palm of her hand. *"Davy, Davy. What do you know?"*

"Fuck you!"

Her mouth lifted in a grin. *"Oh, how I've missed your spunk."*

"My spunk? Here's some more spunk."

Davy began fighting her.

The Immortal frowned. She was distracted and released Lucas from her hold. She rallied, focusing all her attention on the human in her. *"You would dare to fight me?"*

"I'd dare to do more. You took my body, you psycho narcissistic bitch."

"And I will take more. I will take your life," The Immortal sparked back at her. *"Remember that I hold the power of your loved ones in my hand, literally. You will do better to work with me than against me."*

The human wasn't happy. The Immoral felt Davy wanting to fight back, but what she spoke was the truth. The human needed her to help her friends.

"The Mother Wolf."

The Immortal frowned. *"The Mother Wolf?"*

"That's the answer. She's the big bad mother Alpha. I'm guessing she's the key to Jacith. She's a psycho bitch like you, so you better kill her. Don't become besties or something. She'll try to take your power."

The Immortal chuckled softly. No one could take her power. No one was a match to her anymore. She thought, *"Thank you, my human."* Then, she released Davy from her thoughts and pushed her back, as far back into the back of her mind as possible. It was the same jail that she herself had been locked in. Then she opened her eyes once more. She turned again to the battleground before her.

Instead of resuming her search for this Mother Wolf, she saw that Lucas wasn't kneeling before her anymore. She turned, and he was behind her. An army of his vampires behind him. All of them were staring at her, and she could sense their fear and rage all at the same time.

They wanted to kill her.

She smiled. *"I don't fear you."*

Lucas growled, *"You should."* But he was conflicted. She saw the damage that all his memories had done to him. He loved her, or he loved the vessel, but he wasn't sure anymore.

"You shouldn't question yourself. You know who you truly love, Lucas." Her voice dropping to an intimate whisper. Her words acted like a caress to him, trailing over him and filling his mind with the memory of when he made love to Davy. But it was her. He was feeling The Immortal, not the human anymore. He felt The Immortal's power in the vision.

"Stop." He turned away, breaking the connection from her. "Get out of my head."

She whispered, her voice sounding as loud as thunder in his mind alone, *"I cannot. You love me. It was never her."*

He pressed his hands over his ears and roared, "GET OUT!"

His friends started forward, reacting to his plea. They each had varied expressions. Alarm. Fear. Awe. Some were captivated by her, but none of them were a threat.

As they raced around their leader for her, she stepped backwards. Her feet touched air, but she lifted her arms and she was airborne once more. They stopped on the edge of the cliff. There was a woman snarling at her. Her chest was heaving. Her rage was clear and she wanted to murder The Immortal.

"Wren," The Immortal spoke, pulling her name from Davy's memories. "You are in love with Lucas."

The vampire's eyes narrowed and she reached for her, but The Immortal moved back again. She was out of the vampire's reach unless she stepped off the cliff. "There, there," she taunted her. "You cannot fly, the last I remembered."

"I'm going to kill you."

"Yes. You wished the same thing to the human who I share this body with." The Immortal tilted her head to the side. "But you cannot harm either of us. We are both too powerful for you, and you hate it." She flicked her eyes up and down the vampire's body.

She was strong. Long black hair. Fierce dark eyes. Ruby red lips. She had hate and a yearning for power not so unlike The Immortal. She chided, sighing, "I wish that the prophecy had been changed. If I could've merged with you, I think both of us would've been happy with the result."

But no, she had a human in her.

"Davy!"

A new voice sounded and The Immortal lifted herself higher. The voice came from behind the throng in front of her. It was a werewolf, and as she recognized her, she felt Davy fighting once again. This was a friend to her human.

"Pippa."

"Davy." The younger wolf rushed forward. Her sleek hair blowing in the wind. She had recently transformed back to her human body so her clothes were torn. They hung limply from her. The werewolf paid no attention. "Davy, please."

The Immortal didn't say a word. Sympathy filled her and she frowned. Where had that emotion come from? She wasn't keen to human emotions.

Davy. The answer was clear to her. The human in her still had power over her senses. Perhaps that was why she didn't wish to harm this wolf.

She needed to leave. She had to get away from Davy's friends. They had power over her, power that she didn't want anyone to have. She turned her back to the group on the cliff. She could feel Lucas's confusion still. They were linked now, linked even more than they ever had been, but she had to deal with Jacith. He was a problem she didn't want to regret not stopping as soon as she could.

The Mother Wolf. She needed to find her first.

She flew then, searching for her prey.

"Roane."

As soon as The Immortal was gone, Wren dashed to her leader's side. Falling to her knees, she placed a hand on his shoulder. He was pale and trembling. The Immortal had been inside his head. She frowned, worrying about how to help him. What damage had Davy's Immortality done to Roane?

"I'm okay." Lucas touched her hand and raked his other hand over his face. He could feel her. He could see through her eyes as she soared over the trees now. He needed a block to her. He couldn't let her know what he sensed when she had been accosting him with visions of time with Talia and Davy. Sensing that Wren was about to question him, he held a hand up. "Don't ask me questions. She's in my head still. I can't tell you anything."

Wren pulled her hand free and hastily retreated a step. The vampiress's eyebrows were arched high. The others heard his words and followed her lead. They all looked in fear at their leader now.

He couldn't think.

The Immortal was moving farther away. Their link was lessening, but it was still there. He could feel The Immortal's essence in him. It was pure power and he drew in a sharp breath, feeling his body acclimate to the sudden surge in him. It was overwhelming, but he couldn't do a thing to stop The Immortal right now. Turning to the battle, he could do something there instead.

"Lucas!"

Christian Christane had arrived. He pushed his way through Roane's vampires and stopped next to his sister. Glancing at Pippa, he paused a moment. Their heads bent together. She was filling him in on what happened. When she was done, a different expression crossed the Alpha Werewolf's features. It was close to sympathy, but there was caution as well. His eyes held to Roane's with a wariness Lucas felt in his bones.

Christian was gazing at him as if he were an enemy.

He was so far from that, or he hoped to be. Before Christian could speak, Lucas shook his head. "She gave me power. A lot of it. We can use that and launch another attack."

"They're retreating below. We can follow to where their camp is."

Roane nodded. He signaled for Wren to come to him. She did, so did Pippa and her brother. He spoke, already feeling a grave distance starting between him and them. He would be their enemy soon. The Immortal was in his head, and she just proved that she couldn't be trusted.

He said, "She's in my head. She can feel me, but she's distracted right now. Her power is immense and I don't know how long I'll be able to hold onto my own will. Right now, I'm your ally. You can use me against our enemies, but don't trust me."

Pippa's bottom lip trembled. "Davy's gone?"

She wasn't. He felt her inside of The Immortal, but he said, "There's little hope of getting her back."

"Your brother."

They all turned to Wren. She raised her chin up and squared her shoulders back. Her hands went behind her back and her legs stood apart. She took on a soldier's pose. "He used witches to separate the thread from Davy. He could help, perhaps, in weakening her now."

Christian's nostrils flared. Anger pitted deep inside of him. "Are you joking? He's the reason this entire war is happening."

Wren stiffened, but she didn't back down. "He wants the thread. Now that she's loose, he'll be scared of her. He caused her pain. I heard the screams. I've no doubt that he'll be more fearful of The Immortal than he will be of us."

"It's a shot."

Christian's head jerked back to Lucas. "You can't be serious?"

He was, so very much so, but there was more Roane needed to say. He couldn't. She would sense his intentions. As it was, he was trying to keep his thoughts clear. The Immortal couldn't know what he was planning, but while she was in his head, he was in hers. He was there. Davy was there too. It was something, at least.

"Roane."

His name was being called and Lucas looked over. What he saw had him closing his eyes as a surge of hope filled him. He shoved it down, almost as soon as it appeared. Bastion pointed behind him, to Gavin, Tracey, and Gregory. There were two others and he could smell the humanity on them. Before going over to greet them, he turned away. The less The Immortal knew, the better.

He said to Wren, "Fill them in. I will lead a charge to where the Romah and Benshire wolves are holed up. That was their first wave. I know there's more farther in the forest."

"After that?"

Lucas hesitated. "After that, I will venture to my brother, but you must head there yourself. Without me."

"Why?"

"The less all of you have to do with me, the better." He could feel The Immortal still flying. She was nearing wherever she wanted to go. She was intent on her target, and he was taking advantage of his distraction, but he knew there were limits. He couldn't risk too much. He held onto Wren's hand and whispered urgently to her, "I will fight. We can win now. The Immortal is seeking The Mother Wolf. After that, I will seek out my brother. He's our only hope in getting Davy back."

Wren went still. Her eyes sought and held onto his.

He saw the fear appear and he swallowed hard. Wren was never scared. She was only angry or hurt, seeing that vulnerability in one of his most loyal now caused his anger to flicker alive. He had it contained, along with all of his emotions, but as it broke free, that was one emotion he wanted to feel. It would blanket the rest. If he was furious, The Immortal would accept that. She wouldn't search for what else was in his mind.

He started to step away. His head lowered, and he was going to leave without speaking to his friends. He didn't want to, but The Immortal couldn't know they were alive. The less she knew, the safer everyone was.

"Roane." Wren grabbed him again.

He heard the dip in her voice, how it grew husky, and his chest tightened at the sympathy he knew would be in her eyes. He couldn't look at her.

"I have to go."

"But Da—"

He pulled away and rasped out, "I know." He had to stop her. She couldn't say Davy's name, because Davy wasn't really lost. She couldn't be. He couldn't think that way. His voice hardened. "I have to go to kill our enemies."

She started to reach for him again, but he went to the edge and dropped to the bottom. Sensing their leader, his men that had been on the battleground turned toward him. They didn't know yet, but they soon would that he was no longer their leader. He was compromised, but until he really was under The Immortal's power, he had one more battle to wage.

Pulling out his sword, he started in the direction that he saw The Immortal fly. She was seeking The Mother Wolf, that was where the rest of their enemies would be. He didn't look behind him, but he registered that the Christane wolves were turning to follow him. Christian and Pippa had followed him, as everyone did.

Wren, Bastion, and the new arrivals remained behind. They had their own mission.

IT WAS DONE. Roane felt it in his gut. The Immortal had won, and he hadn't even known there was a fight for Davy until she was smack in front of him, kissing him. He knew she was different, but he didn't care. It was Davy. She was finally in front of him. He could hold her. He could taste her, touch her, inhale her. But, it had been too good to be true. There'd been something off about her, he felt that in the back of his mind, but he turned it off. He didn't want to question how Davy came to be. He was just glad she was there.

Then the other shoe dropped. It wasn't her.

And now, as he led his army into the forest with his sword ready in his hand, The Immortal was swirling around inside of himself. He wasn't sure if it was even him in there, or just her. He felt under her control, but there was a small tunnel. He felt Davy before. She was still in The Immortal. If he could get to her, if there was a way of breaking her free, he had to take it, but for now—they crested the last hill and below them, they could hear the screams.

The Immortal had already arrived.

It was chaos. Hundreds of Benshire wolves were dead on the ground. The image was almost as bad as the battleground they just left, but there was an army missing. Roane searched the woods. The Romah vampires were there. It wasn't just the

Benshire line. Jacith had brought his oldest and most powerful vampire family.

"No!"

Christian and Pippa stood next to him, but the rest of the Christane wolves streamed around them. They began to attack the rest that still lived, but before the first could lunge in the air, a bloodcurdling scream went through the air. It went through everyone, sending chills down their spines.

At the top of the next ridge stood The Immortal and The Mother Wolf. One in her white dress and the other in her blue robe.

A deep roar ripped from Christian. "No. She's mine to kill." He surged forward. "NO!"

Davy looked over at them. He hated to call her that, but he loathed to keep referring to her as The Immortal. It was a grand title that she didn't deserve. She wasn't grand. She wasn't anything except a monster, who took the real Davy away.

She was holding The Mother Wolf up with one hand at her throat. Genuine confusion flashed over her features as she looked from Christian to the woman in her grip. She held her up higher. "You wish to kill this one?"

Pippa started crying. Lucas heard her sniffling from the other side of her brother. He closed his eyes—this stranger who had Davy's body was so cold.

Anger was mounting in Christian and he nodded, stiffly. "Yes." His tone softened, but only a little bit. He was holding back the rage.

The Immortal—Roane couldn't call her Davy. It was too painful to think of her name—met his gaze. She was weighing her options. Her head tilted to the side and her long dark hair swept over her face from the wind. She was impervious to the weather. It was normally hot and humid where they were in Central America, but a cold front moved into the air. The temperature dipped low. The werewolves and vampires, who were impervious to weather as well, were starting to shiver. And through it all, The Immortal was immune to all of it, even the blood that seeped around her bare feet.

He looked around—so many bodies, so much death. The river would run red from the blood that night, but this was what they all signed up for.

War. Death. Carnage.

The Immortal still hadn't decided what to do with The Mother Wolf. She turned back and brought the older woman closer to her. She was studying her like she was a new creature for her to understand.

"No." Roane started forward.

Recognizing his voice, The Immortal looked again. More confusion crossed her face, but she didn't say anything. She held her comment and waited.

"What are you doing?" Christian reached for Roane.

"I'm going over there."

"No, Lucas."

"Don't. Please."

The last was a whimper from Pippa, Davy's friend. Roane's stomach clenched, but he moved out of Christian's reach. Lowering his voice, he said, "I'm going to her. Someone has to try to contain her."

"Contain that?" Christian's statement was a whip, lashing at him.

"Yes." She was too powerful to allow on her own, and he had no idea if he could control her. He could try, at least. He had to try. "None of ours can get hurt."

"One of ours already did." Pippa was glaring at Davy's body. Her own growl began to build in the back of her throat.

Roane started forward again, but he said as a goodbye, "I'll ask her to leave The Mother Wolf for you, but return home after that."

"Lucas—"

"I mean it!" He glared at them before turning away once again. "Leave. Go home." "*Go and be alive*," he thought before crossing the distance until the next ridge.

The Immortal was waiting. She had heard his thought and she asked now, in his head still, "*Is that what you think will happen? You will die.*"

He faltered just beneath the hill she stood upon. He held her gaze, never wavering. "*Either my body will die or my soul will. Either way, all is lost.*"

"*Nothing is lost. It's just a new life. That is all.*"

Everything was lost, but he held back those words. She heard them, a darkness flashing in her eyes, but both let it go. He gestured to The Mother Wolf. "*My friend has come this entire way to kill her.*"

He remembered the stories spoken about The Mother Wolf.

"*The Alpha went to The Mother Wolf,*" Pippa said.

The Mother Wolf knew about Davy. She was connected to The Immortal.

He remembered when he first saw her. There, in the middle of five Goliath-sized wolves and four Romah guards in full armor, was a woman.

He knew who she was.

This was The Mother Wolf, the one that Christian told him about. She was stunning. Black hair fell free and loose past her shoulders. She wore a blue and silver robe. The colors were striking, matching the air of strength she was emanating. Her eyes were dark. Her lips were bright red, curved into a half smile, and her head was raised in a confident and authoritative manner, but that wasn't all that clung to her —magic.

She had been so powerful then. And now, her arms hung limply, her head fell back as if she were a doll, and her eyes were dull. They were almost lifeless. The Immortal had done this. It was a shock.

She was nothing now. She was weak.

The enormity of The Immortal's power shouldn't have surprised him, but it did. And with each action that showed even more power, a part of his hope died inside of him. Swallowing painfully, he asked, "Why did you go after her?"

"She has his magic." The Immortal peered at The Mother Wolf again. "It's inside of her. He planted it in her and I need to follow it to where he is. He must die. He is the only one who could be troublesome to me."

Roane continued to feel his insides spilling out over him. "You mean he's the only one who could match your power."

"No." She snapped back to attention. "Never. He is no match. He is beneath me. It's why he is hiding. All his magic, it's everywhere. It's in the wolves. It's in his vampires. It's in the ground." A light gleamed in her eyes. "The ground. He's underground." She focused on Mother Wolf and placed her hand between the woman's breasts. The Immortal leaned closer, peering where her hand was and she began to say under her breath, "You are in her. I can feel your magic. There is a path. I must follow where it goes."

As the last word was spoken,=, the air shifted.

Roane could feel a heaviness, as if something was poured into the atmosphere around them. Then, The Immortal uttered one word, "Ignite," and an explosion happened. He covered his eyes. The light was blinding, but when he looked back, Mother Wolf was hanging in the air. The Immortal had suspended her there and a light shone from inside of her. A string, or a line, moved out from Mother Wolf's body and he turned, tracing it all the way down the hill they stood on, through the valley of the second battle, and past where Christian and Pippa stood.

The Immortal came down to stand beside him. She was watching the trail. "It goes back to the water. He is back there."

She started forward.

A surrealness had come over everyone. There were few of the Benshire werewolves alive, but those who still survived ceased fighting Christian's pack. As The Immortal walked past them, they moved apart. An opening cleared for her and she left, either unmoved or indifferent to the fear that everyone had for her.

He looked back to The Mother Wolf, but she was still in the air. There was no fight left in her.

Christian and Pippa hurried to his side once The Immortal was gone from their eyesight. Christian peered up at his enemy. The corners of his mouth turned down, and he remarked, "The victory in battle has lost its appeal."

Pippa looked up at him. "You need to kill her. You can't let her live through this."

Christian's frown deepened. Roane could hear the regret in his voice when he replied, "I won't, but it's not an honorable death anymore. I'm merely ending her suffering."

"Roane." The Immortal spoke in his head. *"Come."*

He had to go, but he said to Christian, "Thank you for being my ally."

Pippa moved around so she could see him squarely. "You're leaving?"

"Roane."

"The Immortal." He gestured in the direction she had gone. "She's calling me."

"That's annoying," Christian bit out.

Roane laughed. There was nothing else to do. There were no other reactions to feel. All he could do was laugh, because at the very least, it was annoying.

He rested a hand on the Alpha Wolf's shoulder and lowered his head in a small bow. "Our time has come to an end. I hope to see you on the other side one day."

He started to pull back, but Christian covered his hand with his. It was a rare gesture, but before Roane could do anything or say anything, the Alpha Wolf pulled him in for a hug. It was brief. Each clapped the other on the back; they had come a long way. There'd been mistrust and a reluctant aligning with each other.

They loved the same woman, but now they were on the same side. They had another similar enemy.

Christian stepped back. "Go get your woman back."

Roane swallowed a lump.

He couldn't think about her. Those thoughts were erased and he stepped aside to face Pippa. "Thank you. I know you came to help your friend."

Tears were trailing down her face. The younger wolf lifted a hand and wiped at some of them, but they were replaced with new tears. Roane didn't think they would end soon, and he had to admit that he wished he could cry alongside her. Instead, he murmured, "If I can, I will save her."

"*You are lying to them,*" The Immortal chided him. "*You know she is lost. Do not give them false hope.*"

He thought back, "*They will fight otherwise. I am saving their lives.*"

He waited, but there was silence from her end. Pippa hugged him, and then he left them. He walked on the same path The Immortal had gone, and once he was gone from their eyesight, he heard one last bloodcurdling scream.

The Mother Wolf was dead.

26

LUCAN

He stood at the highest point among the Mori lands.
The winds had shifted. What he thought was his greatest enemy was now his greatest ally. Another Mori came to stand beside him and he spoke, knowing it was Jiyama's father, "The thread has become her own entity."

The elder Mori glanced at him. There was a pause and the air was heavy with tension. It was known that Jiyama was gone. Her body was never found. None sensed where her essence was, and stories of how another Mori was killed at the hands of The Immortal had spread fast. Another Mori witnessed the murder, but he had retreated to share the information. He hadn't engaged. When the rest of the Mori realized their new danger, a council had been called. Warriors were placed near the outer edge of their land to report back the events that were unveiling beyond their river's boundary.

Lucan heard about the transformation, and he was told how The Immortal had seemingly cast a spell over his brother.

Jiyama's father, Jeoji, asked, "What will happen now?"

Lucan grunted. "If I had to guess, my brother's friends will want to come here." Jeoji turned to him, but Lucan added, "We created this. We unbalanced the thread inside of her. They'll want us to help fix it."

"We?" A warning growl. "You created this problem. We had nothing to do with this."

Lucan turned and faced the Mori's leader. They were face-to-face, eye-to-eye, and while one held all the power and magic of a Mori vampire, the other was more dangerous. Lucan was human. He remained in his weak vessel because of one thing: the thread. He wanted that thread inside of him, and he knew that he would be told of visitors traveling their way. What he predicted would come true. His brother's friends would seek him out, and he would help them because at this moment, their wishes co-aligned. All of them wanted The Immortal contained. Afterwards, that was another issue, but he said to Jeoji now, "Do not play the ignorant fool. I was one of you. You and your men traveled with me in search of the thread. You and your men, my brothers too, helped me capture my brother's lover. You have known since the beginning my wish for the thread. It is why you allowed the child to come into this clan. Do not act innocent. You have shed blood, just as I have."

Jeoji was older, wiser, but he knew Lucan spoke the truth. Blame fell on his shoulders, perhaps more because he never stopped this one. "My daughter loved you." He let that sentence hang between them. His daughter, who was missing. His daughter, who had been so curious about the thread-holder. His daughter, who would never leave without telling him or her mother. His daughter, who he thought would marry this man standing in front of him.

His regrets were deep, and he added one more to the pile. He pulled his robe tighter over himself and glanced to where the war was still going on. "We have heard their screams. We can smell their blood. We can even feel their pain, and all of them were wiped out by one being that we set free. Capturing The Immortal is on our shoulders. We will assist you by whatever means you find necessary. That creature must not be allowed to remain alive."

There was an unspoken message between them, and Lucan accepted it. There was no proof, but Jeoji suspected him of his daughter's death. They would help him take The Immortal down, but afterwards he would be cast out. It was the way of their clan. He'd be exiled once again, but it wouldn't matter.

Lucan would get the thread. He would get that power, even if he would die in the process. It had become his sole obsession. He turned to go, but said over his shoulder, "Lower the shield. Allow my brother's friends in."

27

ROANE

He trailed behind The Immortal. She kept going, past the first battlegrounds and farther down the beach. The Mother Wolf was killed, but the line that led them to Jacith still existed. He didn't know how that was, but he didn't question it. The less he thought, the better, but he couldn't stop waves of grief from crashing over him. They came one at a time and every one was suffocating. He couldn't breathe so he kept going, sometimes blindly. He kept going. This thing, whatever she was, continued ahead. He knew she was aware of the suffering inside of him, but she paid him no attention.

"It is not because I do not care." She paused, and turned so she could see him from one eye.

He stopped, but he said nothing.

She kept going, "It's because there was no other way. You don't comprehend it. No one does."

"Comprehend what?"

"My existence."

They were coming to a waterfall. Roane heard the water falling earlier, but the sound was nearly deafening now, even to him. Still, he could hear her fine as she walked around a pile of large boulders. They were setting out on the bank, and as she circled them, he saw there was a trail that led underneath the waterfall.

"He's undergound." Her words came back to him, and he understood. Jacith was beneath everything. He was in the cave below the waterfall. The Hunter in him was telling him to pull back, proceed with caution, but The Immortal didn't have the same instincts. She walked freely without a care for herself. She spoke with the same freedom, speaking loudly, "Since I was created, I was always contained and hidden within a human. My creator did that because humans were thought to have the compassion to restrict me. That wasn't true. What they had to restrict me was their weakness. I couldn't exist if they did, and since it was their body, they were the host. They contained me. All that changed with Lucan and his coven. They weren't pulling me free of Davy. They were changing her. She was turning into something that wasn't human anymore. When that happened, I was able to get a foothold in her. I've been steadily gaining a foothold in her ever since."

She dipped underneath the water and held a hand up. There was nothing hanging to be lit, but small bursts of fire floated in the air, lighting their way.

He asked as he followed, stepping onto the damp rock path, "What did you mean before? What is it that no one understands?"

She paused. Just beyond her shoulder, the light was brighter as if they were about to step into a large opening in the cave. A low baritone voice was chanting in there, and Roane could feel the magic all around him. It was thick, sending shivers up and down his back. The hair on his neck stood up, but this was The Immortal's show. If she wasn't worried, he didn't think he needed to be.

Or he hoped.

Her eyes flicked over his face before the corner of her lip

lifted up. "It was never about me becoming one with Davy. It was either me *or* her. That was the question. Always."

He frowned. "What do you mean?"

"I couldn't exist if she did."

She waited, letting that statement linger.

Roane cocked his head to the side. His frown deepened. Understanding and horror dawned on him at the same time. "You —you were planning this the whole time." He felt gutted.

Her slight grin turned smug and she stepped around the corner into the larger open area. "You are right." Her gaze trailed to the man chanting in the middle of the cave.

Roane couldn't move forward. Everything in him was locked in place. He needed to run, but he was the Hunter. He was a vampire. He was Lucas Roane. He did not run, but right there, in the realization that The Immortal had been planning this move all along, he knew survival meant running.

He jerked around, as if he were actually going to go. He tried making himself.

He couldn't.

The Immortal laughed. It was a soft graze against his ears and he winced, instantly hating the sound. "You've been looking for Jacith. You said it was because he was the only one equal to you, but—" He couldn't bring himself to say the rest. His gut was saying otherwise. One didn't seek out their enemies first. No. One would seek out an ally first, and she'd been seeking out the sorcerer since she came to be.

This wasn't enemy territory to her.

She wasn't cowering. She wasn't sneaking. She wasn't even being cautious.

She stood, right in front of one of the most feared sorcerers since Roane had been alive and there was no fear.

He finished as all of his insides threatened to spill out of him, "He's not your enemy, is he?"

"No." A full smile stretched on her face, and she turned around.

Jacith had his eyes closed. He was wearing a similar robe as The Mother Wolf, blue and silver. The hood was pulled low over his face so his eyes were shielded, but his power was immense. It rippled through the cave. His arms were stretched out as he continued to chant, he allowed them to continue their conversation, until he sensed The Immortal's attention. His eyes opened and a smile appeared on his face.

The sight sickened Roane.

Jacith lowered his arms and his head at the same time. He bowed to The Immortal. "As we meet at last."

He held a hand out, and The Immortal took it, letting him hold it as he looked back up. She echoed, "As we meet at last."

The two shared a smile before Jacith removed his hood.

Roane had never met him, but he heard about him. Everyone had. Jacith was tall in his vampire body, but once the hood left his head, he grew in height. He stood at another four inches, towering over the both of them. His hair was black and gray, all mixed together and his eyes were a clear blue. A white line shone around his irises, but Roane had a dreaded guess that that was The Immortal's influence over him. She was assisting him with magic in some way.

"Lucas Roane." Jacith tucked his hands to his chest, his robe's sleeves hanging low to the ground. He moved around The Immortal and approached. He scanned him up and down. "You are every bit as powerful as she said you would be."

Roane needed to get out of there. As fast as possible. He began to move backwards, an inch at time.

The Immortal studied him alongside Jacith. She folded her arms over her chest and nodded. "He is. The Hunters are close by. His tattoo is alive. I can feel it." She glanced to him. "Can you?"

Jacith's eyes narrowed, a mere fraction of an inch. "Of course, I can."

"Really?" Her grin turned smug, just the slightest hint. "He has power. We can draw from it."

As she spoke those words, Jacith's eyes lit up. An eager gleam grew bright, and he moved forward. Roane went still. He was a prey to the sorcerer. He was focused on getting out of there, but at the cold sliver that rang down his back, he reassessed the situation. Hunters. His tattoo. They could draw his power, the last shoe dropped then.

"You promised him my power." Roane didn't even ask. He knew that was what happened. It was the only thing that made sense.

Surprise and pride flashed over her features. "You're smart, Lucas. Yes, I did."

"All that you said before, about how I loved you, all of that was a lie."

"No. That was the truth. You do love me. I've been drawing you to me for decades. The thread-holder before Talia would've found you, too, if she had been smart enough to realize her wishes weren't her own." She spoke dryly, a wry twist at her lips, "She was more accustomed to females so when she began dreaming of you, she knew something was wrong." Her eyes grew hard. "But I will have my time with that thread-holder. I know she is waiting. Her time is soon, but until then, everything else was a lie." She shook her head. "I don't love you, Lucas. I'm not a crazy, besotted weakling like the others. You have power. You have lots of power and you will be giving all of that power to Jacith." She glanced at the sorcerer. "He was very keen to get his hands on you. That was my part of the deal. I was to deliver you to him."

"How?"

Roane wasn't sure he wanted to know, but he asked anyway.

"Your brother helped so much, but I needed more power to break free from Davy. Every time she was unconscious, and there were a lot of times your brother's coven made her pass out from pain, I called onto Jacith. I drew him to me. He loaned his power to me and here I am, returning it to him. You. You are my payout."

"This is a joke, right?"

Jacith was advancing on him. His sick delight was making Roane's stomach roll over. He couldn't defeat the sorcerer and he knew he couldn't defeat The Immortal. A brief thought of ending it his way, his power intact, flashed through his mind.

"Don't!"

He met her gaze. *"Why not?"*

"Because—" she glanced to Jacith, but his back was completely to her. He was focused only on Roane. Her eyes narrowed and a cold wall fell over her face. She thought back to him, *"Because you were my bait for him. That's why."*

"Bait?" He couldn't keep up with the changes. A new alliance was popping up every other minute. He asked her in his mind, *"What do you mean by bait?"*

"Wait." Her voice was calming. *"You will see."*

As Jacith grew closer, Roane was backed up into the wall. He didn't feel the cold wetness of the rock behind him. Jacith's eagerness was rolling over him, overwhelming him. The sorcerer reached up and gripped Roane around the throat. At the contact, Roane gasped. His blood was on fire. Every inch of him was burned and he felt his insides being sucked out. Jacith was drawing on his power.

No matter what she said, this was the end.

Roane closed his eyes. He didn't know if the sorcerer was in his head or not, but he made himself think of Davy. He tried to talk to her. *"Davy. I love you. Can you hear me?"* As he spoke, his hand reached for a dagger tucked behind his back. His hand found the handle and wrapped around it, gripping it tight. A tear slipped from his eye. *"Davy, I don't know if you can hear me or not, but no matter our ending, we'll have the next life together. A new chapter. I promise."*

He imagined she was there. She was standing in front of him.

He could hold her. He could rest his forehead to hers and whisper, *"I love you so very much, to the deepest parts of my soul. You, Davina, you make me an honorable man. You are why I have fought in this life and you are why I will continue to the next. I love you, wherever you are."*

She was there, gripping his hands with hers. Her tears mixed with his and she whispered back, kissing him at the same time, *"I love you, too. I will be there. I'm waiting for you, Lucas. Come to me. Come to me."*

They were kissing. They were hugging. They were happy— and at the last thought, he pulled his dagger out and plunged it into Jacith's stomach. The sorcerer jerked back, a thunderous roar ripping from him. Lucas was unfazed. He pushed up from the wall and held onto the dagger with a better hold, then he pushed it as deep as he could. His hand was inside of the vampire, and knowing it wouldn't be enough, he thrust his other hand and wrapped his fingers around Jacith's heart.

No creature could live without a beating heart.

He yanked it out.

The body crumbled to the floor, but his other hand held onto the dagger. The Immortal screamed, and in the midst of it all, Lucas held the sorcerer's heart in his hand and the dagger in his other. A feral smile adorned his face as he met The Immortal's horrified eyes.

He said, "Oops."

He threw the dagger at her.

28

"NO!"

She deflected the dagger.

It flew right at her, would've landed smack center in her chest, but The Immortal lifted her hand. The dagger stopped and flew right back at him, except it sheathed itself into the cave wall behind it. Roane froze, his eyes wide at how quick her response was. She rushed to Jacith's side, and placed her hands on his chest.

Roane didn't say a word. She could've killed him with the dagger, but didn't. She could still kill him, but after that one scream, she was concentrating. Resting on her knees, her eyes closed, she remained perfectly still.

Roane stood there. He needed to run, but he stayed. He needed to see what she was doing, and when a black coloring formed under her hand and began to move up her arms, he had a good idea. She was absorbing all of Jacith's power.

Roane turned to go. It was time, but before he could even form the thought, she opened her eyes, pure black, and said, "Stay."

An invisible wall slammed in place. He couldn't get through.

Hitting it only hurt his hand. It felt like ten cement walls glued together. Vampire strength couldn't stand up against magic. He waited, leaning against the wall as The Immortal continued to pull the rest of Jacith's magic into her. When she was done, the black coloring was gone except as she stood and opened her eyes once more. They were still black.

Her hair billowed out behind her. She didn't say a word and Roane didn't think she could. The magic was settling inside of her, and another few seconds, her normal chocolate brown eyes snapped back into place. Her hair rested against her back again and her normal coloring came to her face.

Jacith was different. He was a corpse with a giant hole in the chest. A second later, his body burst into flames. He really was dead now. He couldn't come back from that.

Roane grunted. "If I knew it would've been that easy to kill him, I would've done it a long time ago."

"You're a fool," The Immortal spat at him, waving her hand in the air again.

The invisible wall fell from behind him and Roane caught himself. She swept past him, and he followed behind. "What do you mean?" He was waiting for the wrath to come out on him, but she kept heading back toward the waterfall.

She said over her shoulder, "Everyone has a weakness. Jacith's was just like a normal vampire. You had to get close to him in order to kill him, and that was my mistake."

He was still waiting for her wrath.

Sensing his thought, she said, "I wanted to kill Jacith. That was why I gave you my power."

Wait.

"What?"

She glanced back, rolled her eyes, and turned back. "Everything I've said to you was a lie since I broke free. Everything, Lucas."

"You told me that I loved you."

She said, "You don't."

"You told me that Jacith was your enemy."

"He wasn't, but he was at the same time."

"You told me that you were going to offer me to him as a payback."

"I was. That was my plan."

He frowned and stopped walking. "I don't understand."

"You don't have to." She kept going. When he didn't resume following, she gestured to him and commanded, "Come."

His feet and legs started moving. Roane had no control over them. He sighed. There was a lot that he couldn't control anymore, but the one thing he could—his murderous rage. He wanted to kill.

He wanted to kill *her*.

LUCAN

LUCAN STOOD UNDERNEATH A TREE, just behind his brother's friends and downwind from them. They were all lying toward the top of a hill, peering at the Mori on the other side. He had been notified of their presence and circled around, taking a tunnel underneath so he could sneak up, but as they all lay plastered to the ground, he didn't have to be stealth.

They were talking too much. A blind elephant could've have snuck up on them.

"So," one of the humans cleared his throat, speaking up. He pointed over the hill. "Just so I get this straight, the four of you were captured by this dude in there."

No one responded. A beat passed and Gavin said, "Yes."

"He tortured you guys—"

"He tortured Davy."

The human nodded. "The psycho chick that killed that one other cute chick, right?"

Wren glared at him. "Do you have a point?"

"Yeah. I mean, why are we heading back there when we should be leaving?" The human propped himself up on his elbow, lying on his side. The other human was still behind him, but he was facing the rest of the others.

Lucan frowned. There didn't seem to be fear on this human, just curiosity and a dry sarcasm. He sniffed the air. There was another smell to him, too. He couldn't place the smell, but it clung to both of the humans heavily.

Gavin hissed, motioning with his hand. "Get back down. Now."

"Okay." The human rolled to his back and folded his hands over his chest. He gazed up at the sky. "But back to my point. Tell me again why we're seeking out some dude who wants to kill all of you guys."

"Because he doesn't care about us. He cares about the thread." Gavin sat up. His voice raised to a normal volume. "And because that means we have the same enemy."

"What are you doing?" Wren yanked him back down.

"Wren," Gavin started, sitting up and staring behind them.

The last human muttered, "I could go for a smoke. Seriously. Seeking out another bad guy's got me jonesing hardcore."

His friend threw him a grin, kicking his feet. "Don't stress, Cal. The way I figure it we're hanging out with a bunch of vampires."

"We're going into another group of vampires," the one called Cal groaned. "And they aren't friendly."

"But we just escaped an entire army of other vamps and werewolves. Like, holy shit, vampires and werewolves. No one will believe us, but we saw those things."

"We're going to die, Spencer." He shot him a dark look.

"Yeah." Spencer shrugged. "But we sure have lived, haven't we?"

"Shut up," Wren growled at both of them. "We either move or we leave. We need to do something to help Lucas."

Gavin, still looking into the trees behind them, said, "Wren—"

"Let's go." Wren collected her sword and crouched to a crawling position. She could maneuver over the hill, continuing to slink toward the village.

Gavin stood up and Lucan grinned. His brother's best friend was staring right at him, and as the others gasped in shock, Lucan stepped forward. He said, "Welcome." All of them jumped to their feet, grabbing for their weapons, and he turned his smile toward the two on the end. "You brought more humans. My friends will welcome their dinner tonight."

Cal frowned and scratched behind his ear. "Say what?"

29

ROANE

They'd been walking through the forest until it got dark. Roane kept waiting for her to fly away, or go invisible, or do something magical, but she never did. She trekked ahead of him, walking as if she were a human, until they came to a clearing. She stopped and gazed around, sighing. "I suppose we can sleep here tonight."

His eyebrows pinched together. "You sleep?"

"No." She waved her hand in the air and a bonfire appeared. Two sleeping bags were on the floor, on either side of the fire. She dropped down on one of them and crossed her legs. "But you do."

His head moved back an inch. He couldn't bring himself to give her a compliment. She was being nice.

"What?" She laughed. "You're surprised I might have a soul in me? I was inside of Davy for a year. Some of her niceness rubbed off on me."

She had Davy's face. Davy's voice and right now, as she was staring at the fire, it was like she was Davy. His stomach clenched. This was not Davy, and he couldn't forget that. Ever.

She rolled her eyes, lying down on her side. Her hands tucked under her head, acting like a pillow. "I'm not her, but I'm not that bad either, Lucas Roane of the Hunters."

He grunted, dropping down onto the other sleeping bag. "You replaced my girlfriend. I think you are."

Her eyes found his through the fire. A dark and sober expression filled them. "When it comes to the question of you or someone else existing, you might be surprised at the lengths you'll go to live."

"You're not a person."

"And yet here I am." She rolled to her back. "Talking like a person. Breathing. Feeling. I think I'm more human than you are, even."

She was lying. She had no soul. Davy had been the soul in her. He continued to study her, and she let him. He didn't need to sleep that much, maybe a few hours if even that, but after a while his eyes closed, and he slept.

"Lucas."

He stood up. Everything around him was dark, but that was Davy. She was crying. More sobs came from her, and he called out, "Davy? Where are you?"

"Lucas?"

The crying stopped. Her voice grew clearer. "Lucas!"

"I'm here. Where are you?"

"Here." And suddenly, she was. She was smack in front of him. Her dark hair lay straight down her shoulders and her eyes were wide. "What are you doing here?" She touched his shoulders and patted him. "Are you real? Are you really here?"

"Davy." He closed his eyes and groaned. She was right in front of him. He could touch her. Taking her hands in his, he pulled her close and tucked his forehead to the crook of her neck and shoulders. He clasped her tight. "Oh my God. I can feel you."

Her arms wrapped tightly around him and she pressed up on her toes. Her whole body moved even closer against his.

He savored this. He had her. Finally. He could hug her, kiss her, feel her, taste her, inhale her.

"Oh my God."

He felt her tears against his shoulder. He only wanted to hold her longer.

"Oh my God," she repeated. More tears. "Is this a dream?"

Yes. He was asleep. If this was real or not, he didn't want to question it. He just wanted to draw strength from it. If only in his dreams, if that were the only place he could see her, it would be enough. It would be more than enough.

"This is a dream." Her tears lessened. She pulled away, but he held on. He didn't want her to pull all the way away. She leaned back so she could look into his eyes. What he saw there had his rage going again. She knew this moment wouldn't last. He would leave again. She said, "Lucas, if this is real or not, you have to know about her."

He shook his head. "Stop, Davy. I just want to hold you. I don't want to think of her."

She stepped farther back. Her hands fell to his arms. Her fingers dug in, holding onto him with a cement grip. "No, but you have to. This is important. She's going to destroy the only person who is a threat to her. She's an innocent."

He leaned back. "An innocent? She'll never be innocent."

"No. You don't understand." She clenched onto him even harder. Her fingers were turning white. "You think she's all powerful. You think there's no hope, but there is. Someone is missing. Who is missing? Ask yourself why they're missing? And she's not the innocent, but the innocent is the key. There are people coming. They will help. People you have forgotten about. People that you started in motion. Remember, Lucas. Think, Lucas."

Wind started blowing around them. It was growing faster, starting to tug at him. Their time was ending. He was getting pulled away.

He didn't want that. He wanted to only savor her.

"Lucas!" She framed his face with her hands. The wind was like a

tornado. It tripled in power and she was yelling so he could hear her. "I can come back! You can bring me back!"

The wind was too much. It was a vacuum. He was pulled away and their hands held onto each other. He was in the air, but still, his fingers laced with hers. She was trying to keep him there, but right before he was yanked backwards, she yelled again, "Bring me back!"

He was gone.

His eyes snapped open and he jerked upright. "Did you do that?"

The Immortal was on her sleeping bag. It was light out, and she turned her head lazily to him. "Do what?"

"My dream. Davy." His breathing was ragged. "Did you do that?"

Her eyebrows knotted together and the corners of her lip curved down a bit. She sat up, straightening her dress. "No, but now I'm intrigued. What did you dream about?"

"Why do you lie?"

Her eyebrows arched high. "I'm not. I really want to know now. What did she say?" A half grin teased at her lips. "Did she tell you of my demise?"

"Someone is missing . . . the innocent is the key. There are people coming. They will help. People you have forgotten about. People that you started in motion. Remember, Lucas. Think, Lucas."

Davy's words haunted him. They were ricocheting around him, and they felt so real. Her desperation was still with him. He could feel it. He could feel her.

He sat back down.

Davy had been there. Whether real or not, she was there. She was giving him a message. He shook his head and lifted his gaze. The Immortal was watching him. Her eyes were piercing. He asked, "Are you in my head?"

She didn't respond. Her lips pressed together, then she stood up. "Let's go. We've rested long enough. Neither of us is human. We don't need that much sleep."

She wasn't in his head anymore. She started forward, but that realization echoed strong inside of him. She wasn't in his head, and she was pissed about it. Then, did he dare hope, that could mean that Davy had been real?

He swallowed hard, painfully, but hope bloomed inside of his chest. It was small, but it was there.

He could bring her back.

———

Someone missing.

An innocent.

And people were coming back.

That was Davy's message to him, and Roane tried to decipher it. Who was missing? Davy. Everyone. Himself. He couldn't wrap his mind around who she meant and the innocent—no one was innocent. And who was coming back? She was insistent that there was hope, but as he followed The Immortal, he couldn't figure out who Davy meant. The one person who had enough power to defeat The Immortal was Jacith and he was dead. Thinking about it, Roane could've cursed himself. He hadn't been thinking, but The Immortal was in his head. He couldn't have been thinking ahead. She would've known then.

"Okay." They'd been steadily winding up around a mountain and The Immortal stopped. She stepped out on an edge. "We're here."

He looked to where she was gazing and was surprised. "That's the Mori village?"

His mind was racing. Why had she come here? What did this mean? He glanced sideways to her. "Are you here for my brother?"

Her eyes narrowed, but a hint of a grin flashed over her face. It was a glimmer, and it was gone just as quick as it showed. "No, but your brother could become an annoying pest." She leaned forward and said, "Silence. I need to hear."

She was listening to the entire village. He should've been surprised, but nothing surprised him anymore, not when it came to this creature. She could bend the world's rules. She could be in his head. She could do almost anything. It was hard to imagine that Davy could be brought back, and yet, The Immortal was no longer in his head. A small victory happened, and she hadn't gotten into his head since. She had stopped many times on their trek, and she kept glancing back at him. She was trying to understand what happened, how she was locked out. Frustration rippled off her, and he basked in it, but all that was gone as she was eavesdropping on his brother's allies.

"Your friends are there," she murmured.

Alarm spiked in him.

She waved a hand at him. "Of course, they're there. They want to free you." She shot him a warning look. "They won't succeed. They're harmless, right now."

His friends weren't being held captive. She would've told him if they were. That meant they were there on their own accord. They were there to work with his brother, like he told them to do. He needed to distract her.

"Why are we here? If you're not here for my brother, who then?"

She frowned.

He asked further, "My brother's witches? He has a coven. Are you here for vengeance? I can't imagine they're an actual threat to you, not if Jacith hadn't been. He was the most powerful sorcerer on the earth—"

"I know what you're doing." She cut him off. "And it won't work." She turned back for the trail. "I found what I needed to find."

"What?"

She ignored him and began around the mountain once more.

Roane fell in line behind her and they walked in silence until they got to the other side of the mountain. He was mulling everything on his mind when she stopped again. He could hear the sounds of children laughing not far from them. He judged they were a quarter of a mile away. Too close for his liking. She shouldn't be this close, not to children, but he couldn't stop her. *Yet.* He could hear Davy's voice in his head. Yet, but he would.

She closed her eyes, bowed her head, and a second later the air became overwhelming. It pressed down on him, and he couldn't move. He opened his mouth to ask what was going on, but no sound came out. She looked at him and spoke. Her voice sounded like she was on the other side of a wall. He could barely make it out.

"You can't come with me any further."

"Why?" He tried yelling. No sound still came out. He was yelling in his own head.

"You're cloaked. No one will know you're here. They can't sense you either. I will be back once I'm done."

A foreboding sensation tunneled low in him. It was spreading fast and growing in urgency. *"Don't."* But it was useless. She turned her back and left for the village.

All he could do was yell, but no one heard him.

30

TRACEY

Talia had been her sister. Their bloodline was among other thread-holders. She was honored to be Talia's sister. She always had been even when she was taken and hidden by the Roane family. She knew Talia loved Lucas Roane, but she knew that Talia had loved the werewolf as well. Both loves had been true and unconditional. Talia was a gentle soul. She was beautiful in spirit and body. Tracey understood why both men became besotted with her.

And now, as she watched her niece kicking a ball around, she saw similar traits in her. A soft smile spread over her face. It felt alien. Her cheeks were stiff. She hadn't smiled in so long, but this was right. She had come all this way for her niece. Her mission had been the correct one. No matter what happened, she would remain at her side. She would guard this child with her life.

"She looks like her mother?"

Her niece's mother, the Mori who adopted her, sat beside Tracey. Her name was Suhnah, which meant sunny and warm in their language. She explained it to Tracey the first night she welcomed her into her home. When Lucan brought all of them into the village, their reception was much different than the first time. They were captives then. They were visitors now. And being able to walk among the Mori freely, she realized they were good people. They just weren't aware of Lucan's evilness, but that would be corrected soon.

The Immortal was coming. Tracey felt it in her gut. And she was coming for her niece. When The Immortal would arrive, Tracey didn't know what would happen, but she knew there would be chaos, death, and misery. Lucan would no doubt unveil his true self. He wanted the thread for himself, but the thread would never go to a man. It could only go to a female and the Mori had kept her niece human. Suhnah told her that they wouldn't turn her into a true Mori vampire until she decided what age she wanted to be for eternity. They thought that would be her future. That's what they wished anyways. Tracey hoped her niece had a future at this point.

"Lily!" Suhnah called, standing up from where they were sitting on the grass. "It is time for your meal."

Lily stopped in mid-kick. Her cheeks were rosy and her eyes were elated. Her blonde hair was in a mess, sweat-darkening streaks near her forehead, but to Tracey, she had never looked more alive than ever. This was the magic of humans. This was why they were to be treasured and cherished. They were alive in the truest form.

Their heart beat. Their blood warmed their faces. They had a child-like naivety that never left them. Tracey felt the same quality from Davy, even until the end. It was there, like a light that had been dimmed, but it was still there. Tracey yearned for that never to happen to her niece. She always wanted her light to burn bright, no matter what forces of evil were at bay.

"Are you thinking of your sister?" Suhnah asked, holding her arms open as Lily came running. A giggle escaped her niece and she stopped, breathing hard, but smiling so widely as Suhnah closed her arms, folding a robe around her child.

At the mention of 'sister,' some of the glee left Lily. She gazed up at Tracey, like she had since she first arrived as a guest in their home. No words had been exchanged. Suhnah told her that they never explained her connection to a thread-holder or that Tracey was her aunt through blood, but she knew. A look of wonder showed over Lily's face every time she focused on Tracey. She knew deep down, whether she spoke the words or not. Lily knew Tracey was her aunt.

She took her hand, tipping her head back so she could look all the way up the bigger vampire. "You're missing my mommy."

Suhnah gasped, but Tracey felt a burning behind her eyes. She was trying not to cry. "You know who I am."

Lily nodded. Her little hand squeezed Tracey's. "But you know that I knew." Her cheeks puffed out. The color had started to fade, but it pinked again. "My mommy comes to see me. She told me about how nice you are. You came all this way to protect me."

Suhnah's head lifted. She stared at Tracey intensely. "Protect her? From who?"

"The other lady that broke them out, Mom."

The burning moved to her throat. Tracey felt a lump forming. Her niece was trying to reassure her Mori mother, but she looked back to her and when their gazes collided, she knew that the child was aware of so much more than she should've been. Tracey knelt down. Her hands rested on Lily's tiny shoulders. "What do you know about that lady?"

"She's here." Her voice dipped low. She glanced over her shoulder, as if looking for her to arrive right then and there. "She's coming because she's scared that I'll take the thread from her."

"What do you mean? She is the thread."

"Yeah, but if she's turned, she'll come into me. She won't exist anymore. She'll just be the thread again."

Tracey's mind was spinning. There'd been talks about how to stop The Immortal, but no one had come up with anything legit.

All the ideas were too outlandish and failure was a certainty. None had considered asking the child. She had to know more, so much more, but she forced herself to speak calmly. She didn't want to alarm her niece. "Lily, do you know how to stop The Immortal?"

At the mention of her, Lily's face grew alarmed. Her eyes rounded. The ends of her mouth grew tight and her neck stiffened. She looked like she couldn't breathe, but she only shook her head in a clipped motion from right to left and back again. A whispered, "No," came out.

"Stop it." Suhnah rushed forward and pulled Lily away. She lifted her up. Lily buried her head into her Mori mother's neck and held on tight. A whimpering sounded from her. It was low and sent shivers through Tracey, but her niece knew. Her niece knew about The Immortal. She knew she was coming for her. She knew about Tracey. She knew about Talia. She wanted to ask more, know more, but she bit her words back. She wouldn't find anything out that way.

Tracey stepped back and lifted her hands up. "I'm sorry." She faltered, feeling an ominous sadness weighing down on her chest. She was going to lose her niece. Her end was coming, but she didn't know when.

"If you don't mind, I think you should stay with the others for the night." Suhnah cupped the back of Lily's head. Her eyes flashed in anger. "There's a room for you. We can talk tomorrow about what happened today."

Tracey nodded. "Okay."

Suhnah walked away, and she couldn't do a thing to stop her. The ominous feeling grew, and all she could do was watch. Lily lifted her head. The tears were dried up already, but she held her aunt's gaze as she was carried away.

Tracey let out a soft sigh. "Talia, if there's a time for you to perform a miracle and help me save your child, it's now. Help me keep her alive."

TALIA HEARD HER SISTER. She was on the other side. A barrier was between her and the living, but she was there. She knew what was coming and unlike those still alive, she could see what was coming.

Saren stepped next to her, watching Tracey who was watching her niece. "We'll stop her."

Talia glanced at her, sadness emanating from every cell of her spirit. "I hope so. I really hope so."

"The Immortal knows about us. She must've been the one to tell Jacith about us. She'll come for the child and then she'll come for us."

Another thread-holder sister joined them. Others were there as well. One by one, they all came to stand on the other side of that veil. All watched the child and all knew, their end was near.

Sireenia said, "She is the last thread-holder. That means something."

No one looked at her. No one wanted to remind her that it could mean all their spirit deaths were coming, because more than likely, that was the ending for their prophecy. It was their death and not The Immortal's.

Saren was the vessel chosen to fight for them, but it wasn't time yet. She was waiting, and as they remained there, she was coming.

The Immortal had arrived.

31

ROANE

Lucas was stuck, literally.

She froze him in place and all he could do was wait. No matter how much force he tried to break through her invisible boundary, he couldn't. And he was cloaked, but if he did break free, he'd figure a way around being invisible. Another day, another time Davy would've been laughing with glee. She would've loved being invisible. All the pranks she could've pulled on everyone, even her human friends that annoyed her. She really loved torturing them.

He started to grin, imagining it. Then, he was brought back to reality with a resounding crash. There was no Davy and there soon wouldn't be if he didn't do something about it. She said he could break her free. He had to try, but his Hunters' tattoo burned at that moment. It had been burning more and more since the battle. The Immortal said it was because the Hunters were nearby, but it was a lie. They kicked him out and turned off his connection to their power. The tattoo was alive because of her. That was the only reason that made sense, but it was scalding him now.

He tipped his head back and a roar erupted from him. The

pain was blinding, even to him. He glanced around, but there was no Immortal. She wasn't there, so what was happening?

Then, he heard, "Lucas Roane of the Roane bloodline." A deep and bellowing voice spoke from behind him. He turned around, but there wasn't one person. There were a dozen or more.

Shock had him speechless. He got over that real fast, though and scowled. "Blackstock."

Blackstock was the elder of the Hunters' line. He vowed to protect humans from vampires. It was the terms for why the slayers were discontinued. Too many slayers went rogue, and the Hunters were created. He was old, even for being a vampire, and he had gray hair. Not many vampires had gray hair. It spoke to his eternity. He was close to the end that he chose. Gray hair appeared only when a vampire wanted to die.

He folded his hands together. "You've been feeling your connection again?"

He meant the Hunter tattoo. Roane continued to scowl. "I'm guessing that's why you can see me."

"It is. We activated your connection when we learned of your new mission."

"My mission?" Roane clipped out. "You wanted me to kill Davy."

"We had good reason for your order. She is too powerful now."

"I know."

"This is what we feared. A creature too great to exist on our plane."

Lucas groaned. He used to be more professional, but that was when he had been regarded as their best Hunter, before they told him to kill the woman he loved. Since then, since going rogue, he wasn't feeling any inclination to be polite. "Tell me something I don't know." He shot Blackstock a dark look. "Tell me something that's useful." He punched at the invisible wall holding him in place. "Get me out of here. That'd be useful!"

Blackstock frowned, but glanced over his shoulders. The other Hunters nodded. "We will try."

"How?"

"We will give you all of our power."

Roane was stunned. That much power . . . he looked at all of them. There were sixteen Hunters standing there and no one was blinking an eye. There was no hesitation. All were ready, merely staring back at him, and waiting for when it was time.

He said, "This is why you came, isn't it?"

Blackstock nodded. "We had to know what side you were on so we came. We waited. We watched and now, we know. It is time."

He had no words. "You will die."

"It is worth dying for. The Immortal cannot be allowed to live. You must kill her."

"But—"

"There is no time, Lucas of the Roane Bloodline. There is only one more who was created to hold the thread. The Immortal is looking for the child now. She will kill her, and when that happens, there is no more hope." He raised his hands up. It was the signal. All the Hunters placed their hands on the shoulder of the Hunter before them. The two behind Blackstock both touched his shoulders. They were all physically connected and at the last touch, Lucas doubled over again. His tattoo was a line of fire. It was burning, singeing the air, and the pain was slicing through him. It felt like his tattoo was trying to pull him apart.

There was no more time wasted. Blackstock immediately began chanting, and as he kept going, one by one the Hunters began to fall to the ground. It was the last line. They started on the left and went to the right. One down. Two. Three. Four. Then, five, six, seven. Lucas couldn't do anything except watch and count them. Eight. Nine. Ten.

Six left.

They had gotten to the second line of Hunters behind Black-stock. Eleven. Twelve. Thirteen.

It was the last two behind Blackstock.

He kept chanting. Lucas's tattoo was one huge flame. He ceased feeling anything except being burned alive, but he knew it would stop. The higher the flame went meant another Hunter had fallen.

Fourteen.

Fifteen.

It was down to one. Blackstock stopped. He was the last and he lifted his head. His eyes were complete fire. It reminded him of Saren . . . Saren? Lucas frowned. A nagging emotion started, but he couldn't focus on that. Blackstock spoke, "With these last words, I will pass along the last Hunters' power to you. We have lived our lives. We have fulfilled our missions. Our new purpose is to live through you."

"Blackstock." Lucas didn't know what to say. Everything in him was searing pain, but he felt like he should say something. "I'm sorry it came to this."

"It would've come to pass no matter what course of actions you chose. As long as a thread-holder exists, The Immortal would've tried to come alive. It is no one's fault." He paused. The older vampire hesitated, just slightly, before he lifted his head even higher. "Are you ready?"

Lucas nodded. He wasn't asking him. Blackstock was asking himself. It was time for him to die and he said the words needed. As the last one left his mouth, his head fell back. His arms spread out, palms faced to the sky. A burst of light left him, making his body appear like it was going to blow up, but it shot up in the air and then back down right away. It burst through the invisible barrier and slammed into Roane. He cried out, feeling all of their power inside of him. It was too much. His body couldn't contain it. He was going to explode. All would be lost, but as he thought that, it was done.

He was the last Hunter. The power settled into him and he could only stand and watch as one by one, the Hunters' bodies died. They withered to corpses, and then to bones, and then to dust. They became one with the earth.

A last wind raced across the land, sweeping them up, and it grazed over Roane. It was his last goodbye to them, and with that, as they were carried to be scattered over the lands, Roane was alone.

He saw his sword had fallen to the ground. He bent to pick it up, and as he did, another voice spoke, "You got amped up, I see."

It was Saren, but instead of the usual sneer on her face, there was wariness. He finished picking up his sword and sheathed it into place. "You've been missing." She was the one Davy talked about.

She didn't come closer. She remained ten yards away and shifted so her knees were bent and she was on the tips of her toes. She was ready to bolt or fight if necessary. Lucas registered her stance. "Are you fearful of me?"

"She was in your head. She could be speaking through you right now."

She—The Immortal.

It wasn't meant as an insult, but Lucas still felt it was one. His eyes flashed in irritation. "I was never under her control."

"You drank from her. You could've been."

"She forced me to, but I was never under her control. I was still myself."

"She was in your body and your head."

She was. Lucas couldn't argue that. "She's not anymore. Davy did something. I don't know what, but The Immortal isn't in my head anymore. I'm not connected at all to her now."

At the mention of Davy, Saren's head popped up. Her eyes grew more alert. "Davy? You've been in contact with her?"

He nodded. "I don't know how. It was when I was sleeping, but when I woke up, The Immortal wasn't in my head."

"How'd she react to that?"

"She didn't really, but I could tell it bothered her." He shrugged. "It's probably why she didn't let me go with her."

"What else did Davy say?"

"That someone is missing. She said something about being turned and an innocent one." Talia's child. Blackstock said the child, but it all clicked with Lucas right then. Talia's child was here. She was the next thread-holder. It was why they had come to the Mori village in the first place. He couldn't think about Talia's child being murdered. He said to Saren, "You've been missing. Why?"

Saren didn't answer at first. She gazed at him, seemingly studying him for something, Then, she sighed and replied, "Jacith was aware of us. He had cloaked himself to my sisters and me. We didn't proceed until we knew the reason."

"It was The Immortal."

"Yes." Saren nodded, her eyes downcast. "We saw all that transpired. It was alarming to find out that The Immortal betrayed Davy and our sisters. You killed him too early, though."

Lucas frowned. "What do you mean?"

"She was going to use him to help destroy our line. We think that is why she allied with him. That, and because she needed more power to burst free from Davy. Those were the two reasons."

"She said she was going to offer me to him. He wanted the Hunters' power for himself."

"No." She shook her head, moving closer to him. Whatever had been holding her back diminished. Her shoulders relaxed, her words came more freely, and the old Saren spark was revived. He saw the flame light up her eyes, and as she spoke, it burned more and more. "We think that was a ruse. We think she took you and connected you two to keep watch if anyone would plot against her. You are the glue. She knew you sent your friends ahead to plan how to save Davy, but if anyone is able to bring her back, it would be you. We think that was the real reason she took you with her."

"But Jacith."

"If he killed you, her blood would've been in him. She would've had even better access to his power, and he wouldn't have known. We think that was the real plan for her to use him and then destroy him when she didn't need him anymore."

"So she would've killed me?" Lucas's head moved back. That thought didn't sit well with him. "That bitch."

Saren cracked a grin. "Yeah, well, that bitch is going to kill one of my sisters. We will need your help to stop her."

Talia's child. Roane focused again. "What's the plan?"

She didn't skip a beat. "You."

32

They felt her coming.

The winds moved with her. The grass turned toward her. The sun dipped low, as if to light her path better. Clouds formed in the sky, circling over the Mori village. Animals raced for shelter, and a chill went down everyone's backs because they could all feel her power.

The Immortal walked across the grass for where the Mori children played. Suhnah was halfway back to their home when she stopped. She turned, holding Lily, and fear slivered through her like she had never experienced before.

Tracey couldn't move, not at first. The same fear everyone felt was paralyzing her, but then her instincts kicked in and she placed herself in The Immortal's path. She raised her chin up, challenging, and said, "You will not go any further."

The Immortal stopped a few feet away and cocked her head to the side. Her eyes ran over the warrior vampire and then she grinned. "You are Talia's sister. At last, we meet." The way The Immortal stood there, her hair billowing from the wind, flying behind her and around her, the image was beautiful, but chilling at the same time. Her white dress was clean, as if she wasn't a creature of the world. It was like she was above them, a god among them, but Tracey knew that wasn't right. She was beneath them. She had been created and stuffed inside a human to keep her powers controlled. She was a murderer.

The Immortal laughed softly. She shook her head. "You are wrong, Tracey, sister to Talia. I'm fighting for my existence. That is all. You would do the same."

"I wouldn't," she growled back.

"You would." The Immortal's voice dipped to a low warning. "You would kill anything that stood in your way of living. It is the very essence of who you are."

"What are you talking about?"

"You are a vampire. You take blood from those living to live yourself."

"I do not kill them."

"You would if you were starving. You wouldn't be able to control yourself and you would justify it later when you were of sound mind. You had to live. They were the weaker species. It is the hierarchy of life."

She was right. Tracey hated it, but she had killed. When she first turned, before she could control herself, and though she felt guilt, it hadn't stayed with her long. She was fighting to live. "Shut up."

The Immortal laughed again. The sound was eerie. "You're angry because you know I am right. I am only trying to live."

"You are life itself. You will live even if you are inside another human."

"That is not life. That is surviving. That is entrapment." Her eyes flashed in anger. She drew closer, and as she did, the winds picked up. They slammed behind her, rushing past and assaulting Tracey. The Immortal added, "I am only trying to exist. That is all."

"It won't be enough."

Others were gathering. The longer they spoke, Tracey saw

more and more Mori standing around them to watch. All had fear in their eyes. All had a sense of helplessness. Tracey couldn't stomach it. They weren't even going to fight. It came down to her and her alone. Her gut twisted into a knot and the ends were yanked savagely, tightening. For a moment, she felt tears swimming in her eyes. This was the end. She couldn't do anything except try, but she had to. Suhnah had taken her niece away. Tracey only hoped they were hiding the child as she stalled The Immortal.

"But you are not."

She heard The Immortal, and her heart sank. "What do you mean?"

The Immortal tapped her head. "I can hear your thoughts, if you didn't realize it already. They are not hiding the child." She bobbed her head down, indicating behind Tracey's shoulder.

Tracey turned and that knot withered and died.

Suhnah was bringing Lily to them.

"No!" She held her hand out. "Don't. Run. Hide. Try something to save Lily."

Suhnah stopped, still holding onto the child tightly, but The Immortal crooked a finger. She made a motioning signal to her. "Come, Suhnah. Bring me the child." She said to Tracey as Suhnah did as she commanded, "There is no more fight. They can all sense it. They are offering a sacrifice instead for their livelihood."

"How do you know?" Tracey couldn't speak. Her throat was raw. "You can't know." But it was. She saw the resignation and defeat in Suhnah. The Mori vampiress was crying. Tears streamed down her face in a steady line, but she never faltered. She closed the distance until she was right in front of her child's would-be murderer.

"No," Tracey whimpered. She had to try and she shot forward. She reached for Lily. She was going to rip her from Suhnah's arms and run as fast as possible. It wouldn't be enough, but at least she had tried. At least someone had fought back, but her hand only grazed over Lily's leg before she was yanked backwards.

"NO!" The Immortal lifted her in the air. She didn't touch her. She merely held a hand up. The higher the hand went, the higher Tracey was in the air and she turned her hand. She released Tracey from her hold and the warrior vampire was flung to the ground, yards away. Her body broke through the crowd of Mori. They jumped aside so she wouldn't crash into any of them and once she fell to the ground, she tasted blood in her mouth. She rolled over, coughing it out. The Mori closed the gap behind her. She was aware of this in the back of her mind, and she wasn't paying attention to it. The need to try again, to save her niece, was the only thing forefront on her mind, but when she raised herself back up, she realized the Mori wouldn't let her pass. They remained strong, keeping their backs to her. She tried to move past another one, but it was the same. They moved to block her. She couldn't penetrate the circle anymore.

"Stay back."

A hand came to her shoulder and she was lifted once again and moved backwards. A growl ripped from her throat, and she turned, ready to fight, but it wasn't who held her in place. It was the person beside who told her to stay back.

Lucan held her in place, but her eyes fell to the human beside him and she fell back in surprise. "The witch?"

Brown waved, smiling self-consciously. She tucked her hair behind her ears and grabbed her other hand in front of her, pulling and twisting at her sleeves. "Heya. You're Tracey. I remember you."

It was the human witch that Davy was friends with. Tracey said, "You were left behind. Lucas—"

"Lucas put her with Mavic to train her magic."

"Your magic was locked to you."

Brown nodded, dropping her voice to a whisper, "It was. Mavic helped unlock it, and he's been helping me hone it more."

"But why?" She wasn't enough. Tracey knew it would take more than one Bright witch. She turned to Lucan. "Tell me there is more. Tell me you have a plan."

Lucas's twin brother glared at her, his forehead wrinkling and he narrowed his eyes at her. "I would ask you to stop being insulting to me. Right now, you can stop."

Tracey didn't dare hope. "There's more than her?" There had to be, or all was lost. Davy was gone. Her niece was gone. "Lucan, tell me—" She grasped onto him with desperate hands.

"Tracey, stop." Wren ran up to them and pulled her lover's hands away. She held them in her own and said to her, "It's not. There's more. I promise." She twisted back to Lucan. "Do it. Now. We can't wait."

But Lucan wasn't paying attention. Brown and a man in a robe stood beside him. Tracey guessed this was Mavic. She had never heard of the sorcerer, but he was rumored to be the second most powerful, second to Jacith. Some of her dread lifted as she recognized him and hope flickered inside of her. It was small, so small, but it was there. Tears streamed freely from her eyes now. She must've looked as Suhnah had, but she would never relinquish to The Immortal. Never.

She held onto Wren's hands now. "Wren," she gasped.

"I know." Wren pulled her close so their bodies touched. She rested her forehead against Tracey's. "Just hold on. Hold on."

"It's not done." More tears. She gave her lover a watery smile.

"It's not done," Wren soothed her. One of her hands released her and wrapped around Tracey's shoulders. She held the blonde warrior to her chest and ran her hand down her hair. "It's not done. I promise. There's more to come, much, much more."

And then, a new sudden burst of wind ripped across the lands.

Lucan let out a breath. "It's time."

Tracey watched from the crowd. The Mori allowed her to see now, knowing she wouldn't rush in anymore. The Immortal reached for Lily. Both mother and daughter's faces were wet. They were crying steadily, but Lily didn't fight. It broke Tracey's heart. She couldn't imagine the fear her niece was experiencing, but the little girl wore a brave front. Despite the tears, her eyes gleamed with a fierce determination and her hands were balled into tight little fists. When The Immortal pulled her into her arms, Lily didn't wrap her legs or arms around the other. She held limp, making her body dead weight for The Immortal. A twinge of pride tunneled deep into Tracey's chest.

She brushed her own tears away and held onto Wren's hand tighter.

Their roles switched in that moment. Tracey was the solid one. She had been their foundation and Wren was the feisty, more emotional one. Wren was her rock that day. She held her hand and as Tracey couldn't look away from her niece, she continued to smooth a hand down Tracey's hair and back. She was reassuring her, or trying, but the truth was that no one knew what was going to happen.

Even Lucan, who glanced to Mavic and Brown. Both nodded. Both were ready, but they still waited. Mavic felt the thread-holders arriving. He knew the entire line of sisters was going to show, and he felt another power traveling with them. He didn't know who or what that was, and he refrained from telling Lucan. There'd be questions he could not answer, but when they were on the outskirts of the Mori, he lifted a hand to Lucan's shoulder.

Lucan touched Wren's shoulder, who was already touching Tracey. The Mori nearest Tracey touched her shoulder and one by one, a Mori would touch the shoulder of the next one and so forth. Tracey stopped crying. She stopped feeling so helpless, and her tears dried up. Her hope flared brighter. They were all going to fight. She realized that as all the Mori became connected to each other. When they were done, the only Mori who wasn't touching another was Suhnah. It came full circle, rounding back until it was Brown's turn. The last Mori placed his hand on her shoulder, and then they all began to chant.

We are.
We will be.
As one.
Together.
We will
cast out
the imposter.

They repeated those words softly under their breath.

Tracey couldn't help herself. She called in her mind, *"Lily, look at me."*

"I am."

Tracey's eyes snapped open. Her niece was staring right at her and there was no fear. There was only happiness. Her tears dried up too and she added to her aunt, *"I'm going to see my momma. I am so excited, Tracey."*

Tracey gasped silently. Her mother. Talia. Lily was going to die. That was what she meant and she started to say, *"No, Lily. Not that way—"*

"Yes!" Lily cried out. She thrust her hand over The Immortal's shoulder. "Look!"

33

Davy felt them.

She could feel her sisters there. They were with Lucas, who was connected to all the Hunters before him. The Mori were as one being, along with Brown and Mavic. There were so many, but they were all needed. All against one. It was what was needed and as The Immortal turned, distracted, Davy stood up inside of her. She was pushed to the farthest regions of The Immortal's mind, but she was still there. It wasn't over. Not yet.

SAREN STOOD BESIDE HIM, and they strode forward.

They had remained hidden, cloaked from The Immortal until the last second. Everything was set in place. They continued walking forward and he knew the instant the invisible spell fell away. They appeared, a foot, a leg, both legs, the torso, then the arms, shoulders and finally their heads. The full bodies were now visible and The Immortal turned at the child's cry of 'look!' Her eyes first gleamed in amusement. Her top lip curved up in a mocking grin, but her eyes trailed past Saren and soon filled with horror.

"No," she shook her head, saying quietly.

"Yes!" Saren growled.

Lucas glanced behind him and started. All of the thread-holders were there. They weren't in their bodies, but they stood as if ghosts. They were there, though. That was all that mattered, and they were standing behind Saren. He realized now what it meant that she was their vessel. He had the Hunters' power in him and she had all of their power inside of her.

The crowd moved to the left of Saren. The Mori were all still connected, but they were able to maneuver so two that were forgotten came forward.

Brown and Mavic. Lucan followed behind them. Lucas's eyes went flat at seeing his brother, but that was a battle for another time.

Lucan caught his gaze and wore a mirrored mocking grin that The Immortal had moments before. It was as if to say, "Later, brother. Later."

Lucas stifled the growl and swung his head to focus on The Immortal again.

She congregated to them. "What is this?" Her eyes trailed over everyone, seeing the touching hands of the Mori before landing on Lucas. She jerked forward, a growl coming from her. "What is this?"

"It's over." Saren drew her sword. "That's what this is."

"No."

"Yes." And Saren attacked, but as she did, all the thread-holders launched with her. They rained down on The Immortal. It was a whirlwind after that. The Immortal was covered in ghost forms and the wind picked up, swirling around them like a tornado. Lucas stood back. He wasn't sure if he should wade in or hold back, but when he heard the first cry, he knew that wasn't The Immortal. No matter how much he hated it, she still had

Davy's voice. He would've recognized her cry no matter how far away.

He started forward.

"Wait." A hand touched him. It was soft and warm. It was gentle, too.

Brown was there, her eyes were open, but he only saw the whites. Her eyes had rolled into the back of her mind. He said, "Tell me that's magic."

"It is." Her hand clasped tighter onto him. "I am connecting you to everyone to fight her."

"I can't fight if I'm being held back."

"I know. I'm connecting to you mentally." A shift happened inside of him, like a room appeared and the door swung open to let thousands inside. He gasped, but he heard her say, "And I'm done. Go. Fight. Get Davy."

That was all he needed to hear. Gripping his sword, he waded in through the winds.

The Immortal and Saren were trading blows. One would hit, the other retaliated. It would repeat, over and over again. He had to push through more winds and more of the thread-holder sisters. They were there right alongside their sister. They were urging her on, chanting words of magic to her. The Immortal was growing frustrated. She couldn't strike Saren down, but when Saren swung the sword to her head, she grabbed it and yanked it out of her hands.

Saren cried out, losing her weapon.

"Finally," The Immortal growled and swung it herself.

It would've come down on Saren, who was dazed, but Lucas blocked it with his own sword.

"No!" Furious dark eyes snapped to his. They widened at his arrival. "I was going to let you live."

He kicked her sword away and grunted, "You were going to let Jacith kill me."

"Well." She shrugged, rounding back and steadying on her feet. "I was, but then I liked your company after all."

"Bitch," he snarled.

"Vampire," she shot back.

His eyes jumped to hers. Shock spread quickly through him. It was the same insult, said with the same venom that Davy first held for him. He looked into The Immortal's eyes. *Davy?* The Immortal's eyes lit up. A literal light filled them and he heard back in his mind, *"It's me. She can't concentrate on me, but I'm slowing her down. Each time she swings or tries to send magic out, I block her. She hasn't figured out what's going on, but she can't stop me anyway. She's losing her hold. Keep going!"*

He swung his own sword, and The Immortal blocked him, rounding to hit him across his face. It was a slap, but with her strength, it was a launch backwards.

"Vampire!"

He thought it was The Immortal, but it was Saren instead. She jumped in the air, grabbing a dagger that was tucked against his back and she thrust out, slicing The Immortal. It was going to slash her throat, but The Immortal evaded. It cut her arm instead and another unearthly growl came from The Immortal, who retaliated. She swung the sword out. It was quick enough to graze Saren's cheeks.

Blood had been spilled on both ends.

Lucas rebounded and both Saren and he were swinging at The Immortal. They struck at the same time. The Immortal was cut by both, but her efforts doubled. They fought like that, trading blows, until Lucas had lost track of time. He felt like he had been fighting for hours. His body was growing weaker so he closed his eyes and pulled forth more of his power. The Hunters were there. He felt them rallying inside and when he opened his eyes again, he felt all of them with him. He swung, but they were all swinging with him.

His sword hit hers. It held and he leaned forward, pushing on it. He was going to overpower her. He had to.

Sensing the renewed strength, she dropped her sword and hit at him with magic. "Enough!" she roared.

The magic hit him like a two-ton semi. It hit him hard and he was winded. He could see, but he couldn't stop her as she turned on Saren. The wind went to her feet and began circling her. It picked up speed as it started up over her feet, her calves, her legs, her waist. She was drawing power from the ground.

She was going to kill Saren. He felt her intent and tried to help. "No!" he yelled.

It was too late.

The Immortal shot Saren with a blast of magic.

The blue-leathered warrior fell back, stunned by the hit. Her eyes rolled to the side and she began to fall.

"No!"

Lucas thought that was him. He was shouting in his mind, but it wasn't. It was the other sisters. They surged ahead and Talia stepped into Saren's body. He blinked by the sudden transformation. The blue leather was gone, and instead the red hair grew and a similar white dress formed over the thread-holder.

The Immortal stepped back, shocked, too.

"MOM!"

Talia's eyes widened. She paled and turned. The Immortal did as well. Lucas saw the little girl run past him. He didn't know what had happened to her. The Immortal must've placed her down, but she ran right by him. Her arms and legs were pumping as hard as she could and her eyes and mouth were flat, looking determined. "MOM! Mom!"

"No!" Talia gasped.

She lifted horrified eyes to Lucas. "Stop her—"

But she was past him. It was too late. Talia moved to scoop her daughter up, but The Immortal was there. She grabbed the child before Talia could and swung her away. She lifted up in the air and laughed down. "It is too late now. I will end all of this fool-ishness."

"NO!"

The Immortal placed a hand against the child's cheek and closed her eyes.

"No, no, no." Talia was whimpering. "She can't kill her. It's all over for us then."

"Lucas!"

He heard Davy shouting to him. *"What?"*

"Throw Talia up here."

"What?"

Talia turned to him, hearing him. "What?"

He ignored her. *"What, Davy?"*

"Throw my sister up here. Just do it. The child has a knife. She's going to plunge it into my body. The Immortal's distracted. Now's your chance to free me."

"Davy, I don't know—"

"DO IT!"

So, he did. He hurried to Talia. "I'm only doing what I'm told." His fingers wrapped around her arm and he circled once, gaining enough momentum and then he let loose. Talia was launched in the air.

"Mom!" The child saw her coming and like Davy said, she pulled out a dagger that was inside of her shirt. He recognized it as one that he had given Wren as a gift. Then, right as The Immortal saw it, it was too late. It was plunged into her stomach.

"NOOOO!" she screamed, crashing back down to the ground, but he didn't have time to figure why that one cut held so much more power than the others. The Immortal's body was writhing on the ground and he stepped forward. A hand touched his. Brown was beside him. She said, "They need magic for this so hope you're ready."

"Wha—"

Again. He didn't have time to question anything. He was overtaken by her magic, but it wasn't just hers. He sensed all of the Mori as one. He sensed his friends. Gavin. Gregory. Wren. Tracey. Bastion. They were all connected. His brother, too. Mavic. Everyone. A moment later, he felt all the thread-holders, too. Brown must've connected to them, or to Talia, and they were all being channeled into him.

"Come in, Lucas!" Davy was calling him. He was on another plane. He wasn't in his body form anymore. He had become his mind, but he followed her voice. *"Davy, lead me!"* he shouted back.

"I am. I'm pulling you to me."

He stepped forward, feeling intense power all around him. It wasn't his. It wasn't Davy's. It was angry, but it was distracted. It was blind to him until he was in front of Davy. He reached for her hand. Relief pouring through him. *"Davy!"*

His hand went through hers. He frowned, pulling it back. *"I can't touch you."*

"I know." She was concentrating on his hand, her eyebrow bunched together. Her mouth turned down and she said, with authority in her voice, *"But I'm going to grab you."*

He waited, holding his hand up, and as he held his breath, she started to lift her hand to his. He felt an immense pressure pushing back against him, but he held strong. Davy was breaking through whatever was holding her in.

A gasp.

He heard it in his ear. It wasn't him. It wasn't Davy.

A reeling sensation zipped around them. An anchor began to sink inside of him. The Immortal knew what they were doing.

"Davy, you have to hur—" Her fingers touched his and the last of his sentence fell from his lips, *"—ry."*

That was all the connection she needed. Her eyes closed and he felt the power radiate from her. It was like a blanket coming from her, one thread at a time. It was covering The Immortal around them and he felt a shift in gravity. They were going down.

Davy's palm fit against his. She tightened her hold on him and grunted out, pain laced in her tone, *"It's working. She's weakening."*

She kept breaking through the barrier until her other hand was holding onto his, then her arms, her elbows, her legs, her knees, her feet, her waist, then her entire body. They were crashing to the ground. It was The Immortal, not them. He realized that now until he was holding Davy in his arms again. As the entirety of her body fit against his, perfectly and how it always had, he was back in his own mind. He was in his own body and he really was holding Davy.

She opened her eyes. Tears burst forth, and she smiled at him. "Hi."

Hi. She said hi. Lucas felt a stupid grin on his face. He grabbed her face, rested his forehead to hers, and asked, "Is it done?"

Her smile spread as wide as his and she nodded, bobbing their heads together. "Yeah." Happy tears slid down her face. "It really is." She grasped his head too and dipped so her lips met his. One kiss. Two. Three—he couldn't let go. It'd been so long, so damn long. He groaned, his hands going around her. He pulled her in. He just wanted to hold her and reassure himself that she wasn't going anywhere anymore.

"I'm here," she gasped against his lips. "I'm not going anywhere. She can't break free. She doesn't have the power. I do. I'll never let her have it again."

As they kept kissing and hugging, they began to hear sounds of sobbing. He didn't want to pull away, but he did with reluctance.

Lily was kneeling on the ground beside Talia. Tracey was next to her, and Wren was standing on Tracey's other side.

"Momma." Lily stroked Talia's cheek. She bent down and pressed her forehead to her mother's. She whispered, "Momma, I love you."

"Talia." Tracey was moaning, rocking back and forth. Her hand went to touch her sister's cheek, then lifted away. She started to touch her niece's cheek, but her hand raised once again and began to go back to her sister. She couldn't decide who to touch and in the end, she merely bent forward and pressed her forehead to Talia's stomach. She grabbed ahold of her on both sides and cried.

Wren let out a soft breath and stroked Tracey's back.

"Oh no." Davy's hand found Lucas's. "They're gone."

Brown stepped forward. She told Davy and Lucas, "They gave their power to Davy—"

Davy finished, "I needed more. I couldn't break through the barrier. They gave everything to me so I could. It cost them." She lifted her haunted gaze to him. "They died so I could live."

"No." Brown grabbed one of Davy's hands. She held it to her chest. "They died so The Immortal would be defeated. If it was another thread-holder, if it was another time, you would've done the same."

"I'm alive, though." Tears were fast falling down Davy's face again but the celebration had gone. There were losses to mourn.

"And they won't be forgotten," Brown said. She readjusted her hold on Davy's hand, holding even tighter. "I promise, Davy. They will never be forgotten. We will remember. We will live for them now."

Lucan joined the circle. His face was a mask. His lips were in a flat line. His eyebrows were fixed. He wore a bland expression before he turned to Brown. "I hate to strike while there are grieving ones here." He lifted his eyes to his brother. A smirk showed and a chill sliced through Lucas once again.

He growled, his hands forming fists. "What are you doing, Lucan?"

"Well." He let out a frustrated breath. "You see, everyone forgot why I was helping. I mean, yes. Take down The Immortal. Hear, hear. All cheers for her demise, but," he cringed, smiling at the same time. "No one thought about the afterwards, and well . . ." His hand gestured to Talia and to Davy. "I have to strike while I can, and the time is now."

He stared at Davy, but Brown gasped. Her head flew back and her chest arched up. Her hands spread out. She cried out, "Davy!"

"Brown!"

"There's pain." A bloodcurdling scream ripped from her. She cried out, hoarsely, "Something's happening inside of me. I can't —oh my God! I can't—Davy!"

"What?" Davy grabbed both of her hands. "What is going on? Lucan! Stop it. Whatever you're doing, stop it!"

Lucas started for his brother, but he was grabbed and hauled backwards. Five Mori warriors restrained him. He scanned the group, and all of his warriors were being held back by Mori. A high-pitched scream sounded from Lily as she was picked up and handed off to her mother. "Mom!" She hit at the Mori mother, but her futile attempts were ignored. She was whisked away.

Tracey kicked out. She tried to break free, an animal-like growl coming from her. She couldn't. She was too weak. So was everyone else, Lucas himself, and his eyes found Davy's, too. She was the weakest of all.

All that power, everything that had been given to them would be for nothing.

Lucan double-crossed them. As Brown kept screaming, Mavic moved around so he was standing in front of Brown and Davy both.

"Yes. Yes." Lucan stood in front of his twin. His breath was hot as he was laughing. "You're starting to piece it all together now, aren't you? You were my way of breaking the thread from exis-tence, but you're my enemy. You were my weapons against her and it all couldn't have worked better for me if I had planned it myself." He leaned close and said softly, "Thank you, brother. Thank you for putting one of my own coven members in touch with a Bright witch. Thank you for allowing him to mold her into his own weapon, because you see, her magic wasn't released at all. No, no. He's not able to perform miracles, but he was able to channel other magic inside of her. She was the trusted one. She was sent here to help you and one of mine traveled with her. So while she was in The Immortal's head with you and Davy, she thought she was helping you free Davy, but she wasn't. Her magic wasn't created to do that. Her magic was weakening Davy so that now I can kill her. Finally. The thread will jump to Brown, and then right to me. It's all been planned. I'll get what I wanted. I'll be the first and only male thread-holder. I'll be the final thread-holder."

His brother's delight repulsed him.

Lucas shook his head. If the thread were pulled from her, she would die. The thread made her immortal and as he watched, it was happening. Brown was connected to Davy still and Mavic was performing a spell on both. Davy's skin was literally jerking. The thread was going to be ripped from inside of her.

Think, Lucas. He had to think. He had to calm down and just think!

Turned. That was the last piece that Davy told him in his dream. Everything else had come true. The innocent. The forgotten. The one would come back, but she said she would have to be turned.

His brother had everything planned.

But what if she died *before* the spell was completed? That would stop it from going to his brother. No. The thought sickened him. Davy wanted to be human. That was all she dreamt about, to be normal. He couldn't . . . no, no. He couldn't take that away, but as he continued to watch—he couldn't see any other way. Davy would die. He had no doubt his brother would kill everyone else.

He had to do it.

He closed his eyes and focused. He needed to call upon all the Hunters again, but there was other power in him still. The

Immortal gave him her power. He used most of it up, but he still felt it in him. He needed to use all of it. He had to make it count.

"Davy," he thought.

Her eyes found his, so terrified.

He said, *"I'm going to kill you."*

"What?"

"Don't be afraid. I have to do it. It's the only way."

She nodded, moving her head only a tiny bit. She was held captive by the spell, but at her signal, Roane erupted into motion. He launched himself backwards and then jumped over his five captors. They were too slow. Everyone was too slow.

He was at Davy's side within the blink of an eye and in the next, his fangs were in her neck. There had been blood trickling down his arm and he raised his thumb to her lips. He brushed it over her mouth, and her tongue darted out to swallow a drop. His other hand grasped the back of her neck, and as she drank, he told her, *"Turn, Davy. Turn for me."*

He snapped her neck.

34

DAVY

They told me I slept for three days and I started laughing. Three days. How cliché was that, but it was true. It had been three days since my final death. And I say final because it felt like I had died a thousand times over, but three days ago had been my last time. I was no longer The Immortal. I was no longer even a thread-holder. I wasn't empathic, and I wasn't a human.

I was a vampire.

Lucas told me when he killed me, the thread jumped out of me. It hadn't been in enough time for Lucan's spell to do whatever it had intended to do. It went straight to the nearest thread-holder, Lily. Talia's little girl was the newest and according to a prophecy that I never knew about, she was the last thread-holder. Tracey explained that Lily would always be the thread-holder. She doubted anyone would try to separate the thread again, not after word spread far and wide how powerful The Immortal had been.

I felt horrible. I felt Talia's second death. I felt all of my sisters' second deaths, but in the moment I hadn't realized what the impending doom was that I was feeling. I had been selfish. I had been so happy to be in Lucas's arms again, for real, but Tracey reassured me that Lily isn't a normal thread-holder. Apparently she was still able to see her other sisters, Talia too. Because she grew up among the Mori, who had their own magic, her body wasn't normal. I was thankful to hear the sisters still lived on another plane, but I wouldn't see Saren again or hear her annoying voice in my head.

It was done. All of it. Even Lucan.

When she became the thread, Lily saw Jiyama's death. She told the Mori leader that Lucan killed her and where he had deposited the body. Any assistance Lucan got from the Mori was done. Apparently, there had been suspicion, but there was proof now. One of their own saw it. Lucan was hauled into their prison while Lucas and the rest of us were treated as guests. Tracey laughed. The Mori were never going to harm any of us, but they were following what Lucan had promised—that they still needed to complete what they had originally set to do, which is to destroy the thread. They weren't aware of Lucan's secret plan of putting the thread into himself. They were ashamed once they found out the truth. Kates was set free, as well. It was realized that Lucan forced her to turn on us. When the others discovered the torture she endured from Lucan, she was welcomed back, but I knew it would be a long time till she was trusted.

I was in bed waiting for Lucas to come back. He went to see his brother, one last time, and we were leaving for home the next day. Lucan was going to be executed at the same time, but Lucas didn't want to stay for it. He knew it would happen. That was good enough for him. All the killing had been too much. He had kissed me and told me, "I just want to get home. I want to get you home. Finally."

Home.

I never thought I would be going home again. That night, the first night that I woke as a vampire, Lucas made love to me. I cried the whole time because I never thought I would be in his arms again. I never thought I would have a second chance at life.

The opening to our tent lifted, and Roane slipped inside. I sat up and smiled. "Goddess." I shook my head. "I will never get used to seeing you. I'll never take it for granted. I will never," I paused as he came over, a grin teasing the corners of his lips and I laid back. He started to fall on top of me, but switched to rest beside me. One of his elbows propped him up and his eyes traced all over me, from my eyes, forehead, cheeks, and to my lips. He lingered there. "I will never take it for granted myself." He leaned down and touched his lips to mine.

I sighed, happily. It was like coming home. I caught the side of his face and whispered, "Have I told you how much I love you?"

He nodded, moving his lips over mine. "Say it again. I like hearing it."

"I love you."

His eyes darkened, and he shifted so he was lying on top of me. "And again." His mouth dipped to my throat.

An ache was forming between my legs. I knew he would soon be there, filling me, making me feel whole again, and I sighed as his lips moved up my jawline to find my mouth again. "I love you."

"And again." He kissed me. Long. Lingering. And so damn lovingly.

"I love you." I would never stop telling him, just like he had done the same to me the night before.

After he was inside of me, after we were moving together, after we reminded each other that we could still touch one another, he lifted his head and gazed down. "You mentioned last night that you wanted a new name?"

I laughed, arching my back and pressing against him. "Is now the right time for this?"

He smiled down at me. "I want to know what name to call you when I make you scream tonight."

"Oh my God." I laughed, but then sobered up. "Davina."

"Davina?"

I nodded. It was my full name, one that I hated, but I was different. I was changed. I was no longer the happy and giddy college girl, only hoping to deal with being empathic. I would find that girl again, but it would be a while. It might be a long while, but it felt right. My hands splayed out over the side of his face. I looked up into his depths as he gazed down to mine. I murmured, "It's a new life for me. I'm no longer Davy. She died when The Immortal took hold of me, but I can still be Davina. That's my name."

"Okay." He leaned down, and his lips lovingly moved over mine. "Have I told you how much I love you today, Davina?"

I laughed and then relished as he proceeded to, over and over again. We were still showing our love for each other as the sun dipped down, the moon came out, and still when the early morning started to peek out again.

When it was morning, I fell asleep, but there were no more worries anymore. I was in Roane's arms again and I knew if I stayed there, all could be handled. When we woke, we packed up. The rest of our group was waiting for us. The goodbyes were spoken. Lily hugged me tightly and I barely managed to hold back tears. She was such a little girl, but I was reassured that she was protected by an entire village. Tracey and Wren said goodbye. Wren decided to stay with the Mori. She would help protect the newest thread-holder and she wouldn't have to leave her lover again. There was a special goodbye between Lucas and Wren. She had been one of his best warriors for centuries. She would be missed, but it was a good goodbye, not a sad one. He was holding back some of his own tears as he stepped next to me and took my hand. After the last goodbye, the Mori headed for the center of their village. The bells began to toll. Lucan's execution was near. As the Mori headed past us, we walked the other way.

We left.

We were outside of the village, and the bells had almost faded when a sudden cheer filled the air.

We all stopped. Gavin, Bastion, and Brown. Gregory found his daughter, so she came with us. We glanced back, and then to Lucas.

His brother was dead.

We traveled another mile when we heard a bush rustling. Both Gavin and Bastion drew their swords, but then we heard, "Hey, man. Shit. What's with the swords? I thought we were all friends."

"Yeah," a second voice crawled out. "You told us to stay put and we did. We've been chilling for a week and holy cripes," a pair of eyes found me and widened, "the psycho bitch is back."

It was Cal and Spencer.

Gavin's mouth fell open. He groaned, hitting his hand to his forehead. "We completely forgot about these guys."

Lucas frowned. "Who are these guys?"

All eyes came to me and I laughed, nervously. "So, it's a long story, you see."

And, as we continued home, I held his hand and told him everything that happened, and it was a long story indeed, but it was a good story. In fact, it was a great story and while Spencer and Cal were finally sent home, I knew this was a story that I would tell our child. The one thing I never told anyone since the beginning was that I was pregnant, and even though I was a vampire now, with Mori magic in me, I was able to give birth to a healthy little girl.

We named her Saren.

EPILOGUE

L ucas said the wedding could be in his restaurant or the new hotel he bought, but the idea of being indoors hadn't sat right with me. It hadn't sat right with me ever since we returned to Benshire. Being captured by Lucan and then again by The Immortal, I'd been yearning more and more to remain outside. It was wintertime, but I still did. The winter didn't touch me, which was one of the nicer qualities about being a vampire. Still. I was transitioning to my new state in life. I was free. I was a vampire. I was going to be a wife, and feeling my hair getting tugged, I looked down at the best transition in my life. I was a mother.

Saren waved her plump hands in the air and started to tip back, laughing. She didn't go far. I had her tucked in my arm so her head hit my arm lightly, but she loved it. Peals of more laughter filled the air.

"Is she hungry?"

Pippa asked the question, eager, but Brown was right next to her. Since we got back, Brown had been wonderful. She'd been by my side the entire time, making sure I was okay. Pippa came for Saren's birth, and she stuck around. She was going to try college again. So was Brown. Both had dropped out because of my captivity. I knew that was the elephant in the room. They wanted me to go with them, but neither asked yet. Vampires could go. It's where I met Lucas. We could walk in the light. We could do almost everything a human did, but it was different.

I had to mourn not being a human. Going to college—it would be in my face every day. I would never grow old, weak, diseased and I was an idiot. I was grieving? I was a vampire. They were always gorgeous and since my transformation, I'd gotten the gloss over too. It wasn't that my looks were totally changed, but my skin was clearer. My eyes darker. My hair was shinier. I was already slender, but I became more toned.

Saren started kicking her legs and gurgling.

This one, my hold on her tightened, she was worth it. Everything. If I hadn't spent so much time with the Mori, Lucas's sperm in me wouldn't have taken root. I was human, but he wasn't. It was their magic, just being in their lands, that helped make Saren possible.

"You should get your dress on." Pippa came forward. Her hands were already up and she was smiling at Saren. "I'll take the little one."

Brown jumped beside her. "I can't wait. A bridesmaid. I'm a bridesmaid. I've never been a bridesmaid."

Pippa slid her hands under Saren and stepped back with her. She grinned at Brown. "You're a Bright bridesmaid."

"And you." Brown clapped her on the shoulder. "You're a werewolf bridesmaid. I can't wait till I get drunk. You're nursing, Davy—in a . . ." She trailed off, glancing away.

That was another transition.

I told her, "It's fine, Brown. You're not the only one. Trust me."

Pippa groaned, rocking Saren back and forth. "Oh yeah. I've been calling her Davy since I arrived."

Both sobered and gazed at me. Brown sighed. "It's not that we don't want to call you Davina."

They were torn. They loved Davy. I was alive. I reached for

both of their hands and squeezed them. "I'm different. I know, but I'll get back to my old self."

The Immortal.

Lucan.

Losing my humanity—the last year before Lucas broke me free had been hard, but I felt the old me coming back. The old me *would* come back. I squeezed once more. "I love you guys, and you are helping the old Davy spark to life again. Thank you. And thank you for being a part of my wedding."

"Well, hell yeah. Of course." Brown gestured outside my bedroom window. We were back at Lucas's house, the one by the cliff where Lucan captured us in the first place. There weren't great memories, but each night Lucas helped push those bad ones away as he made new ones with me. And there was land. There was lots and lots of land. I didn't feel so 'constricted' here. The cliff was where the wedding would take place. Emily was the wedding planner and she was utilizing everyone to help. The entire backyard was transformed so it looked like a magical forest. Trees had been relocated and spelled to grow tall. Flowers hung everywhere. Logs made up the seats. It didn't look like it was next to a cliff at all. And within a few hours, it would be filled with vampires, werewolves, witches, and a few humans (those who were either clueless or brave.) There would be a few slayers as well. A group of them were waiting for us when we returned. They took Kates with them. I knew they were going to help her heal. Her time in captivity had been the worst of all of us. There'd been a few correspondents between the two of us. We were both getting better, and I was excited to see her again. She'd been my childhood nolstage. I wanted to get to know my best friend once again, well not my real best friend. That was Lucas now, but Kates held a special place in my heart. She always would.

Brown said, "This wedding is a dream wedding and hello, Roane in a tuxedo." She fanned herself. "Swoon right there."

Pippa frowned. "He's going to be her husband."

"But he's gorgeous. I can see. I can appreciate." Brown nudged Pippa with her shoulder. "Just like I can appreciate the hotness of your brother. Hubba hubba. Come to me Christian Christane." She leaned over and grabbed Saren's thumb, but paused and asked, "Does he have to be betrothed to another werewolf? Is that a thing? What about a witch? You think I got a shot? He can be my Alpha any night of the week."

Pippa's frown deepened and she turned, giving Brown a curt response. Brown retaliated, another laughing joke. It had been like this over the last few months and I sighed, listening, but I loved it. The teases were flying. The jokes were sent back and forth. Pippa would huff about something, and Brown would follow with one more outrageous suggestion, all the while trying to hide her grin.

This was normal. This had been my life, and I knew it would be again.

The old Davy was rearing up. She wanted to join in, but the slight tease I had was held back. If I joined in with the joking, they would be quieted in shock. Then, they'd want more. They'd start looking for the old Davy every minute, every hour, every time they were around me and she wasn't there. Not yet. But she was coming. I felt her in me again.

I turned back to the window and gazed down. Roane was there, listening to Emily who was pointing at a post that was covered with flowers. Her hand movements were sharp, and his frown grew, even as I watched.

Emily never wanted to bother me with anything, so she bothered him. I thought it was hilarious.

"Having fun?" I asked him.

He looked up, knowing exactly where I was. He thought back, *"Your old roommate still drives me crazy."*

"Remember when she had a crush on you?"

He groaned. *"I was using her to get to you. I should've known better."*

Resting a hand to the window frame, I leaned closer. I teased back, *"Oh, come on. Don't be so hard on yourself. You're a stud."*

"Don't start."

I laughed under my breath. *"You're the last living Hunter. You're a legend, Lucas."*

"Davina." He sighed.

I was loving the sweet torment. *"I know you're a legend in my mind. A legend in bed."*

His eyes flashed a warning. *"If you keep going, I'll come up there and show you how legendary you can be, too."*

My hands curled around the frame. *"Promise?"*

He groaned again, shaking his head. Emily quieted, and stared at him blankly. Her eyes trailed up, following his, and when she saw me, understanding flared over her face. She lifted a hand, giving me an impish grin, and said, "I'll let you two be alone. Davina, dress."

I opened the window and hollered down, "Aye, aye, Staff Sergeant."

I didn't think, but as soon as the words left my mouth, I cringed. Emily's eyes widened and she sucked in her breath. That was the old Davy. Sarcastic. Teasing. Still grimacing, I waved back. "I will. Thank you, Emily."

A sheen of tears showed and her hand waved again. Her smile softened. "I'll be up in a bit. Your hair looks beautiful."

She darted around Lucas, hurrying and waving at someone else. Lucas was still there, and my eyes found his again. He asked, *"You okay?"*

I nodded. *"I am."*

"I love you."

Warmth rushed through me. *"I love you, too."*

"You're going to be my wife in an hour."

I gave him a half-grin. *"You have an hour to run away. You've been warned."*

"Never." His eyes glittered, his love shone brightly there.

"*Never, Davina of the Roane Bloodline. You are mine forever. You are in my heart. You are in my soul. We are of one now.*"

Saren shrieked behind me and both of us grinned at the other.

Roane thought to me, "*One day we'll explain why she'll age older than us.*"

I barked out a laugh. "*It's a hell of a story.*"

"*Yes,*" he answered. "*It was, wasn't it?*"

I held his gaze and let out a soft sigh. He was right. It really was.

THE END

If you enjoyed the Davy Harwood trilogy, please consider leaving a review! They truly help so much.

For more stories, go to:

www.tijansbooks.com

ACKNOWLEDGMENTS

Wow! I can't believe I'm writing this part, and for this book. This series was one of my first that I was really proud of. I had written other stories before Davy, but all of them were while I was trying to 'learn' how to write. Davy was the first story where I felt ready. I didn't know what I was ready for. I had no idea what to do after I wrote the story, but I was ready for something. I was so proud of myself. I had gone up another level in writing. Man. Davy was always so near and dear to me. I want to thank all the readers that started with me in my Fictionpress days, followed me to Livejournal, and stuck with me when I began publishing. I know so many of you have been waiting years for this conclusion. I truly hope I did it justice.

Thank you to the Tijanettes! You, ladies, make me smile daily! Thank you to the admins, to my betas, to my editors, proofreaders, to my formatter, to my agent. Thank you to Erica Adams and Ali Oop. I know both of you have really cheered for Davy and it always meant so much to me. Thank you to all my author friends who I might've pasted something in their inbox to quick read over for me, or patted me on the back when I needed it. Thank you, thank you, thank you. I don't know if I can say it enough.

ALSO BY TIJAN

More Paranormal Standalones:

Evil

Micaela's Big Bad

Mafia novels:

Carter Reed Series

Cole

Bennett Mafia

Jonah Bennett

Canary

More of the Fallen Crest/Roussou world:

Fallen Crest/Roussou Universe

Fallen Crest Series

Crew Series

The Boy I Grew Up With (standalone)

Rich Prick (standalone)

Nate

Kess

Other series:

Davy Harwood Series (paranormal)

Broken and Screwed Series (YA/NA)

Jaded Series (YA/NA suspense)

The Insiders (trilogy)

Sports Romance Standalones:

Enemies

Teardrop Shot

Hate To Love You

The Not-Outcast

Young Adult Standalones:

Ryan's Bed

A Whole New Crowd

Brady Remington Landed Me in Jail

College Standalones:

Antistepbrother

Kian

Contemporary Romances:

Bad Boy Brody

Home Tears

Fighter

Rockstar Romance Standalone:

Sustain

An MC short story:

Kess

More books to come!

Lightning Source UK Ltd.
Milton Keynes UK
UKHW042128080223
416676UK00004B/219